TRAINS TO FREEDOM TRAINS TO HELL

ERICH BEER

Translated from the German by
Lisa Beer-Alon

gefen גפן
publishing house בית הוצאה לאור
JERUSALEM ◆ NEW YORK

Typesetting: Raphaël Freeman, Jerusalem Typesetting
Cover Design: S. Kim Glassman

First Published in Germany, 1977.
Ner Tamid Publishing Erlangen.
…und sie leben denmoch

ISBN 9789652293312

1   3   5   7   9   8   6   4   2

Gefen Publishing House
6 Hatzvi Street, Jerusalem 91360, Israel
972-2-538-0247 • orders@gefenpublishing.com

Gefen Books
600 Broadway, Lynbrook, NY 11563, USA
1-800-477-5257 • orders@gefenpublishing.com

www.israelbooks.com

Printed in Israel

Send for our free catalogue

ABOUT THE AUTHOR
ERICH BEER, 1903–1977

ERICH BEER was born in Velka Kriva, then Hungary, in 1903 and went to live in Berlin as a young boy. He was a businessman and died in Berlin in December 1977.

He went through two very hard eras in his adult life. One was the Holocaust, when he lost his wife and had to escape with his two children from Berlin. The other was his time in a prison camp in Siberia and in Russia after the Second World War, until he returned to Berlin.

He wrote two novels about these times, one about the era of the Holocaust and one about his experiences in the USSR.

ABOUT THE BOOK

STORIES OF LOVE and of hate, of fortune and misfortune, of survival and destruction are intertwined in this moving novel about a group of people and their experiences during the Holocaust. Erich Beer describes people and their fates in the most terrible era of the last century. He preaches neither hatred nor revenge, but exposes the hell that was created by human beings in order to annihilate people because of their religion, nationality or political beliefs.

Through his touching recounting of the stories of Bernhard and his children, Rachel and Yankel, Haim and Feigele, the author tries to prove that faith, love and hope can help to overcome even the worst hell ever created by mankind. Despite merciless prosecution, these people did not give up – they survived the horror and remained alive. Fortunate in their misfortune, they found the reserves within themselves not only to physically survive, but to emerge without hatred in their hearts.

1.

A T FIRST THERE was a buzzing sound from the speakers at the railway station, then came the rasping voice of the station manager from the semidarkness of the timber-frame construction:

"The Prague–Bucharest fast train scheduled to arrive in Khust at three fifteen will be delayed by ten minutes."

It was Thursday afternoon in this small town in the Carpathian Mountains in the southeastern part of Europe. It was summer 1938; the sun was shining strongly out of a bright blue sky, and the cool winds of the evening had not yet blown over the land, making it hard to bear the heat. At this railway station in Khust, one could witness a scene common to all stations.

Parting.

People coming together, standing around in tight clusters, exchanging last warnings, wishes and greetings, kisses and words of hope. Abandoned pieces of luggage lying around. Embraces, restlessness, confusion and tears…

Yet this parting scene differed from the many others taking place all the time all over the world. The *Halutzim*, the young men and women who were parting from their entire families, had packed for a hard task and a long trip, a journey to their old-new land. They didn't know at this separation what the future was holding in store for them. Hope and confidence showed on the young faces, anguish and fear on the wrinkled faces of the old. The sounds of sobbing grew more intense as the time of the arrival of the awaited train approached. Again and again the old ones called out the names of the *Halutzim* and caressed the young heated faces on which now, minutes before the arrival of the train, some signs of nervousness could be seen.

These young people, raised by their families in poverty and love, were trained to rebuild the Promised Land. They would help cultivate the land, establish the civilization and make space for a new homeland for the Jewish nation, whose people had been dispersed all over the world for centuries.

*

David Gutmann and his wife were waiting at the Khust railway station that afternoon. They had come to meet a friend who was arriving on the same train on which the *Halutzim* were leaving.

The couple knew almost all of the young men and women, for David's father ran the *Hachshara*, the experimental Kibbutz, outside the town, where the young people had been trained. Now David and Sara took advantage of the delay to say good-bye to some of the people.

Suddenly someone from the group called out, "Look, the train is coming!"

For a second everybody was silent; only the loud quarrelsome chirping of birds and reverberating sounds of work from the nearby forge could be heard. Then the din of voices started again. Everybody edged nearer to the railway track in order to better see and personally affirm the arrival of the train. And indeed there was a cloud of steam in the distance, growing bigger and bigger and quickly approaching, coming nearer.

There came the stamping and roaring black iron monster, the wailing siren, the whistling valves and the squealing brakes, until it passed the crowd and the green passenger cars stopped at the ramp level.

Voices full of distress could be heard once again, as the moment of parting had finally arrived.

Quick strong embraces, sounds of mothers crying and elders' moans could be heard, as the first *Halutzim* began climbing into the cars and the clerk on duty announced the arrival of the train and its impending departure in a scratchy voice through the metal loudspeaker.

Doors clacked, luggage was loaded into the cars, windows were lowered, handkerchiefs, which were supposed to wipe away tears, were waved, last calls were made and then the last touching of hands, which were stretched out through the open windows to the people remaining behind.

The whistle of the clerk on duty could hardly be heard, but the passengers felt the train begin to move slowly and jerkily, leaving the platform of Khust with creaking noises and wrapped in big steam clouds. It soon disappeared from the onlookers entirely. But even so, the people remaining behind kept waving to the *Halutzim* for a long time.

*

From the last car of the train, the only passenger alighted. Until the train departed, he stood unnoticed near some piles of luggage, observing the scene at the station.

Now Bernhard Rosen walked slowly over to the station house. He held a big brown traveling bag in his right hand, and over his left arm he had draped a light summer coat. He smiled a little tiredly when he discovered his friend David.

"Bernhard, how wonderful to see you again!" David and his wife Sara hurried over to his friend.

"David, how are you? And this must be your wife, Sara?" Bernhard shook hands warmly with both.

"How was your trip, Bernhard? Probably quite interesting but rather strenuous, wasn't it? We have already prepared a room for you. You will surely recover at our place." said Sara with a smile.

"Thank you very much. But if it is all right with you, I would rather stay with your father at the farm, David. Would this be possible? Please don't be disappointed. I am so thrilled to get acquainted with the Kibbutz. You don't mind, do you?" asked Bernhard.

"Of course not," replied David, and took Bernhard's traveling bag. They left the station and climbed onto a waiting carriage, which took them straight to David's parents' home outside the town. They talked excitedly on the way and did not notice how quickly the time passed.

Upon their arrival at the farm, Sara went ahead to the residential house. David and Bernhard went looking for David's father, Hershel. They found him in the cowshed where he was helping with the birth of a little calf.

Hershel was a tall slim man with friendly eyes, around fifty-five years of age, a man prepared to help vigorously anywhere a helping hand was needed.

"Shalom Papa," said David, "I bring you my old friend and study colleague Bernhard Rosen from Berlin. He has come here to rest after a long stubborn cold, and would like to stay at your place outside the town, rather than with us. You will find in him a good partner for talking about your most beloved subject, 'Eretz Israel'!"

"Welcome to our Kibbutz, my dear Bernhard," said Hershel. "Please feel at home here with us. Ah, let's speak informally right away, as we Jews are one big family. Perhaps I'll yet see with my own eyes the rebirth of our old homeland Israel! For that purpose I raise the young here. They are our hope and future!" Heatedly he went on: "If only the Arabs, who are actually Semites like we are, didn't attack the Jewish settlements all the time!" Hershel looked at Bernhard excitedly.

"If only they would leave us in peace! They have more land than they could ever cultivate!"

Hershel wiped his eyes and looked at Bernhard with a sigh. Full of thoughts, he turned, reached for a bundle of straw and went on rubbing the calf dry.

"Until later then, Papa," called David, and with a smile pulled Bernhard away from the cowshed. "One cannot talk to him now, Bernhard. Now he is, in his thoughts, in *Eretz Israel* with the Jewish settlers. Believe me, if my father were ten years younger, he would emigrate to *Eretz Israel* right away!"

"So why didn't he go years ago?" asked Bernhard as they strolled over to the residential house.

"My grandfather wouldn't allow it! His whole life, he waited for the Messiah. For him, what the Zionists did in Israel was a sacrilege. My father showed consideration for the old man and remained here, but even while his father was alive, he began to prepare the farm for a *Hachshara* in order to train young people for Israel. Look, there are my mother and Sara!" David pointed to a group of trees in front of the main house. Bernhard looked in that direction and saw a dainty slim woman in her mid years standing beside Sara.

"Really, but she still looks very young!" said an astonished Bernhard.

"Yes, she is quite a few years younger than my father," replied David proudly. "She is very efficient. She not only takes care of all the housework, but also looks after all the financial matters of the farm; she collects the bills and pays the wages, and even though she is so occupied, she still has time for a friendly word for each person. You will surely like her, Bernhard. Hello, Mama, may I present...."

"I know, you flatterer!" answered David's mother, Hanna, smilingly and approached Bernhard. "Welcome, dear Bernhard. Sara has already told me everything!" While she was shaking his hand warmly, he noticed the many silver strands that ran through her full dark hair. Yet instead of making her look older, it gave her a certain dignity. The dimples in her cheeks and the fine lines around the corners of her eyes revealed that she enjoyed laughing. This immediately made Bernhard like her.

"Come, Bernhard!" called Hanna as she led him into the house. "I am going to show you your room. Your luggage has already been taken up there. You must be awfully tired after this long journey, right?"

"Thank you," smiled Bernhard. In his room, he refreshed himself a little and went down again to join the others.

They all drank some coffee and then Bernhard was shown around the house. The most fascinating part for Bernhard was the richly filled library. He knew at once that in the days to come he would be spending many hours in this room. Here he could really relax.

*

Bernhard spent the next morning becoming acquainted with Hershel's Kibbutz, of which he was very proud.

It was a Friday, and in the evening began the Sabbath, which was prepared in a special festive way in honor of the guest from Berlin. David and Sara came, and most of the *Halutzim* were also present, the girls dressed in blue skirts and white blouses, the boys in trousers and shirts, also in blue and white.

"*Haverim!*" called David. "Come and greet my old friend Bernhard Rosen from Berlin!"

The lively group came from every part of the room to surround and greet Bernhard. Each one wanted to speak a few words with him: "*Shalom Bernhard!*"

"How do you like it here, in our Kibbutz?"

"Have you already visited in Khust?"

"How long are you going to stay here for?"

"Will you also go to Israel?"

Bernhard's head was whirling from all these questions, and he did not know which ones to answer first. David's mother saved him from his embarrassment.

"Doesn't anybody want to help me?" she called, and looked at the cheerful group reproachfully.

"Yes! Immediately!" were the answers. One of the girls sat down at the piano and started playing Jewish songs while the others set the tables festively. Food and beverages were brought in and everybody sat down for dinner. The Sabbath began with Hershel Gutmann blessing the wine and breaking the bread, and then everybody began to eat the meal. Later in the evening some musicians played dance music. Sara came over to Bernhard and David. "Now you two are sitting together again and talking and talking!" she scolded them. "And you have so much time for all that later! Bernhard will be staying here for quite a while, and you will have ample time to speak of old memories. Don't you want to dance at all?" she said sulkily to David.

"There you have it, Bernhard!" sighed David, "how marvelous were the old bachelor days in Berlin when one could talk undisturbed with one's friends!" At the same time he winked at Bernhard with a smile.

"Ho! That's it!" scolded Sara indignantly and set her hands on her hips. David got up and took her in his arms.

"I am sorry, darling!" David kissed Sara on the tip of her nose. "You know, when one begins to plunge into old memories…!"

"All right," she waved him off generously, "but the matter regarding the bachelor days in Berlin – that you will have to explain to me more specifically!"

"What?" asked David, grinning and pulled her strongly against his body. "Right now, or later…?"

Sara's cheeks went red; she left her husband's arms in embarrassment. Returning to Bernhard, she introduced him to the pretty girl who had been playing the piano earlier. "Bernhard, this is Rachel."

"Pleased to meet you, Rachel." Bernhard stood up. "Shall we dance?"

"Yes!" Rachel took hold of Bernhard's hand, ready to follow him to the dance floor.

David detained her. "Take care, Bernhard," he joked, "not to step on her feet! Her intended is standing over there and looking at you!"

"Is your fiancé so jealous?" asked Bernhard, astonished, but Rachel reassured him: "Don't fret, we are not even engaged! Yankel's father, Leib Goldenbaum, doesn't want any liberal Zionist like me for his daughter-in-law. He is, like David's grandfather, a real old *Hassid*!" They danced silently; then Bernhard asked: "And Yankel? What does he say to that? If he loves you, he can go away with you!"

"Oh, he would do that without delay, but he cannot leave! His father is old and Yankel has many younger brothers and sisters, for whom he feels responsible. It is a sad story! But let him tell it to you himself."

After the dance, Rachel introduced her Yankel to the guest from Berlin. They were around the same age and hit it off immediately. Bernhard told him about Berlin and his family, and then they spoke about Yankel's problem.

"Should I perhaps speak to your father, Yankel?"

Bernhard did not expect much out of it, but at least he wanted to try and help Yankel and Rachel.

"If you really want to try, I would appreciate it," said Yankel. "Come and visit me any day next week if you have enough time for it. Then you can meet my wonderful mother, my brothers and sisters and my stubborn old father."

Yankel gave Bernhard directions to his parents' house and finished with these words: "You can't miss it! Every child can show you the way!"

"Bernhard!" Sara came over with a peeved look on her face. "David is again occupied in an endless discussion! Come and dance with me!" Bernhard was delighted to be pulled away to the dance floor by the pretty woman.

"But I must say, I'm awfully tired," he confessed. "I would have said good-night to you shortly, anyway."

"The journey must have tired you," said Sara, while she led Bernhard to the dance floor. "I was wondering how you've managed to stay awake so long! Yesterday you had the long trip on the train and then today a whole program of sightseeing on the farm and the Sabbath festivities in the evening. I certainly would have been worn out hours ago!"

"How could I have gone to bed, without having had at least one dance with you?" Bernhard flattered her. Sara laughed. They danced that dance to the end, and then Bernhard went up to his room.

*

The next morning, after a long stroll, Bernhard visited the library. Among the shelves of books, he found Goethe's *Faust* and became absorbed by it.

Until then he had never understood *Faust* as well as he felt he did that morning, in that small Slovakian town of Khust, and above all, Goethe's warning not to deal with the devil. It seemed to him that this warning was being ignored by Goethe's own people. If the poets of humanism could rise again, they would probably be suffering inside some concentration camp. But the admonishers of the past remained only in the consciousness of a small minority – a minority which was being eliminated by force. The ignorant masses were being manipulated with the help of a hypocritical cultural propaganda in such a way that the humanists, who certainly condemned any tyranny, were being celebrated as the "Forerunners" of the "National Revolution of 1933!"

Stirred by these thoughts, Bernhard put aside *Faust* and went out into the fresh air. From the direction of the Tisza River, flowing through the foothills of the Carpathian Mountains, there blew a cool summer wind over the fields on which the midday sun was shining that brought with it the fresh smell of hay over the land. Bernhard felt himself light as a feather, a feeling he had not felt for a long time! Only his tie and collar seemed to stifle him. So he removed these remnants of city life with a fierce movement in order to be able to breathe freely. With that movement, a newspaper that he had bought in Prague fell out of the pocket of his jacket. Immediately a big headline, underlined in red, caught his attention: "New threats of Hitler against Czechoslovakia!"

'Is there going to be a war?' Bernhard asked himself thoughtfully. Shaking his head, he put the newspaper back into his pocket and let his eyes roam over the peaceful countryside. It seemed unreal to him that perhaps in a short while this peace would be shattered by war.

*

On this Sunday morning, the surroundings of the small town of Khust looked, to Bernhard, like the Garden of Eden. He was on his way into town to visit Yankel and his family. The peasants were singing during the bountiful harvest and they seemed to be rather happy with the abundant presents from nature. Everybody was moving about merrily. Even the colorful songbirds joined the chorus that rose up as if to ward off the dark clouds arriving from the northwest.

At first glance, Khust was like any other small town. Narrow streets and bumpy lanes on which oxcarts and horse-drawn carts and carriages ambled along; houses full of life surrounded by vegetable and fruit gardens in which children, poultry and goats romped about in a colorful muddle; an idyll that could be found anywhere in the southeast of Europe.

Only someone living longer in Khust could feel the special rhythm of this small town, a place where, over hundreds of years, different groups of people had lived peacefully together. Hungarians, Ruthenes, Jews, Rumanians and Czechs lived there in harmony with the Swabian peasants and skilled manual workers who had immigrated from the south of Germany.

A peaceful, cheerful and seemingly carefree atmosphere predominated in Khust – just the mood in which a big city dweller could recover spiritually and physically.

Bernhard felt this as he walked through the old alleys looking for the Goldenbaums' house. In a short while he found it in a lively street not far from the railway station, just as Yankel had described it. Over the door to the shop there hung a small nameplate, declaring in old-fashioned golden letters: "Leib Goldenbaum, Food and Groceries."

Bernhard entered the garden and passed through beds of dazzling red and yellow asters and dahlias into the backyard, where the noise of a lively group of hens and geese, scurrying all over, competed with the shouting of some children rollicking around a dog's kennel. In the middle of this jolly muddle, the white shaggy mongrel lay like a resting pole and did not let anything disturb his peace.

Entering the house through the back door, Bernhard right away met "Mother Golda," the spirit of the house. He was not sure if that was her real name or if they just named her thus, because as the mother and personified living center of the Goldenbaum family she had a heart of gold.

Yankel had told him that she spent most of the day in the shop, sitting amongst boxes, sacks full of sugar, salt and flour, baskets filled with eggs and cardboard boxes with chocolates, everything piled up to the ceiling. No. She was not just sitting there, she was sitting enthroned like a mild queen, smiling graciously, and even though she was well over forty years of age, still looking beautiful, with her imposing figure and her thick black hair.

Yes, it was hard to believe that this woman, who moved about from early in the morning until late at night with such youthful agility, was really the mother of eight children. The eldest was the already adult Yakob –

Yankel – and the youngest was a chubby creature named Miriam, who was caught out by Bernhard, sitting in a dark corner of the hall picking her nose, lost in thought; good that Mother Golda did not catch her doing that! In spite of so many responsibilities Mother Golda reigned over her group of children with a soft smile and with wise instructions, and only in very extreme cases with a friendly slap on their behinds.

"*Shalom*! Do you want to buy anything? The shop is in the front, just straight ahead at the end of the corridor," Mother Golda greeted Bernhard in a friendly way.

"No, I don't want to buy anything. I came to visit Yankel. My name is Bernhard Rosen." Bernhard bowed to her.

"Ah, you are the gentleman from Berlin who is a guest at the Gutmanns, am I right? Yankel already told us about you. Please come with me, I shall lead you to him! Yankel, here is Mister Rosen from Berlin."

She continued, "You have to excuse me, I have to get back to the shop. But you are staying for coffee, aren't you? Then we shall have some time to chat."

"Yes, with pleasure," replied Bernhard, and turned to greet Yankel.

"*Shalom* Yankel, how are you?"

"Fine, thank you. So you have fulfilled your promise and come to talk with my father?"

"Of course! I keep my promises!"

Yankel called his brothers and sisters to come in, and the time went by quickly and merrily, with laughter and jokes.

Then, when the family gathered and sat down for coffee around the long table, the real head of the Goldenbaums, old Leib Goldenbaum, arrived. He was a man who had grown old before his time and looked extremely aged, with his white wisps of hair, the long thin temple locks, which he wore in the *Hassidic* way, and his long gray beard. He looked like a rabbi from the old Jewish past, and yet at the same time, because of the big black cap on the back of his head and his yellowish sunken cheeks, like an ascetic priest. This appearance was deceptive, though; he was not a great speaker. But every word that he did speak was well thought out and showed his deep religious conviction.

"All my ancestors, as far as I know, were deeply religious Jews! They read the Holy Scriptures all their lives and waited for the arrival of the Messiah sent by God!" the old man told them during the conversation.

"Did your family always have a shop here?" asked Bernhard, in order to change the subject for the time being, but the old man could not be moved away from this theme.

"No! My wife's family had the shop. My father and all those before him devoted all their lives to the study of the Torah, as I do myself. Only my son Yankel wants to break the family tradition!" said the old Goldenbaum excitedly. "He doesn't believe in the Messiah any more! He, together with some other infidels, wants to build a new Israel in Palestine! But I shall not allow him this! Never, never, never!"

The liberal-thinking Bernhard could understand the old tradition-ally-minded thinking man, but he nevertheless wanted to try and defend Yankel's and his own point of view. "See here, Leib Goldenbaum. Don't condemn your son, only because he represents the opinion of the new era! The majority of the Jews have realized meanwhile that times have changed, and that it is impossible to live in this modern fast moving world strictly by the rules of our ancestors. And if we go on and just sit back passively, we are going to be a nation scattered by the four winds forever! But we do have a homeland, where we can purchase the land and soil to rebuild the old Israel! A land in which we all, the whole Jewish people, can find a home and shelter and from where nobody can drive us out any more! And this is the reason why we liberals don't want to just sit back without doing anything and wait for the Messiah, but to take the initiative and…"

Bernhard could not go on, because Leib Goldenbaum suddenly collapsed. From the excitement over Bernhard's fiery speech, he suffered a sudden seizure.

"Father, *Tatte!*" cried the children and surrounded the old man in order to help him. Golda jumped up frightened and ran to bring his cardiac medicine drops. She gave Bernhard and Yankel a sign to leave the sick man and let him rest. "You had better go to your room for a while, Yankel, so that your father doesn't see you right away upon coming round!"

"I am very sorry, Mrs. Goldenbaum," said Bernhard, distressed, "I shouldn't have gotten so worked up. I should have been more considerate of your husband's poor health!"

"You are not to blame, dear Bernhard. Leib often has attacks such as this one. You only wanted to defend Yankel. Oh, the poor boy, he is suffering a lot from his stern father!" Mrs. Goldenbaum shook Bernhard's hand and quickly went away.

Yankel and Bernhard left the house, for Bernhard saw that his mission had failed and he wanted to leave. Yankel wanted to accompany him, so they made their way to the Gutmanns' farm together.

Yankel said: "Now you can surely imagine, Bernhard, how much my work at the Kibbutz annoys and infuriates him. Mostly I don't tell him that I go there at all. Everything we do there is a sin in his eyes. More than anything, he dislikes the fact that young men and women work together at the Kibbutz, and even play music and dance together! If only you knew," Yankel went on, "how sorry I am, not to be able to see things my father's way! Oh, if only he wasn't so ill, Rachel and I would have been in *Eretz Israel* for a long time by now!"

"If only I could help you," said Bernhard, depressed.

Suddenly they heard the sound of horses' clopping and from behind, there came a horse and cart. Up in the front sat a muscular tanned fellow, humming a little song to himself. He seemed thoroughly lost in thought, as he did not take notice of the two men.

"Hey, Beryl! Do you want to earn some Korunas? Come and take us with you!" called out Yankel to him.

The young man pulled the reins, stopped the two small, strong horses and laughed. "Today I was lucky!" he called. "I have just earned a full hundred Korunas at the market, by helping some farmers with their work!" He pulled a note of one hundred Korunas out of his pocket and waved it triumphantly in the air above his head. "Nu, Yankel, where to?" he asked, after putting his money back carefully into the pocket of his jacket.

"To the Gutmann family, outside the city."

"Oh," he remarked, and looked Bernhard over thoroughly. "So this must be the gentleman from Berlin? A 'Zionist' too, probably! Well, it's all the same to me who I earn the money from," he finally said. "Up you go!"

"Bernhard is not a comrade of yours, I'm afraid," answered Yankel, while they climbed onto the cart. He turned to Bernhard and went on: "Beryl wanted to explain to everybody his ideas of communism and fell in love with a Christian Swabian young girl."

"Well, when love strikes…!" nodded Bernhard, with full understanding.

"But her parents and brothers were against it and beat him up so severely that he almost became a cripple! They threatened to kill him if he ever went near the girl again!"

"That's hard," replied Bernhard. "Actually, Beryl why are you a communist?"

"Because communism condemns the exploitation of people and will give us, the Jews, equal rights!" replied Beryl, rather unwillingly.

"But with this you declare yourself to be a member of the Jewish community, don't you?"

"Of course I am a Jew, but not a religious one."

"Then, Beryl, I want to give you some good advice: Come with us to Israel and establish the communist party there, if it doesn't exist by now! There you may be a Jew and a communist. Here in the Diaspora, the party members will never accept you with equal rights!"

Beryl waved this off: "I am staying where I am. And you, Yankel, mind your own business! And I want to say something to you. I really loved Christel, and we would have been a happy couple a long time ago, if only there hadn't been any Henleins who were enticed by the Nazis, and who are now spreading around anti-Jewish inciting leaflets, here among the Swabians! And this, while we all lived together harmoniously as neighbors!"

Almost threateningly, he went on: "But the Reds will certainly beat the anti-Semitism out of the stupid brains of the Nazi followers and the Henleins!"

Beryl spoke so loudly, as if he himself was not so sure of his words and as if he had to underline them by the power of his own voice. After a while he asked Bernhard: "You must be fleeing from the Nazis?"

"No, surely somebody told you that I am here at the Gutmanns to recover."

Beryl shook his head, not understanding, and thought: 'A German Jew, who in this critical time just goes for a holiday! He must have absolutely no idea about politics!'

Indeed such a man could not be understood by Beryl, the manual worker, who in his free time read political papers and who eagerly studied Marx, Engels and Lenin! He could hardly hide his agitation as he stopped his horses in front of his Aunt Gittel's house.

"So," he said dryly, "it is not so far from here to the Gutmanns. You can walk the rest of the way on foot!"

"Good," said Bernhard, "here, this is for you." He wanted to give Beryl a twenty-Korunas-note, but Beryl waved him off. "No, from you I don't take money!" he said loudly and went with big steps towards his aunt's house.

"Come," said Yankel, "let's give the money to his Aunt Gittel. She needs it more than many others." But Aunt Gittel also did not want to accept money from the German-Jewish capitalist and Zionist. Nevertheless, she invited the guests in and chatted with them. She told them about some periods of her life, and more than anything she talked about her late husband, Moishe Kahan. "He was such a good man, my Moishe. He left me too early in life! Without him I manage pitifully. Beryl is such a good boy and he takes care of me as if he were my own son, but I feel so lost without my Moishe…"

While the old woman spoke, Bernhard looked around furtively at the small neglected house and the poor furniture. The bed of the late Moishe Kahan seemed to not have been used since the time of his death. But Gittel Kahan did not live only in the past. She was very interested in all that happened in the world and in politics. As Bernhard tuned back into the conversation, she was just predicting the communists' victory over the whole world.

*

Arriving at the Kibbutz at last, Yankel was told that he and Rachel would take part in the next *Aliya*, which was set to leave a few weeks later on its way to Israel. He parted from Bernhard excitedly and hurried to look for Rachel in order to tell her the great news immediately.

"Rachel, darling, we are going to Israel!" Yankel grabbed Rachel round her waist and whirled her around in a circle. "Just imagine, in a few weeks' time both of us, you and me, are going to be in Israel!" Yankel pulled her to him and kissed her passionately.

Rachel laughed and cried at the same time and could not believe that she would be so soon joined with her Yankel, until the end of time. She did not say anything; she just leaned on Yankel's shoulder, crying. But suddenly Yankel freed himself from her arms and said quietly: "No, I cannot! I have to stay here. There is no other way. My family needs me! How should my mother cope with everything alone, educating my brothers and sisters, the household and the shop…! That is too much for her, and she doesn't get any help from my ailing father. He lives in a different world and clings with all his soul's strength to the promise of the Messiah. Even the ominous messages of disaster of the last years, the threats of Hitler and his thugs, all this cannot frighten him! 'God will protect us and will destroy our enemies, the Nazis!' Time and again he says to us these words in which he believes thoroughly!"

Yankel wiped his hand excitedly over his forehead and went on: "Can I allow myself to let my parents and brothers and sisters down? Even if I cannot help them in their misery, I would act irresponsibly to leave them to fend for themselves in these unsure and critical times!" Yankel sighed.

"But I would be glad to know that at least you are safe. Please, Rachel, you go ahead alone, all right?"

"No, never!" said Rachel fiercely. "No, Yankel. We both go together, or we stay here and bear together what God has burdened us with!"

Silently they went on their way to Khust. They did not feel the chill of the dew under their feet, but when they began to see the first houses of the city they quickened their steps without noticing. It seemed as if they wanted to leave the darkness, as if the warm gleam of the lights could somehow brighten their gloomy thoughts and uncertain future!

At last, walking through the deserted streets, they arrived at the house where Rachel lived with her family. Yankel drew her into his arms. Still they did not speak a word; only Rachel's sobbing could be heard from time to time. They stood some time in silence under the tall old ash tree in front of the house, consoling one another by the nearness of their bodies, until they heard the click of a window being shut. Startled, Rachel freed herself from Yankel's arms, gave him a farewell kiss and ran into the house. She ran breathlessly and with her face drenched in tears into her mother's room.

"Mama, Mama!" she sobbed and threw herself upon the bed, directly into her mother's arms, who started upon seeing her joyful and self-confident daughter burst into the room with a tearstained face.

"Child, what is it? What happened to you?" But as much as she tried, she could not get a word out of Rachel. She hugged her daughter tenderly and caressed her to calm her down. Rachel's tears stopped, she calmed down and gradually fell asleep, nestled entirely against her mother, like she had done as a little girl when some beautiful experience had excited her or when she had felt threatened by something.

Meanwhile, Yankel walked sadly back home. Suddenly he heard steps behind him. He turned around startled, but calmed down when he recognized his friend Haim, the son of the preacher Samuel.

"Hey, Haim!" he called out to him, "What are you doing in the street so late at night? You must have gone to your bride's house, am I right?"

"As for my 'bride'!" said Haim, and uttered a sigh. "You do remember that two weeks ago I went to Feigele's father, Mordechai, and asked for the hand of his daughter, don't you? The old *Hassid* threw me out, without listening to me at all! Then he forbade his daughter to speak with me. Nevertheless we met, of course, and today Feigele tried once again to persuade her father to allow our marriage and *Aliya* to Israel. And do you know what he said? He became hopping mad and screamed at Feigele: 'I prefer beating you to death than giving you away as a wife to this bum Zionist!'"

"Oh, oh," said Yankel, "then you are in the same situation as I am! With you it is the father of your bride, and with me it is my own father who stands in the way of my life's happiness. Tell me, Haim, what shall we do?"

"I don't know either, Yankel," answered Haim sadly, "we can only wait and hope that the future will have more consideration in store for us than the present! Good-night, Yankel!"

"So be it! Good-night, Haim!"

The friends separated and each one went on his way.

*

That evening Bernhard talked with Hershel for a long time.

"You know, Bernhard, for you this place looks like the Garden of Eden, as if we don't have any worries and live untouched by the political events in the world. But this is only partially true."

"What do you mean by this, Hershel?"

"You see, time does not stand still in our corner either. Sure, the citizens of Khust are working, some hard, others less, and in spite of different opinions they get along quite well and many are more or less satisfied with their lives. But there are always some fights going on among the various ethnic groups. The Ruthenes want to establish a sovereign Ruthenian state, the 'Carpatho-Ukraina'; the Hungarians strive for a connection to their motherland Hungary; the Wallachs for a connection to Rumania. Most of the ethnic Swabians are Nazis due to the propaganda of the Henleins, and they incite the other ethnic groups against the Jews and feel themselves the lords of the future."

"And what is the opinion of the Jews in this matter?" asked Bernhard, interested.

Hershel sighed and smoked his pipe thoughtfully.

"Well, Bernhard," he continued after a while and blew a big blue cloud of smoke into the air, "what opinion could we present here in this place where we are only tolerated, which is actually the case everywhere! We, the Jewish people, have really only one wish: to live in peace with the other people. As long as the Czechoslovakian state which is divided into so many minorities can hold on, we are still living as free citizens in a free land! But I say to you, Bernhard, this will not go on for long! If only a small part of Hitler's threats come true, then we shall all have to fear for our necks!"

Worried, Hershel brushed off the ash of his cigarette and drank some wine.

"Yes," said Bernhard, full of thoughts, "I can imagine this well!"

Lately, he had been having some strange presentiments, but he did not want to speak about them to anybody. He was sure that nobody would understand him. So, each time he pushed aside his thoughts and forced himself to be occupied with some different matters.

*

In these late summer days, Bernhard spent many hours in the library and took long walks in the beautiful countryside. Sometimes David came and accompanied him.

Bernhard also spent many hours with the *Halutzim*; one day he even helped with the apple harvest. Of course, this was an unusual occupation for him and that evening he fell onto his bed half dead. That night Bernhard slept through for the first time, deeply and dreamlessly, until the morning. Other nights, he lay awake for hours, thinking and drawing his future in the darkest colors.

One day, a letter arrived from Berlin in which his wife dropped some odd hints and asked him to return home as soon as possible. Bernhard did not hesitate and prepared himself at once for the journey home. Hershel and Hanna would have liked him to stay and be with them for a longer time. But they understood that he was worried about his family. So they called together all the friends and arranged a farewell party for Bernhard. There was a strange mood at this party, because they were all weighed down by the uncertainty of the future. They laughed and cried at the same time and played some music and danced. Bernhard caught some pitying looks from the *Halutzim* and he thought with a heavy heart: 'Who knows what is waiting for me at home…?' Nevertheless, they drank together "*Lehaim*" and said upon parting: "See you again in Israel!"

After all the guests had left, Bernhard sat for a while together with Hershel and Hanna before going up to his room.

"We are so sorry, Bernhard, that you cannot stay here any longer," said Hershel. "I have enjoyed sitting with you and having a comfortable evening, playing some chess or just chatting for a while."

"Yes, I am sad too, Bernhard! I have taken you into my heart like a second son." Hanna patted Bernhard's hand. "It was delightful to have in the house a grown-up son again whom I could spoil like a mother!"

"I like it here very much too and would love to stay on, but I cannot! I just have to get back to my wife and the children! Who knows what is going on there!"

Bernhard sighed worriedly.

*

The next morning, Bernhard again stood together with David and Sara on the platform of the small railway station of Khust. This time there were almost no passengers to be seen, no crowd who would wave upon parting, and this time the train was also on time.

"Farewell, David, farewell, Sara! Thank you so much for everything. I hope that you will come to Berlin soon!"

"So long, Bernhard! Have a nice journey! Please greet Lea and the children for us. We are going to visit you in Berlin soon!" called David and Sara to Bernhard as he boarded the train. But the three friends knew that it could be a long time until they met again. Nevertheless, each one of them tried to cheer the other up and not let a sad mood take hold of them. Bernhard stood in the corridor and leaned out of a window.

"Look in the compartment on your right side. There is a pretty young lady sitting near the window. Wouldn't she be a good travel companion for you?" asked David with an innocent smile. He tried to dispel Bernhard's worries.

As the three of them laughed, they missed the railway clerk's whistle; they only felt the sudden movement of the train.

Bernhard shook his friends' hands once more.

"Good-bye, see you again soon!" he called to them, and David and Sara waved farewell to him until the train disappeared in the distance.

2.

Bernhard settled himself into a compartment, his forced cheerfulness immediately fading away.

The train had already left Khust behind, and as it moved through the wide plain near the slopes of the Carpathian Mountains he brooded over Lea's words.

What did his wife mean in her letter as she wrote "...sultry weather in the air..."? He would know soon enough, as he was on his way to Berlin where Lea and the children were waiting for him.

He thought about how much he would like to follow the *Halutzim* and go with his family to Israel. But his parents considered themselves to be true Germans and were too connected to Germany in their hearts to even think about leaving. And, like Yankel, consideration of his parents held him back.

His father had left his wife and child behind in 1914 in order to go to the war and defend Germany. At the end of 1917 he came back, decorated with the iron cross, but without his right leg which he lost in the fight against the French.

Bernhard's father-in-law was killed in France right at the beginning of the invasion. The two children, Arnold and Lea, were too young to even remember him.

Bernhard thought back and his early youth appeared before his mind's eye again, like a movie.

They had met at the *Gymnasium*, the high school. It was love at first sight. They used to go on trips, Lea and he, to Potsdam, Grünau, to the Müggelturm and to Bad Schandau.

Then, on their trip to Switzerland, she had said: "Yes!"

"Mama, Mama! We are engaged!" he called home on the telephone.

"With whom?" asked his mother.

"With the most beautiful girl in the world!"

Now his mother knew: "With Leachen!"

"Yes, Mama! We are so happy and in everlasting love!"

"Then, your father and I wish you a *Mazel-Tov* from the bottom of our hearts! Come home soon so that we can celebrate together!"

Many relatives and friends attended their wedding, both Jewish and non-Jewish, all of whom regarded Germany as their homeland. Bernhard's father also invited a few friends from the war, each of whom brought a small present as a sign of their unforgotten friendship. They all, Jews and Christians, celebrated the wedding joyfully together until after midnight.

So how could Bernhard's parents believe that these friends could change to foes? After all, his father was a former soldier of war! This could surely never be forgotten!

Abruptly, Bernhard was disrupted from his thoughts as the train stopped. Bernhard looked out of the window and saw that they had already reached the German border.

Suddenly the door opened, and a young girl entered the compartment. Her eyes were slanted and this gave her face an exotic appearance. Bernhard was not sure if she was a European or an Asian.

"*Guten Tag!*" (Good day) said Bernhard, jumping up and helping the young lady to store her bags.

"*Danke schön!*" (Thank you) she answered with a friendly smile.

'She speaks German,' Bernhard thought, astonished.

They were just sitting down when the Czechoslovakian passport control officers entered the compartment. They stamped the passports without delay.

Then came the German officers. One of them turned to Bernhard and asked him: "Heil Hitler! Do you have something to declare for customs?"

"No," said Bernhard, and handed over his passport. After carefully looking at it, the officer returned the passport with the words: "Here, Israel! Your passport!"

Then he turned to the young lady. After checking her passport, he clicked his heels together and said:

"You come from Japan, young lady? You are in the second-class compartment, but you are entitled to travel in first class. Please come, I shall lead you there! You do not have to share a compartment with a Jew!"

"Thank you," answered the small Japanese lady politely, "but I would like to stay in my seat for the few hours left to Berlin."

The officer wanted to say something else, but he turned around outraged and left the compartment, followed by his colleague. A few minutes later he came back and told Bernhard brusquely to follow him with his luggage. He led him off the train to a customs officer, into whose ears he whispered something, and then he left.

"Come with me," whispered the customs officer to Bernhard and took him back to his compartment aboard the train, without searching in his luggage.

"Look," he told Bernhard, "the passport control officer is a dangerous Nazi! He has just told me to hand you over to the Gestapo for smuggling. But as an old officer who had served under the Kaiser, I am not going to participate in such nonsense!"

Bernhard thanked the old man, deeply moved, and the officer left the train quickly. When the train began to move Bernhard heaved a sigh of relief. He could not comprehend the whole thing yet, everything had just happened too quickly! Only now he understood how close he had been to an arrest. He began to tremble and belatedly he became absolutely dripping with cold sweat. He was ashamed in front of the young Japanese lady, but she looked at him in such a friendly and understanding way that he just had to smile back at her.

This incident roused Bernhard's consciousness brutally to the present situation in Germany. A foreign citizen was now given a higher standing and more freedom than a German Jew whose family was living in Germany, deeply rooted for generations.

'Dear God, what will this lead to?' brooded Bernhard. He could not think further about it and leaned back exhaustedly to relax a little.

He must have fallen asleep, because he woke up with a start when a group of young girls, members of the BDM (a German Hitler-youth organization for girls), stormed into the compartment and one of the girls tried, giggling, to sit on his lap. There were disappointed faces when he stood up and offered his seat politely to the girl. Then he went out of the compartment into the corridor.

The Japanese lady followed him and said: "My name is Yosui Sakai; my father is the Japanese Consul in Berlin and we have been living in Germany for a few years now." She stopped and, shaking her head, continued: "But I think that we are not going to stay much longer. If the Nazi regime is going to go on like this, there will surely be a war. And after seeing what happened today on the train, I think that you and your fellow Jews are going to have an even harder time!"

She looked at Bernhard with pity in her eyes and gave him a piece of paper.

"Here, take this card with my address on it. Come to me if you are in trouble and need help. I shall then do what I can!"

Bernhard could not find sufficient words to thank her. He pulled out his wallet, out of which he took a family picture, wrote his address on the back and passed it to the girl. Yosui looked at the picture attentively and asked him about each of the people in the picture.

"This here is my wife Lea, and she is holding our youngest offspring, our little daughter Judith. She is now six months old. And this is my son Daniel, four years old, that is my brother-in-law Arnold and here, as you can see, am I. Nobody can be mistaken about that."

While they were talking, the train was already reaching the outskirts of Berlin. The noise of the train reverberated back from the facades of the houses like hammer blows, as the train entered the densely populated area. A short while after that they reached their destination, the "Zoo" station.

Bernhard handed down her luggage onto the platform and parted warmly from his travel companion. He saw that two Japanese gentlemen had arrived for her welcome reception.

'Probably officers from the consulate', he thought to himself.

Then Yosui and her escorts departed and Bernhard could not see her anymore.

*

Bernhard let his eyes roam searchingly over the crowd and he spotted his wife Lea and his little son Daniel.

"Lea, Daniel!" he called, and hurried over to them.

"Papi, Papi," cried the little boy and tugged at the corner of his jacket.

Bernhard picked him up into his arms and greeted Lea with a long kiss. Then the three of them left the railway station and got into a taxi which took them to their apartment in Momsen Street.

"How good that you are here again," said Lea, her face beaming with joy, and she caressed his hands. At the railway station she had been so happy to see him again that she could not say a word, but only looked upon her husband again and again, silently.

"Yes, I am also happy to be with you again," smiled Bernhard and rubbed his nose on her cheek. He looked at Lea inquiringly. Signs of increasing fright and worry could be seen quite clearly on her face.

"What is the matter, dearest?" asked Bernhard. "You look so tired and weary!"

"No wonder! The situation of the Jews is getting worse from day to day. All the campaigns of incitement naturally affect our business. On top of that, the children were sick, and so I had to be a nurse in addition to the daily work at the shop!"

"My poor darling! Now, before anything else, you must take a rest and get stronger."

"How, with these losses in the business?" asked Lea, shaking her head.

"Nu, we shall see," Bernhard appeased her. "For today, let us first forget our troubles and celebrate our reunion, yes? Our troubles are not going to run away."

He caressed her hair lovingly.

"Let's have a pleasant evening today!" And in his thoughts he added: 'as long as we still can!'

Lea smiled and agreed to that.

*

The next morning Bernhard Rosen stood stunned in front of his shop. The shop windows and facade were smeared with anti-Jewish slogans, with words like: "People who buy here are traitors!" and: "Pictures will be taken of any person buying here!" and: "Out with the Jews!"

Bernhard's body trembled from top to bottom and he just wanted to leave, when a police officer arrived. He at once understood the situation and ordered intimidatingly:

"Come on, open your shop now! And then clean up here, or do you want me to arrest you?"

Bernhard had no choice but to open the shop.

The policeman had just left when the first shoppers entered and bought quickly. Some of them whispered to Bernhard that they had heard that shortly before Christmas all the Jewish shops were going to be closed down. Bernhard sighed.

"What is going to happen then?"

Originally, the firm "Rosen & Co." had had its own textile factory in the Vogtland and a branch in Berlin. By means of the anti-Jewish actions of the Nazis they had already lost the factory; only the shop in the Wilmersdorfer Street was still preserved. And this was also to be closed?

And only two years before, the old Rosen had handed over the management of the business to his son.

"Yes, Papa," said Bernhard silently into the empty shop before him, "so I shall probably be the last Rosen to manage the shop!"

*

That same day, just before closing time, a policeman entered the shop and asked Bernhard to come with him.

"Where to?" asked Bernhard, startled.

"You will find out, Mister Rosen! Don't make any difficulties!" answered the officer. "Here is the official order. Close the shop and follow me, but quickly, please!"

"Yes, but…"

"No but! I am not responsible for answering questions! Do you understand?"

"Yes," said Bernhard, giving up. He removed his smock and hung it up in the locker. Then he locked the cash-box, took his coat and followed the policeman, who had already gone out to the pavement.

He bolted the shop door carefully and turned around. The policeman began to walk and Bernhard followed him hesitantly. Desperately he asked himself what was going to happen to him.

The officer led Bernhard into a big schoolyard, where there were already about three hundred Jewish men and women standing in rows of four.

Soon there came a young police officer who stopped in front of the rows and read out loudly from a paper. The collected Jews were accused, in sarcastic words, of causing so-called unrest in Czechoslovakia. After this, names were read out, and those people whose names were called out had to answer "Yes," and their names were marked with a V.

After all this was finished, they were allowed to go home.

Bernhard sighed with relief. However, he felt as if something was stuck in his throat. He felt that something was wrong with what had occurred that day. The policeman's accusation was, of course, absurd. There must be some other reason behind it! But what…?

*

From then on there were daily roll calls in which, each time, new insults were read out to the Jews. Bernhard noticed that each day some twenty to thirty people were arrested by the Gestapo for absurd, obviously invented accusations. A few days after that, the unsuspecting surviving relatives would receive a small urn of ashes.

So, from call to call there were more and more Jews missing, people whose names were simply no longer read out by the counting officers. Bernhard was one of the lucky ones who were spared.

But among the victims were his uncle and his cousin Breslauer from the shop for ladies' dresses at the Hausvogteiplatz. How long would Bernhard still be spared?

This question weighed heavily upon his mind and overshadowed everything. Now, the Rosen family, like most of the other Jews, tried to emigrate from Germany.

Bernhard's father finally realized that his friends' attitude had changed. Even if they did not actually join the Nazi party, they clearly behaved in a more reserved manner to him; some of them even reacted definitely in a negative way upon being greeted by him in the street. Therefore, the old Rosen said he was now ready to emigrate with them to Israel, although he would never feel himself at home there during the remainder of his life.

But it was already too late. After the failed Evian Conference, in which the admission of Jews from Germany to the colonies abroad was discussed, England had stopped the sparse immigration of Jews to Palestine.

There were, in this muggy weather before the thunderstorm in September 1938, many people like Bernhard who asked themselves: "What is going to happen to us?"

The war psychosis, spread around by the Nazis, had caused the Prime

Ministers of England, France and Italy to go to München in October 1938, where they – believing they served the peace – gave their agreement to split up Czechoslovakia.

In those days it seemed as if time stood still for a moment, to give the people another chance to breathe, a hope of peace. But then the wheel of history began to turn around again, without mercy…!

Then came that night which would be entered into history as the "*Reichskristallnacht,*" Crystal Night. That night, in Berlin, incited mobs of people shattered windows, ravaged shops and workshops of Jewish fellow citizens and destroyed synagogues. The summoned Nazi mob looted mercilessly and bawled: "Jewish blood splashes from the knife, it's very good for our life!"

*

Bernhard Rosen was among the stricken businessmen who lost the whole basis of their livelihood.

Like all the other Jewish shop-owners whose shops were closed down by order of the Nazi regime, Bernhard had to give up his shop too. With his bare hands he had to clear away the broken glass pieces. On top of this, they were ordered to hand over all the leftover merchandise, which had not been looted, to Aryan businessmen for a ridiculously low price.

*

In addition to their extreme financial distress, a further family tragedy occurred. Lea's mother was stopped by young SS men and beaten up, during which she fell, her head hitting the edge of the pavement. Two days later she died in the Jewish hospital in Iranische Street, without ever regaining consciousness.

Almost daily, Jews were victims of such tragic occurrences, and then it was difficult to find ten Jewish men to go to the burial and say the *Kaddish* prayer. Many of them had already been abducted, and most of those who still remained in Germany had been assigned to forced labor.

Bernhard was able to gather enough men for the burial to be held traditionally. Friends and relatives went to the Jewish cemetery in Weissensee to pay their last respect to the deceased. Lea's tears accompanied her mother to the grave.

Later, they brought Bernhard's parents home. The rest of his relatives gathered in Bernhard's apartment in order to decide how they could help each other. The dreadful murder, of which Bernhard's mother-in-law was victim, shook up the last people of the family who were still in doubt. They all now wanted to leave Germany, but at the moment Lea's brother was the only one who was able to do so, as he did not have to take care of his mother anymore. So it was decided to first help Arnold with his emigration.

After a short while Bernhard found out that it was almost impossible to get the required documents for the emigration from the German authorities.

Realizing what a helpless situation they had fallen into, he suddenly remembered the small Japanese lady from the train, Yosui Sakai.

'If I have any luck, she is still in Berlin,' Bernhard said to himself. 'Anyway, I have to take this chance!'

And, as it turned out, indeed Yosui still lived in Berlin. She recognized Bernhard immediately and was willing to help him. A few weeks later she had not only arranged a passport for Arnold, but also a visa for the United States of America. Some good friends from Switzerland had helped her with it.

Now there was nothing to delay Arnold's departure. Some weeks later they received their first letter from the USA in which they read that he would try, with help from American relatives, to obtain immigration papers for Lea and Bernhard too. This news put them into an ecstasy of joy. They could hardly believe it. They were going to America!

But their joy was quickly dampened, as the situation of the Jews in Germany worsened more and more because of the threatening danger of war.

Lea wrote long letters to her brother Arnold, in which she always expressed her fear of an even darker future. And Bernhard went daily from one department to another to get the emigration papers – always in vain.

Yosui Sakai had already returned to Japan, the Jewish Relief Organization could not help him and the competent consulates did not show any goodwill.

To Bernhard, their situation seemed really hopeless now. But he did not want to accept this role of an enslaved, slandered man without rights of the lowest class. He decided to emigrate and it did not matter where to. The most important thing for him was that he and his family would be able to live as free people.

He felt bad, but he gradually lost contact with his parents, as they still lived in the past and clung to the foolish hope that the Kaiser would return to power and get rid of Hitler and all the Nazis.

Only Lea, his faithful life companion, stood strongly by his side as always and earned a living for them with her work. She had, in the meantime, become a competent seamstress. At first she only sewed for her household needs, but later she began making alterations for a manufacturer of dresses. Bernhard helped her with ironing and deliveries.

For the moment it looked as if Lea had accepted both their fates. She and Bernhard now had much more time for their children and for themselves. They went on short trips to Treptow and Grünau, which brought a little variety into their dark and strained everyday life. All the family members, except Lea, were blond and had blue eyes, so they did not stand out as Jews. With Lea, though, some people had their doubts because of her dark hair and dark eyes, and sometimes it happened that somebody called to them "*Rassenschänder*" (race disgracer). But this was seldom and it almost did not touch them.

They felt constantly that a much bigger danger surrounded them; therefore they enjoyed each day as a present. It could be the last day on which the little family was allowed to spend time together…!

Arnold had, meanwhile, not forgotten his sister and brother-in-law. With the help of relatives in America, he had paid a deposit of five thousand dollars in cash, and he wrote to them on 28 August 1939 that the tickets for their journey by ship were already on their way.

*

After this news Bernhard hastened to the police headquarters to try a last desperate effort and perhaps get the emigration papers, in spite of everything.

"Wait outside!" was the answer to his knock. Shortly after that, Bernhard was called to come in.

The man, an officer in SS uniform, sat at a big desk, his head bent deeply over his papers. Without looking up, he asked: "What do you want?"

"I want to get an emigration visa!" said Bernhard calmly. "I filed the application for it a few weeks ago."

"Name?"

"Bernhard Rosen."

The SS man looked up. "Ah, you are a Jew?"

He got up, came around the desk and stood before Bernhard with his legs apart, his hands on his hips.

"So you want to clear off, do you?"

"But it is demanded from us Jews to leave Germany!" answered Bernhard hesitantly.

The Gestapo man began to roar: "That would suit you, right? First to incite war and then to push off! No, no! You are going to perish here! Do you know where your application is? There, in the wastebasket!" He grinned maliciously. "And now shove off, Jewish pig, or I'm going to put you behind bars!"

Despairing, Bernhard left the headquarters and wandered aimlessly through the city. He stumbled over a stone and did not know if it was thrown at him or if it had been lying on the pavement before he had arrived there.

He staggered on through the streets, until he suddenly realized that he was walking within a group of marching reservists! All these young men held different kinds of personal bags in their hands; they marched in a determined manner, but there was neither singing nor jubilation.

Near them, a long train was just rolling by, loaded with war equipment and vehicles. Many soldiers sat in the open cars; they were singing, whistling and waving – they were going to the east! Bernhard freed himself from the group and went home, entirely lost in gloomy thoughts.

*

"Nu, did you achieve something?" asked Lea as Bernhard got home.

"Unfortunately not," answered Bernhard, distressed. "It makes one despair! The officer just threw me out. What are we going to do now? Without emigration papers we cannot get a visa!"

"Don't reproach yourself! You are not to blame!" Lea consoled him and stroked his hair. "You have done your utmost."

"And what is going to happen now?"

"We will find some solution," said Lea confidently, and kissed Bernhard affectionately.

*

Next day, Bernhard had to appear at the employment exchange for Jews in the Fontane-Promenade. There he was assigned to work, together with other companions in fate, at the Civil Engineering Company "Polens & Dedlow."

He had to buy himself a shovel and was from then on a Jewish forced laborer. There he was, a member of the gray depressed mass of people who had to render services for the front, for a state that was going to annihilate them entirely.

The majority of the Jewish employees, with the exception of some manual workers, were businessmen and intellectuals. The hard work, like carrying big iron tubes, was extremely hard for them. It was no wonder that there were some accidents every day. But nobody shirked from the hard manual work; even small, slight men did everything possible according to their strength.

At lunch hour, the Jewish workers sat separate from their Aryan colleagues, at a long temporary table made out of boards. They took out their thin and meager pieces of bread and ate them silently. Nobody felt like chatting.

Bernhard had a special relationship with Landau, who was a good colleague to everyone. One day, upon lifting a heavy iron tube, Landau suffered a sudden rupture.

"What is it, Landau? What happened to you?" called Bernhard as he stared anxiously at the man who was bent over in pain.

"Aaah, I don't know! I suddenly felt such a pain down here, in my groin…" sighed Landau.

"Come on, I'm supporting you!" said Bernhard, and accompanied him to the shed of the construction work manager.

"Go to the doctor, Landau," said the manager. "You have seriously injured yourself, as it seems. Can you go by yourself?"

"Yes, yes!" answered Landau with a pain-racked face and hobbled away. The next day, he returned to work, although he felt a severe pain with every movement and was almost incapable of working. His comrades tried to hush this up, but it did not help.

By the afternoon of that same day, the Gestapo came and took Landau away with them, and five days later his wife received an urn with his ashes…

This incident aroused deep indignation, not only among the Jewish workers, but also among their Aryan colleagues.

*

When one day the Gestapo appeared again and this time took Bernhard from his work, his coworkers were not less annoyed, and even the non-Jewish colleagues stopped their work and looked at him with pity in their eyes.

But Bernhard did not pay attention to them. Inside the police car, hemmed in on both sides by Gestapo men, he felt that his life had come to an end. He thought that he was going to disappear in the same way as Landau had. And then, what was going to happen to Lea and the children? Tormented, he slumped down into himself.

The car reached the police headquarters in Dirksen Street. The policemen led Bernhard to the second floor as if he were a serious criminal. They opened a concertina barrier, entered a long corridor and ordered Bernhard to sit down on a bench. Then they went from door to door.

'Probably they are searching for someone to whom they can hand over their booty'.

Suddenly he heard his wife's voice through an open door. She was crying.

He jumped up outraged and wanted to rush over to that room, but the uniformed men promptly pushed him back.

"Sit down there and don't move at all until you are called!" shouted both policemen, and pushed him back onto the bench. They did not take notice of his protests.

"Ach, stop the bawling!" said one of them sharply, a beefy bull-necked young officer with a fat red face and cold blue eyes.

"But what are they doing with my wife? Why is she crying? And where are the children?" called out Bernhard in despair. Fear and uncertainty tormented him.

"This you will find out in time!" answered one of the SS men.

A long agonizing hour went by until he was called and brought into a room, where there were already a few officers around a desk.

"You are Bernhard Rosen?"

"Yes!"

"You are guilty of high treason and incitement against the state! You had better confess now, it will be better for you!" said one of the men, an elder police officer, in a rasping voice.

Bernhard stared at him aghast and did not utter a word.

"Well?" asked the officer. "We don't have time to waste, are you going to talk soon?"

"But I haven't done anything! Everything you said is not true! To what am I to confess if I didn't do anything…?" stammered Bernhard, confused.

"So you deny having met a young man of Belgian nationality in your apartment fourteen days ago?"

"No, I don't deny that. He wanted to bring us over the Belgian border, and from there we would have been able to go to Palestine."

"Tell us more!" shouted the officer.

"There was nothing more," answered Bernhard.

"We are going to get the truth out of you, my friend!" called out one of the men from around the desk and winked at Bernhard's two guards.

The two beat Bernhard up and then they kicked him several times until he fell down, only half conscious. Then they lifted him up quickly.

Again he was asked: "Can you remember now?"

"But I have already told you that there was nothing more! This is the truth…!" groaned Bernhard, wiping away blood from his chapped lips with the back of his hand.

Again they went at him with punches and kicks. The questioning officer sat back with pleasure, comfortable in his seat, and asked Bernhard from time to time if he had had enough yet and was ready to confess. But Bernhard protested again and again, declaring his innocence, until, by a well-aimed blow, he fell unconscious.

"Away with him!"

They dragged him out of the room into the corridor. There he regained consciousness and swayed along between the two policemen. Suddenly he saw Lea sitting on the bench. He stumbled over to her. Lea jumped up.

"Bernhard, my love! What have they done to you?" She called out, sobbing, as he staggered to her with his smashed up face and broke down in her arms. But he was immediately grabbed brutally by the officers and dragged away.

For two weeks Bernhard and his wife were kept in separate bleak cells, and when they were at last released from custody without any explanation, Bernhard had contracted pneumonia because of the impossible conditions in the prison cell.

Although Lea could barely stand on her feet, she immediately brought the children home from the neighbors, who had been taking care of them during all that time, and took care of Bernhard devotedly. The fever went down gradually and Bernhard recuperated slowly. But his health remained weakened, which meant that he could not do any hard work.

With the help of a physician he knew, he eventually succeeded in finding work in a factory of textile manufacturers. It was called the "Jews-factory" because only Jews were employed there.

At this firm, Bernhard functioned as the "Man Friday." He worked as a laborer, fitter or messenger, depending on what was needed at the time. He did not let it disturb him that he worked for a weekly payment of only twenty Marks. Like all the Jews, he hoped to make himself indispensable and in this way be spared from being taken for deportation.

The boss, weighing more than a hundred kilograms, was friendly to everybody as long as he had sufficient alcohol to drink. But in a sober state he was nervous and capable of anything.

So it was quite often that Bernhard, who was afraid for his and his colleagues' security, went out and got some Schnapps for the thirsty man. Then the big fat man would reach out his hand and greedily take the bottle and empty it within a short time. After that he would once again be friendly and tolerant to his Jewish slave laborers.

*

Many Jews committed suicide out of desperation and fear of deportation. In the Jewish home for the elderly in Berlin at the Schönhauser Tor alone, all forty-four inmates hanged themselves before the Gestapo could take them away.

These suicides threatened to arouse too much attention publicly.

Therefore the Gestapo used a trick. The deported people were forced to send home postcards on which were printed in advance the words: "We are feeling fine!"

Bernhard also received such a postcard – as a last greeting from his parents...

3.

WHAT HAD HAPPENED in the meantime in Khust, to the friends in the Carpathes?

Here, too, the shop windows had been smashed and shrill voices, distorted by hate, had shouted "*Juden raus!*" (Out with the Jews).

Then, in the fateful days of March 1939, under the immense pressure of the German dictator Hitler, the Czechoslovakian republic broke into pieces; Böhmen and Mähren became protectorates of the German Reich. Slovakia declared her independence, and a new state came into being, "Carpatho-Ukraina." But a few days after that they were told: "Carpatho-Ukraina is going to be Hungarian!"

The people of Khust were thrown to and fro like a ball during this confusion. Within one week, the small town was part of three different states.

The inhabitants of Khust experienced a strange, tragic-comic drama. Half-naked, ragged mobs, armed with rifles, moved through the streets of Khust and shouted: "Out with the Czechs, out with the Jews! Kill them all!"

Stones flew through the windows and into the apartments of Czechs and Jews. Incited masses destroyed displays and looted shops; they were searching everywhere for alcoholic drinks in order to get drunk.

Woe to any Jew who fell into the hands of such a mob! They beat him with fists and sticks! They tore the caftans of the *Hassidim*, who were coming out of the synagogues, to shreds and cut off their long beards, laughing mockingly.

35

The Kibbutz outside the city was also not spared. They smashed the furniture and machines of the Jewish workers, crushed the seeds and chased the *Halutzim* through the fields.

At last, Hungarian soldiers came as the representatives of the authorities. But they were not exactly polite, and the Jews soon found out that they could not expect any protection from this side. On the contrary, before long the Jews could tell some frightening stories of searches in houses and arrests, the reason for which nobody really knew. Fear and helplessness prevailed among them, and only the *Hassidim* consoled themselves with the old promise of the people of Israel: "Do not be frightened! The Messiah will come and with him deliverance from all anguish and pain!"

*

But not all of them believed those words of consolation. Beryl, the Jewish communist, took his fate into his own hands. He did not trust the Hungarian gendarmes an inch and therefore he fled into the woods together with some friends.

It took them a year to make it over the border into the Soviet Union, where they met other refugees. Then, they were taken by the Russian authorities to Central Asia for their safety.

Beryl and his friends succeeded in finding work in Tashkent as employees of a big national transport enterprise. They also found lodgings with an Uzbek family.

Their landlord, a pious Muslim, had two wives and six children, four of them girls who still lived at home. Leila, the eldest, and Nathan, one of Beryl's comrades, soon started to like each other, and as they could hardly communicate with words, they let their feelings speak more and more for them.

Beryl and Levi did not approve of this, and so they separated from Nathan. They moved into the house of a Russian officer and rather quickly became friendly with both the officer and his wife. They spent most evenings together, playing cards.

One evening their landlord said: "Why do you have such ugly names? 'Beryl, Levi'! They sound so Jewish! But I don't like Jews. I hate them!"

Outraged, Beryl and Levi looked at each other and said: "But we are Jews."

"Ha, ha, ha," laughed their landlord. "That's a good joke! Two 'Jewish communists' are living in my house."

"This is no joke, comrade! We are really Jews."

"Ah, Jews or not Jews! What is the difference?" intervened his wife, as she did not like this dispute. "The comrades are decent workers and good people."

"No, I don't want to have Jews in my house!" raged the man and jumped up. "Out with you! Go and look for a new place to stay!" and with these words he showed Beryl and Levi the door.

The two of them left the room furiously.

As they reached their room, Levi said: "We should really report this to the party."

"Nonsense!" answered Beryl. "We should not impose ourselves on anybody. If he doesn't like us, we'll just leave."

The following day they moved to the rooms of a colleague from work. It was not as comfortable as their last accommodation, but they got along with their landlord and his little daughter.

Beryl and Levi were faring very well in Tashkent. They had work and accommodation and had even found friends.

However, their thoughts kept returning to their homeland, to their families, whom they had left behind, and to their old friends. They wrote letters back home but never received any replies. They began to think about their relatives and friends with growing worry.

4.

ONE DAY IN September 1941, hundreds of Jews from Khust were dragged out of their homes. Hungarian gendarmes pushed the confused and shocked people, beating them from behind with sticks, in the direction of the railway station and crammed them into the waiting freight wagons. No consideration was shown to children or old people or weak and sick ones.

Lamenting calls, outraged screams, cries for help and loud prayers filled the air. Powerless, the people had to let everything happen to them. The gendarmes called mockingly to the unfortunates:

"Be happy! You are being sent straight to the land of your ancestors, to Palestine!"

Of course this was pure irony, but among the desperate, frightened Jews there were some who believed this and who grabbed at this last hope as one clutches at straw. Only the thought of Israel held them standing upright.

"The Hungarian government wants to get rid of us, so they are sending us to Israel."

These and similar assumptions could be heard in the narrow, dark prison-wagons.

And the train began to move, accompanied by horrified cries from the locked-up people, who suddenly noticed that the train did not move in the southern direction but to the east, to the Ukraine.

Sounds of agitated voices filled the stifling air in the wagon: "Where are they taking us?"

"What are they going to do with us?"

"Why do they do this to us? We didn't do anything!"

But nobody knew the answer…!

In the general chaos, it seemed like a miracle to Yankel that he succeeded to get into the same wagon as Rachel and her family. Full of disturbing presentiments, he looked through the small barred hatch of the wagon into the gray morning. Then he turned around resignedly and confirmed what they had been afraid of: "Yes, I can see it clearly now; we are going to the east."

"Perhaps the train only makes a detour and will later be diverted back south," objected Rachel. "Nowadays there are so many routes closed because of military transports…" In this way Rachel tried to find some explanation with which she could calm her family and friends.

But Yankel shrugged his shoulder.

"Could be," he said. "It is more likely that they are taking us behind the lines to work for the armament."

But Rachel had her doubts about it and said that for this task they needed only young people. "And among us there are so many old people and children. Perhaps we shall go to *Eretz Israel*, or they will settle us in some other land!"

Yankel pressed his bride's hand and said with a forced smile:

"Yes, that's it, my dear! We must build a new homeland for us with our hands. It will not be easy, but in *Eretz Israel* too, hard work would have awaited us. Perhaps some day when the war has ended, we can emigrate to *Eretz Israel*."

Yankel did not believe a word of all the things he tried to tell his beloved girl. He just could not imagine that they would lead the Jews to peaceful construction work in the middle of the war. He saw a black future for them, but that this transport would bring them straight to hell, even Yankel could not foresee!

They rolled forward for hours, through the Carpathian Mountains, until they came at last to the wide waste plain between the rivers Pruth and Dnjestr.

The train stopped many times on the open stretch, but they were not allowed to get out at all, even for a short time. Armed guards with dogs patrolled the train lengthwise and made sure that nobody left the train. Once it seemed to Yankel as if the guards pursued some fugitives, because the sound of barking dogs concentrated at one place and then moved away from the train in a certain direction.

Yankel felt that the train had halted before at a regular station. Then it had started to move again and had halted again, a few minutes later. This is when the barking of the dogs had begun.

Yankel hoped the poor devils had got away.

A short time later the train moved on.

Meanwhile, inside the wagons it was becoming almost unbearable. So many people were huddled close together for many hours in the smallest space, without being let out even once. And the ventilation of the wagons was entirely insufficient. So there were already many dead among them.

In the late afternoon, at last, the doors were suddenly pushed open. Uniformed men, Hungarian gendarmes and German SS men, surrounded the whole train.

With brusque voices and loud curses they ordered the densely crammed people in the wagons:

"Come on, Come on! Get out, damned riffraff! Na, get on with it! Quick, quickly!"

"You have yet to take a bath today, to get to the land of your ancestors nice and clean!" called out a young gendarme to Yankel and Rachel, as they climbed out of the wagon. At the same time he grinned so maliciously that it gave Rachel an eerie feeling. What did he mean?

But she did not have any time to think about it.

All the Khustian Jews had hardly left the wagons, when they were driven on under curses and new shouted orders. Then, after a few minutes, they began to move in a long column. Again and again, whipped up by the brutal orders of the uniformed slave drivers, they moved forward, the old hobbling, crying and sighing, the sick dragging themselves, moaning painfully, the children stumbling on, crying…! But where did the way lead to…?

Nobody foresaw…

From time to time Yankel searched for Rachel's hand and took care not to let his loved one's mother and eleven-year-old brother Shlomo out of his sight.

Around them, reaching the evening horizon, the flat steppe was stretched out, and behind its dark edge, just at that time, the sun – like a big ball of fire – disappeared. There were no houses to be seen, to accommodate so many people. And still they drove them on, to an unknown destination. The exhausted dragged themselves on, leaving behind them large clouds of dark gray dust.

Then they saw some glittering water in the distance.

"Is that over there the sea where our ship is waiting, on which we are supposed to go to Israel?" asked Rachel's brother expectantly. "Perhaps, we shall see soon," answered Yankel hesitantly. Why frighten the child unnecessarily and tell him that they were still far away from the Black Sea, and that this water could be the river Dnjestr, at most.

"Yankel, shall we really, this very same evening, bathe in that water over there, as the gendarme had said? But it is rather cold already!" Shlomo kept on speaking to him.

"Don't fret, my boy. You are not going to catch a cold," answered Yankel absent-mindedly, because something disconcerting took all his attention.

Did they not hear some shots and screams from over there...?

The armed soldiers who guarded the transport began to make loud noises now, as if they wanted to drown out the noise from afar.

They drove the long column on to hurry more, with brutal shouts:

"Hey there, you lazy pack! You waddle along like lame ducks! On the double! Move, move!"

Woe to him who did not move forward quickly enough! The rowdies pushed the old and sick forward, punching them with their fists and beating them with sticks without any consideration.

A few hundred meters before the riverbank, a loud order sounded: "Haaaalt!"

An officer went along the lines and ordered:

"Remove all outer clothing! Quickly, Quickly! You are going to take a bath now!"

"But we cannot undress here before the men! This is against our customs!" protested some women timidly.

But the team of guards beat them with the butts of their rifles and shouted at the hesitant ones: "Shut your traps, blockheads, and be quick about it, or you'll be too late to get to the land of your ancestors. It's almost dark, already!"

In a sneering manner, they forced the Orthodox Jews from Khust to remove most of their clothes and then drove them on towards the river.

Arriving at the bank of the river, a cry of horror arose immediately through the lines of the people.

Were there not lying corpses? Human bodies red with blood? Blood, everywhere blood! Even the water of the river Dnjestr was glimmering in a reddish color. So, this was the meaning of the uniformed men's strange talk about the "Land of the ancestors"!

Behind them they heard the commands: "In with you, into the water, move, move!"

The people turned around desperately, they tried to flee in the direction they had come from, but it was in vain. Suddenly, more and more men in black and gray uniforms appeared from behind the chain of the steppe's hillocks. They looked like real emissaries of death.

And then the submachine guns rattled…!

Shots whipped through the air and tore the bodies of the densely crowded Jews of Khust to shreds. Some of them collapsed with a sudden outcry, others shrieked shrilly in their agony.

Children howled. The air was full of agonized shrieks, sobs, cries for help and tears. A few of the unfortunates tried to rush upon the murdering machine guns in order to grab some of the soldiers and pull them into death with them. However, this way they only ran more into the line of fire and nearer to the weapons' muzzles, and it was even easier for the murderers to shoot them.

Soon the ground was densely covered with corpses and human bodies, writhing in horrible pain, into which the soldiers shot their salvos again and again, until even the last whimper stopped…

Silence reigned suddenly. Only the water glugged quietly. The moon had risen and shone now upon the gruesome scene. Slowly, some of the uniform clad soldiers came nearer, wandered between the heaps of the corpses and stabbed with their bayonets here and there in order to be sure that they had really extinguished all sparks of life.

But they had not been able to kill them all off.

Some of them, among them Yankel and Rachel, had tried to run into the river. They ducked under water as long and as deep as they could, to escape from the bullets.

When the massacre had started, Yankel had abruptly seized his bride and her little brother Shlomo.

"Let's go, quickly into the water! This is our only chance!" he had called to them and dragged them with him into the water. But so many people pushed after them that the little boy's hand was torn out of Yankel's and he was immediately lost in the confused mass of people.

Hundreds of people – dead or wounded and frightened to death – drifted, floated, dived or swam in a mess in the cold water of the river.

Yankel clung desperately to Rachel's hand and called to her: "Take a breath and dive as deeply as you can!"

Under the water too, they held on to each other's hands in order not to lose each other. Again and again they hit against the bodies of the dead or the escapees who, like themselves, fought for their lives.

Gradually they got away from the bank of death. The shots could hardly be heard, and the shouts of the tortured turned weaker and were finally lost in the twilight…

"Quickly, again under the water! We are not safe yet!" pressed Yankel when they again surfaced to breathe. "There must still be death-hunters along the riverbank!"

They swam for more than half an hour down the Dnjestr River, and only when they could not hear any shots at all did they dare to crawl onto the ground cautiously. Bending over, they crept along the riverbank – at last some bushes and trees!

They let themselves fall onto the ground, their bodies shivering all over, taking deep breaths and lying there together, devoid of any feeling. Before their eyes they still saw the overpowering picture of the horrible massacre, which they had escaped so narrowly.

Rachel began to sob convulsively.

"These murderers!" she uttered. Tears flew over her face. Yankel pulled her against him and kissed her tenderly.

"Tell me, what do you have here?" asked Rachel and stroked her hand over his forehead. Blood stuck to her fingers as she withdrew her hand. "You are wounded!"

Rachel quickly tore off a piece of her underskirt and dressed Yankel's wound with it. He must have been grazed by a bullet, but could not remember when. He had been so busy saving his bride and himself.

Rachel stroked over his bandaged forehead, trembling, and sobbed: "You have saved both our lives, Yankel! Alone, I would have certainly stopped or run into the machine guns! But you dragged me into the river and didn't let go of me!"

"In the terrible muddle I didn't have any time to think it over," answered Yankel, breathing heavily. "I acted like an animal, in a pure natural instinct to survive. Therefore we are saved, for now, anyhow. But all the others…? Your mother, Shlomele, my parents and brothers and sisters, they were in the marching column so near us! Perhaps they…?"

He fell silent and bit his lip. Both of them remained silent, despairing.

Only after a long pause Yankel said slowly: "Yes, Rachel, right now we are saved. But for how long? When the sun is up tomorrow, the search-patrols will search the ground along the riverbanks. We are certainly not the only ones who have escaped, and they will send patrols with dogs. We have to get away from here as quickly as possible! Each kilometer we get away from the river gives us a better chance to escape!"

Rachel nodded. "You are right, we must get away. Besides, it is better if we move. You are wounded and have to keep warm."

"Oh, I am not really wounded! It's only a small scratch," said Yankel.

They stood up and crept through the bushes and shrubs along the riverbank as silently as they could. At the smallest sound, the snap of a twig under their feet or the rustle or hiss of trees, they stood still as if rooted to the spot and listened. Yankel, who held Rachel's hand, felt that she began to shiver in moments like these, and he had to control himself not to show his fear too.

Yes, they were afraid. They still could hear the cries of agony and the sounds of shots ringing in their ears…!

Perhaps there were already patrols with their dogs on the way in order to catch the survivors and eliminate them?

Finally they reached the edge of a wide plain and from the faint glow of the stars saw a black stripe at the horizon.

"That must be a wood," whispered Yankel. "We have to get through the big field as quickly as we can! Soon everything will be entirely starlit, and then we are going to be visible from far away!"

They moved rapidly over a meadow and along a wheat field. Yankel was right. It was a wood, a wood of high protecting trees under which they could feel safe, for the time being. Again and again the wood was interrupted by fields which they had to cross. But the breaking dawn found them in a marshy wood with thick undergrowth.

"Let's stop here!"

Yankel pointed to a small clearing, surrounded by shrubs. "We are going to rest a little and will go on at daybreak," he said.

They were very cold now, as they too had been forced to shed their outer clothing. Rachel was wearing her torn underskirt and Yankel was naked from the waist up.

"You are going to lie down now and try to sleep," said Yankel. "In the meantime, I am going to be on watch and rest afterwards."

But Rachel only shook her head.

"Do you really think that I could close even one eye after all that happened today? No, I shall be on watch with you!"

But it took only a little while and Rachel began to fall asleep, nestled closely on Yankel's wide chest.

She murmured to herself: "Are we ever going to see Khust again?"

"Rachel, Rachel!" whispered Yankel, gently, and shook her shoulder.

"Wake up, come on, wake up!"

Rachel yawned half asleep and looked at Yankel, confused, but suddenly she was wide awake.

"What is the matter, Yankel?" she whispered agitatedly.

Then she herself heard it: Voices! She started.

"What shall we do, Yankel?" she asked, frightened.

"Silence!"

Yankel listened carefully. Indeed, there were some people approaching from the left. Yankel clasped the wooden stick which he had picked up while running through the wood and held Rachel's hand tightly.

"This is the only weapon we have. If this fails…! If only the brutes do not walk off the lane! I hope they don't have a dog with them which will sniff our scent and begin to bark!" said Yankel.

Both of them listened very carefully to the voices, which came nearer and nearer. A man talked rather excitedly and was only interrupted a few times by a female voice. A child whimpered.

"Did you hear that?" cried Rachel. "They are speaking Yiddish!"

"You are right," gasped Yankel, "they must be some of us!"

They rushed quickly through the shrubs in the direction of the voices.

"Yankel!" stammered Rachel. "Why, it is Esther, from Khust, and here are Mayer and Mendel! I know them all!"

The thirteen-year-old Esther crouched on the ground and held a child on her lap. This child was a boy who had been wounded by a shot and had been drifting helplessly in the water. She had pulled the boy out of the water to the riverbank and dragged him with her to the bushes. But trying to carry him further, she herself had collapsed. Mayer and Mendel had found the two children like this. At first they wanted to take only Esther with them, because they saw the situation of the boy was hopeless, but Esther had refused to leave the boy behind.

"Shlomele!" called Esther now to the boy.

"Shlomele!" cried out Rachel at the same moment. "My little dear Shlomele!"

But she saw to her horror that her brother hardly showed any signs of life; his face, smeared with blood, did not show any reaction when she leaned down over him.

She asked hesitantly: "Is Shlomele...?" She could not speak.

"No, he is still alive," answered Mayer, "but he has a nasty bullet wound in his chest. Maybe we can find a pitying farmer who will take him..."

"Let me see!" Rachel carefully picked up her brother with trembling hands, laid him down on the grass and opened his shirt. The right side of his chest was covered with blood. Rachel put her ear to his chest and could hear a heartbeat, but a very weak one. At that moment Shlomele opened his eyes once more and a tremble went through his weakened body, as he whispered using all his remaining strength:

"Rachel!"

A shy smile glided over his strained features.

"You are alive...!" he breathed. "All the others are dead, Mama...and... I...".

Upon the last word a shiver went through his body, a gurgle came out of his breast, a bloodstream welled out of his mouth, and slowly his head fell to the side...

It seemed as if he wanted to sleep; the onlookers understood that this was a sleep from which there was no awakening.

Rachel wiped away some of the blood and listened for a heartbeat in a last desperate attempt, but the young child's heart remained silent. Sobbing, Rachel dropped down over her dead little brother.

The men looked at each other in silence. Yankel took Rachel into his arms. They had in the last hours lived with death and had escaped it. For a few moments, the whole flight looked to them so senseless and their strength was about to abandon them entirely. But then they straightened themselves up and turned to the tasks at hand without delay. Mayer and Mendel dug a shallow hole, using their bare hands and some small sticks. The others laid Shlomele into it and piled earth over him. Esther brought stones and twigs.

After a while, Mayer and Mendel pressed for a prompt departure.

"We are still in danger, we have to go on. Let's go!"

After a march of two hours they were completely exhausted and had to stop again. The night seemed endlessly long to them; they crouched together, cold and hungry. They helped keep themselves warm with the few garments which they had left. Then Mayer guarded the girls and Yankel and Mendel went to look for some food. They actually came back with some fruits and roots. After everybody ate something, they lay down to sleep.

But Rachel could not sleep. The horrible events of that day came back to her again and again and would not let her rest. Yankel's words of comfort also could not calm her down; she preferred to get up and walk around.

"Are we going to stay in this wood for long?" she asked. "How easy for the patrols to find us here!"

"You are right, I'd rather not think about that," answered Yankel. "This region around the Dnjestr belongs to the hinterland of the Germans. They have set up the field police and the Waffen-SS who are hunting for the partisans here."

"So where can we escape to?"

"Perhaps the most secure place to be in is the Carpathian woods. If necessary, we can hide in the caves during winter. Besides, the mountain region is not densely inhabited and the few people there are mostly on our side. Also, the roads are so tough there that larger police units can hardly advance. It's a better option than to go to the Ukraine because in the Ukraine there are also many enemies of Jews whom the SS can set upon us."

"That may be so, but the Carpathes are far away," said Rachel.

"Nevertheless, we must try to reach them," answered Yankel, determined.

The others agreed with this plan. They did not rest any longer, but went on again.

*

To their luck, the following nights were also starlit and moonlit. They could march by night and did not need to be seen by day. Upon the wide, open area between the rivers Dnjestr and Pruth they would have been quickly discovered. They moved forward as silently as they could, and before crossroads and turnings one of the men always advanced to look out for pursuers. They made a big curve around every village in order not to be seen by anyone.

They could probably have found some food in those villages, but they preferred to be content with some fruit and field crops in order not to fall into a trap. Around the tenth day of their flight they finally reached the mountains. As it was just getting lighter and they were searching for a safe place to rest, they suddenly saw a stray sheep standing in a small hollow, a small frail animal that had probably lost its way. In an instant, they caught it. It looked to them like a present from heaven, and to the men, thinking of a juicy roast, it was mouth-watering.

Rachel and Esther were sorry for the poor animal, but they understood that their sentimental feelings were out of place in the present situation.

"We haven't eaten real food for over ten days!"

With these words Mayer turned around and searched for a remote place between the surrounding hills. There, he thought, they could dare to light a fire; the risk of the rising smoke betraying them would be small.

They were just in the middle of hanging the sheep over a crackling fire of twigs, when suddenly two men with weapons burst through the bushes.

"Don't fret, we are not going harm to you!" they called as the two girls cried out frightened. They came nearer and greeted the surprised group with a "*Shalom!*"

"How do you know that we are Jews?" asked Yankel, baffled.

"Small wonder!" smiled one of the men, a black-bearded giant. "We have been eavesdropping on you for quite a while now and have decided that you are children of Israel."

He pointed to the fire and asked: "Where did you get the sheep from?"

Mayer grinned. "We took that on credit. It will be paid for when we have the required cash."

"But," said the bearded one, "why did you light such a huge fire? That's how we found you, and we came nearer in order to find out who you were. You should be happy that we are not gendarmes! How long have you been on the road?"

"For two weeks, approximately," answered Yankel and told in a few words what had happened to them.

The black-bearded man listened attentively and said after a while: "If you want to, then come along with us to our place. Our people too escaped the massacres of the fascists with difficulties; some of them went to the woods even earlier, because they foresaw what would happen to them. I shall introduce you to our commandant and if he agrees to it, you can stay."

"Your commandant…?" asked Yankel.

"Yes," exclaimed the giant, "we are now a group of thirty-five men and twenty women. Our commandant is a Jew whose name is Leib. He will not have any objection to you joining us. You also won't go hungry with us; you already seem to be experienced in organizing food. You just have to learn how to be more careful."

"Are you partisans?"

"More or less. We live in the woods like they do, but we only attack in self-defense. And besides, we are happy to be left alone."

The bearded one smiled.

"That's good," replied Yankel. "We are peaceful Jews and not military heroes, you see. In fact, we don't even have any experience in shooting!"

"Well, you will have to learn it at our camp, of course. You must be able to defend yourselves. But now we have chatted enough. Come now, and take the little sheep with you. You will have to share it with us!"

That did not matter to the Khustians. In return for sharing, they were being offered life in a protected community, something they had not dared dream about since their escape.

The two people of the woods led the group to their camp and introduced them to their leader Leib. He listened to their story, called the people of the woods together, and by general consent it was agreed that the Khustian group could join them and stay.

Yankel, Rachel, Esther, Mayer and Mendel fell with relief into each other's arms.

Then the bearded giant, their first friend and helper, came over and led them with a smile to their new companions.

5.

WITH ALL THE other Khustian Jews, Haim and Feigele were also crammed into a wagon. Only once the train was already moving did Haim see that Feigele stood in one of the corners at the back of the same wagon.

He immediately squeezed himself through to her.

"Feigele!" he called out to her. "What luck that we are together at least!"

"Haim, my dearest!" stammered Feigele, sobbing, and fell into his arms. They stayed like this for a while, hand in hand without speaking a word and looking at each other.

They and the people around them, just like Yankel and Rachel who were at the same time in another wagon at the front of the train, had the same questions: "What are they going to do with us?"

"Where are they taking us?"

And the same assumptions were also voiced, as in the other wagons.

A young carpenter named Baruch stood near Haim.

"Ha, just listen to what they are saying!" he called. "I know better! They are supposed to bring us to Israel? Never! Mind you, at the Ukrainian border there is the SS waiting for us, and there they are going to kill us all!"

"Where did you say you know all this from?" asked Haim, horrified.

"A gendarme that I once worked for told me this yesterday evening. He warned me secretly and said: 'Baruch, I advise you, go into the woods at once and don't show yourself any more!' When I asked why, he told me something terrible…!"

"What, what, tell me!" pressed Haim.

"He said that they were going to drag us away and then kill us!"

"What?

But why?"

"I don't know. In Poland and Hungary the Nazis have already got *Vernichtungslager* (extermination camps), as they call them!" answered Baruch. "And I, the stupid blockhead, did not take this seriously!"

"My God, I just cannot believe this!" Haim's hair stood on end.

"You see, Haim," continued Baruch, "there is only one way out for us, to escape!"

"If this is true…!" Haim trembled, deeply disturbed. "If it's really like that…! You are right, Baruch, we must escape! But with Feigele!"

"Out of the question," protested Baruch vehemently. "We cannot take a girl with us! The whole thing is too difficult for a girl. She would only bring unnecessary danger upon us!"

"Without Feigele I'm not joining you!"

"Ach, all right!" grumbled Baruch compliantly. "Let her come with us! But I'm not going to carry her when she breaks down!"

"Indeed, you won't have to," replied Haim.

Then they quickly planned their escape. They decided to jump off the train at a suitable place. For this they had to prevent the wagon door from being closed by the soldiers after having been opened by them at one of the stations.

"I have a good device for this, a little surprise for our guards!" grinned Baruch and pulled out a gun from under his shirt. "This will certainly be very useful, right?"

They wanted to carry out their plan at the next stop. And at last the time came. The train stopped at a small station, where they were going to add more wagons filled with forced deportees.

The guards opened the door only for a few moments in order to push more Jews into the already overfilled wagon. Then the door was pushed closed at once.

But the few minutes were enough for Haim to see that only one of the guards remained behind to close the door. Quickly, like a flash of lightning, he flung open the door, pulled the guard inside and held his hand over the surprised man's mouth.

Baruch immediately closed the door and kept the guard covered with the gun while Haim disarmed him.

Some fearful minutes passed, in which Haim and Baruch paid penance for all the sins they had done in their whole life. But… really! The train moved again…!

Baruch let out an audible sigh of relief and wiped away the sweat from his forehead. The people around them did not notice the incident; they were too angry with more people being pushed into the car again. Haim looked out anxiously through the slightly opened door. The train moved slowly around a curve.

There could not have been a better opportunity.

Quickly Haim gave Baruch the sign they had agreed upon. Baruch opened the door, and like a sudden gust of wind, Baruch, Haim and Feigele sprung out of the train.

Within seconds, shots from the alarmed soldiers whipped through the night. They had seen the escapees. But it took some minutes until the engine driver was informed and the train at last came to a standstill.

So the fleeing escapees had a slight advantage. Encouraged by the shade of the surrounding trees and shrubs, they ran like hunted hares through the wood and stopped only after about an hour in order to catch their breath.

"Come on, take off your shoes! We are going to wade in the brook for a while!" ordered Baruch.

"Must we?" asked Feigele, shivering. "The water is too cold!"

"We'll have to endure much more cold if they catch us!" replied Baruch. "Probably our nice traveling companions set their watchdogs after us. But these clever little animals can follow our scent only to the brook. In the water our scent is lost right away. There their noses will be of no use, and we won't have to fear the police-dogs any more!"

In the meantime they had removed their shoes and Baruch entered the ice-cold water with a curse. He had taken over the lead silently.

Feigele followed him in and cried out as the soles of her feet touched the water.

Haim followed last. Being a former medicine student and an incorrigible bookworm, he was no leader by nature. He was the planner type rather than the practical one. So it was not hard for him to follow without any resistance the leading Baruch who radiated so much assurance with his big strong body and giant fists.

Without further ado, Haim entered the ice-cold water of the brook resolutely, clenched his teeth, shivered and followed the other two.

"And how are we going to continue now?" asked Feigele, chattering with cold.

"First, a little while on through the brook. And then – well, I don't know either…! The whole region around the Carpathes is dangerous in the same way for us Jews. The most important thing is that we must not be seen in bigger towns or villages. There are gendarmes everywhere and they are under the control of the SS."

"Perhaps we should try to reach Bukovina. I've heard that around Czernovitz it should still be proportionally secure for us," they could hear Haim's voice from the background.

Baruch agreed. It was common knowledge that the Nazis were not as strong there yet as they were already in Carpatho-Ukraina.

"I cannot hold on much longer in this ice-cold water," panted Feigele. "My feet are already numb up to the knees!"

"Mine too!" answered Baruch, unmoved. But he took Feigele's hand and pulled her forward with him.

They trudged on like this, until at last Baruch let them leave the brook. But even now they only rested long enough to massage their numb feet and to let their blood circulation get back to normal.

Then Baruch gave the sign to move on again, without mercy. He was frightened out of his wits that the henchmen would catch them, and it pressed him to hurry.

Fear, pure fear! That was what pushed them for the next days. So they stumbled on and on...

They could not find anything to eat. Baruch succeeded again and again to drive the tired to death and totally exhausted friends onto their way to Czernovitz.

*

One day they came upon a herd of sheep that were tended by a fifteen-year-old boy. At first, the boy looked at them with a rather frightened look.

This was understandable, as Baruch, Feigele and Haim looked rather unkempt after moving and sleeping out in the open air during the last days.

Baruch asked him: "Could you please tell us how to get to Czernovitz from here?"

Now his face brightened up.

"You want to get to Czernovitz? Then you must be Jews or partisans, right?" he said, smiling.

"Why do you think so?" answered Haim, feigning to be outraged. "We are wandering farm workers from…from Carpatho-Ukraina."

"Am I supposed to believe that?" asked the boy mischievously. "Almost all the wandering farm workers have bundles on their backs, and you don't even have a woolen coat although autumn is coming soon! – But I'm going to tell you something," said the boy, suddenly serious. "My mother is a Jew and the Nazis have deported her! – And because of that, come with me to my father whether you are Jews or not. He can certainly help you in some way."

"Where does your father live?" asked Baruch suspiciously, as he did not want to go into a village where people could discern them as refugees. But he worried in vain. The house to which the boy led them was situated outside the village. The man who came out to them had such an open face, they at once felt they could trust him.

Nevertheless, they introduced themselves as land workers.

"Listen," said the man, smiling. "Who and what you are makes no difference to me, you don't look very well. One can see that immediately. First, sit down a little and eat something, and then we shall see."

He put a big pot on the table, filled with corn-kasha, added a big jug of milk and watched as the starved people ate. When they were full, they told the friendly farmer their true story and the farmer told them of the similar fate of his wife:

"She was a Jew like you. They demanded that I divorce her. But she was a good wife to me for over twenty years; why should I suddenly expel her? – Then one evening, the gendarmes came and just took her with them."

The farmer wiped his moist eyes.

"I begged and pleaded, raged and roared, but all in vain! They took her to the railway station. I ran after them and saw that they pushed her into one of the wagons, together with many more other Jews from the surroundings. Then the train moved away, and I was left there, alone..."

The farmer wept, unashamed of his tears. He knew that the three strangers would understand him. When he had calmed down a little he went on:

"But you went through all this yourselves! That you were Jews, I understood right away. Jews from Khust...! – Even if I am not a Jew, I try to help every innocent man or woman who is persecuted. By the way, you can do something for me too."

"Anything you wish!" said Baruch, and the three of them nodded. They wanted very much to show their gratitude to the farmer.

"You wouldn't do anything directly for me," said the old man. "For a few days now, I have hidden a poor woman with her two children in my cellar. She is a Jew running from the Nazis. They cannot stay like this indefinitely, of course. It is too dangerous for us all...!"

"Yes, indeed the woman cannot stay with you for long," said Baruch, "we have to find a safe place for her."

"That's it," nodded the farmer eagerly. "I thought of Czernovitz! Take her with you to Czernovitz, where she has a better chance of being put up."

"All right, we'll take her with us," replied Baruch, after reaching an understanding with his friends through eye contact. "We shall manage!"

"But you have to move on soon, if possible, even tonight," said the old farmer, satisfied. "My neighbors mustn't see you! I'll also give you enough food and warm Bushlats for the way!"

"Bushlats...?" echoed Feigele not understanding. "What are those?"

"Those are jackets lined with wool, like the farmers here wear," explained the old man. "If you wear them nobody will think of you as strangers."

The friends agreed. They would rest a little more, while the farmer brought the woman and her two children from their hiding-place and prepared the food and the coats. As it became dark, they said good-bye to their friendly helper, who urged them once again to watch out for the patrols at the Rumanian border. Then he showed them the direction.

They started on their way to Czernovitz, well supplied.

*

"We have to be doubly careful," whispered Haim to Baruch.

"Yes, you are right!" answered Baruch. "We are already a whole caravan: Two men, two women and two children! One of us has to walk ahead a little and give signs of alarm, if men in uniform appear. More than three people always look suspicious!"

Gradually the friends realized what a burden the old farmer had charged them with. The children were so little, and they were afraid to walk through the woods in the dark. They whined and whimpered and stumbled forward unwillingly. After a short while they did not want to walk at all any more.

Baruch and Haim each had to carry a child on their backs. The children soon fell asleep on the wide backs of the men, swaying to and fro. Silently the adults trudged on. They went over narrow paths, past meadows and fields.

The mother of the two children, a rather careworn woman, was walking silently and only after they asked her some questions did she begin to tell her story:

"I come from the Carpathian city of Kossov. The Nazis took my husband away. I saved myself with the children just in time. We escaped and then the farmer hid us."

The woman remained silent for a while, shaken.

"My grandfather," she continued, "was a wise rabbi to whom the Jews of Kossov went for advice many times. God also gave him the gift to be able to look into the future. He said that just a short time before the Messiah would arrive a bad time of persecution for the Jews would come. I think that now we are living in the middle of that time! Will I still live and see the end of it?"

"Don't you have any relatives outside of Kossov?" asked Feigele with pity.

"No, nobody at all. My parents and grandparents, my brother, all of them lived in Kossov. I don't know if all of them were deported or if some of them escaped. If I only knew what happened to my husband…!"

The woman fell silent again, gloomily; only her big eyes gleamed in the starlight, full of grief and sorrow.

The three companions, Baruch, Feigele and Haim, marched on, also lost in thoughts. In their mind's eye they were with their loved ones whom they had left on the train, in the dark rolling prison-wagon! What happened to them?

*

They went on and on silently.

Only after a full day's march from their destination did the refugees finally stop in order to let themselves sit down and rest, entirely exhausted, in a meadow which was safely surrounded by bushes. The children were not hungry, but the adults' stomachs rumbled from want of food. They ate and then, after a short rest, they continued their march because they wanted to reach Czernovitz as soon as possible. But the entirely overtired and frightened children began to cry pitifully.

"You don't have to fear anything! I am here with you!" their mother comforted them. "Come on, walk a little!"

The little ones had to walk a little, as Baruch and Haim could hardly hold themselves up on their feet.

The two children took each other by the hand and began to walk forward slowly, still sniffling and sobbing. They were the first to walk out of the bushes onto the meadow, and their crying stopped at once.

Before them stood an SS patrol of two soldiers!

The two men took hold of the children and threw them aside. One of them pointed his weapon at the two little ones, and the other called out to the comrades who had just come out of the bushes:

"Hands up! And don't move, or we shoot the children!"

"No, my God! My children!" shouted the mother in a shrill voice and jumped towards the little ones. She wanted to throw herself on the SS man who kept the children covered. But the other soldier raised his gun. With one movement, Baruch jumped at him and pushed him to the ground. At the same time two shots whipped through the air and the children fell to the ground. The soldier turned with his weapon, shot once again and the mother fell dead over her children.

Haim woke out of his shocked stiffness and jumped onto the murderer. He tried to beat the gun out of his hand.

Meanwhile, Baruch fought with the other man. He raised his hand and knocked out this enemy's brains with his own gun. Then he hurried to help Haim who was bent over the SS man. That man was still holding onto his gun and suddenly a shot went off. Haim was hit and sank aside.

With a cry, Feigele jumped upon the uniformed man, and Baruch too came to her aid.

Finally, they were able to finish off this soldier too.

"Haim, Haim!" shouted Feigele, frightened, and went down on her knees beside her unconscious friend. He was bleeding but was breathing normally.

Baruch stood up and made a quick search of the dead bodies of the enemy. On one of them he found bandages and on the other an almost full flask of alcohol.

So they put a temporary bandage on Haim's head; then they gave him some alcohol to drink, which brought him back to his senses. Baruch dug a pit and they buried the dead.

Haim's wound forced them to remain there until the morning.

At last they started to leave, looking down sadly upon the grave and thinking of the dangers that still awaited them. They did not feel any satisfaction over the death of their enemies. They were human beings, and the three had until now never killed anybody.

The old rabbi had been right. The bad times had come!

After losing their way a few times, they found at long last the right way to the city. They could not advance quickly, because Haim had developed a high fever. However, they soon saw the first houses of Czernovitz from afar.

Feigele supported Haim on one side and Baruch on the other. In this way they reached the edge of the city. They had not gone more than a few minutes, when a pitying man turned to them:

"Can I help you somehow? The wounded man surely needs a doctor, right?"

The friends recognized from his words that the man was a fellow Jew, and they let him know they were Jews too:

"We are Jews escaping from the Nazis. Haim was hit during an incident with two SS men!"

The friendly stranger led them quickly to the house of a family of friends and arranged a carriage to take Haim to the Jewish hospital. There they did an X-ray and operated on him.

Feigele walked around desperately in the waiting-room and prayed:

"God, my God! Please do not take away the only thing I still have! Let Haim be well again! Why did you let us escape from the train if everything was in vain?"

At last – it seemed as if they had been waiting for ages – the surgeon came out and said:

"Calm yourself. You are Feigele, right? Everything went quite well. We have extracted the piece of lead and he is already awake after the anesthetic. You can enter now and talk with him, but not for too long. He is still very weak and needs to rest now!"

Feigele did not even hear the last words. She had already slipped past the surgeon and was now standing beside her loved one, who, still only half awake, smiled at her weakly.

*

Haim recovered quickly. While Feigele waited for his recovery, she made herself useful at the hospital.

The Jews of Czernovitz were shocked to hear about the fate of the Khustian Jews, but there too some of them had been deported. A few thousand of them still lived there. To the friends they proved helpful in many ways and they arranged new documents, work and accommodation for them. Feigele was allowed to work at the hospital as an assistant nurse, and Haim also found work there after regaining his health completely.

Baruch found work and lodging at the house of a carpenter, and so they were provided for, for the time being.

After a while, the senior physician found out that Haim had quite a lot of medical knowledge and was not surprised to hear that Haim was a former medical student in the advanced semesters. He liked the attentive young man, and as Dr. Bernstein was a widower for quite a long time and had a big apartment, he took him into his house and put the extensive library at his disposal. He enjoyed having an understanding partner for conversations and discussions, but he also took care that enough time was left for Haim to meet with Feigele. They seldom saw each other during the day, as Haim was allowed to accompany the senior physician on all his visits.

One day, while visiting the ward for internal diseases, Dr. Bernstein asked an old Jewish woman:

"What ails you?"

"I am fretting, because so many Jewish people are being exterminated so cruelly!" answered the old woman. When the physician was silent, she added reproachfully: "Well, are those not troubles?"

"Yes, but what is hurting you?' said Dr. Bernstein. "We only want to help you!"

"Oy," said the old Jewish woman, "the heart, the stomach, the gallbladder, also the liver, the head, the small of my back and the legs – oh, simply the whole body. And I myself am sick too!"

"Physically she is entirely healthy," said Dr. Bernstein to Haim afterwards. "Nevertheless, my dear Haim, this woman is very ill, psychologically ill! Yes, in reality her illness consists of her knowing the suffering of the Jewish people, and this knowledge of the sad fate of many fellow Jews slowly takes away her vitality and causes her physical pains…"

*

One evening, as Feigele once again visited her Haim, he said to her:

"You know, Feigele, as I look at you now, I really believe that one day we shall go to Israel together. And then you are going to be my wife!"

He drew her into his arms and kissed her, full of love.

On this evening they were joined by their host. He seemed to be unusually serious, but he did not say a word about what was worrying him. He did not want to ruin the evening for the young couple.

After Haim returned from bringing the girl home, the doctor called the young man to come to his study and told him what had happened:

"Two officers called on me just as I was about to go out for a break. 'You have to vacate the whole Jewish hospital in three days! Here is the written order! The hospital will be needed as a military hospital!' they said to me."

Dr. Bernstein rubbed his forehead, sighing.

"What shall I do now?"

Haim remained silent, concerned. He did not know any way out of this situation.

"I don't know either! But perhaps the Jewish community could do something?"

"We have to try it anyway."

The next morning, Dr. Bernstein hurried without delay to the Jewish community center to arrange for them to send a delegate to the military governor of the town. This way, they at least managed to leave half of the hospital in their hands. And in order to take care of all the patients they arranged an additional clinic in a private house.

But exactly three days after their first visit, the two officers appeared again and now ordered the immediate evacuation of the hospital. Then they set a final deadline: "Tomorrow, tomorrow we are going to come back, and then we don't want to see any of you here!"

The dream of a peaceful life and safe existence had ended all at once.

Haim and Feigele asked themselves despairingly:

"What now...? What if the hospital was going to be shut down?..."

6.

I N BERLIN TOO the situation was becoming more and more aggravated.
Lea and Bernhard were put to work at the Siemens factory, which
delayed their transport for the time being.

Every evening, as their small family came together, they felt as if they
had been awarded some big prize. Even the children knew exactly what
was happening in their neighborhood.

"You know, Papa, they have taken away Siegfried with his parents and
brothers, and Peter said they were never coming back and maybe they were
all dead already!"

Startled by these words, Bernhard tried to talk the children out of it.
But Lea escaped into the bathroom, where she stayed for a long time, until
she had regained her composure.

They went to bed with heavy hearts in the evening, and in the same
depressed mood they parted again in the morning.

Then, in the factory, they noticed that some people had not arrived
on that day either.

Nevertheless, each of them hoped to be spared.

Bernhard and Lea had gotten used to the work and managed to ac-
complish more than the usual quota, but it soon showed that this too was
no guarantee for their safety.

*

One day before noon, the Gestapo took Bernhard and Lea, brought them
to Dirksen Street again and put them into separate cells.

And for three days they were tortured and maltreated by never-ending interrogations. As at their first arrest, it was about the visit of the Belgian in Bernhard's apartment.

One day they put Bernhard and Lea together opposite the Belgian. Both remembered his visit exactly. The young man had brought them a letter – a letter from Lea's friend from Brussels.

At that time, they had met a young, good-looking man who wanted to help them escape.

Shocked, they now looked upon a gray man, broken in body and mind, whom they could identify as "their Belgian" only by his voice.

However, they could not say any more than at their first arrest.

In a rage, the two SS men beat both of them. Lea fainted and one of the uniformed men took her out of the room.

Bernhard pulled himself up and wanted to follow the two but was immediately referred to in sharp words:

"Stop, my friend, you stay here!"

The thugs occupied themselves again with the Belgian. Searching for help, Bernhard looked out of the window and saw down at the Alexander train station people moving to and fro busily. A yearning for such a free life gripped him. He felt like an exile without rights.

How could this possibly be that in the twentieth century they took away the "*Bürgerliches Ehrenrecht*" (honorable civil rights), so correctly written in the official German, from thousands of civilized people and branded them criminals? What had they done? The people down there at the railway station certainly did not think about this. They seemed to think only about their own matters and apparently did not know anything about the crimes that were being committed against thousands of innocent Jews who were tortured and murdered.

One of the SS men took hold of Bernhard's arm and pulled him back into the room.

"Come on!" he called and pushed Bernhard in front of him through the room.

"Stop, don't lock him up again!" protested the Belgian. "I shall say the truth! The Rosens are innocent! They don't know anything! I…!"

But nobody listened to him…

"Shut up and sit down!" an officer bellowed at him.

That was the last thing Bernhard heard before the door was closed behind him. He was locked away again into his cell, where he brooded desperately over the fate of his wife and children. But his thoughts were moving in a circle all the time and showed him that his hands were tied.

"I want to get out! Let me out!!!"

He shouted himself hoarse and hit the door of his cell in powerless despair. But here in the cellar of the police headquarters nobody listened to his shouts. The guard only raised his eyes from his newspaper for a second, shook his head and returned to his reading. 'Let him shout,' he thought.

And Bernhard screamed and raged until he almost lost consciousness.

When the guard later opened the flap in order to pass through a bowl of thin, watery soup, he saw Bernhard sitting in the most remote corner of the cell and looking into space lethargically. He did not even raise his head when the guard called out to him later. He had given up...!

A few days later they brought Bernhard up again, this time without handcuffs, and brought him into a room in which he had not been before. The voice that offered him a seat seemed familiar to him. He raised his eyes and looked straight into the eyes of a former customer who was known to be decent, even though he held a high position as a member of the Nazi party. Bernhard could hardly hold back his cry of surprise, as the man spoke to him in a low voice:

"I am sorry about what happened to you, Mister Rosen! Your wife has been hospitalized at the Jewish hospital." He handed a discharge certificate over to Bernhard and continued: "And you will return to your place of work. If I had been informed earlier of your arrest, you would have been free much sooner. With this I do something which is, of course, forbidden and could cost me my neck. Normally, I should have sent you to a transport. Because of that, you must remain strictly silent about your stay here!"

Then the officer brought Bernhard to the entrance gate and released him, warning him again insistently to be cautious. Bernhard could not grasp it yet. Minutes before, he had still been sitting down in the cellar in a bleak, dark cell without any hope, and now he was sitting in a taxi on his way to the Jewish hospital to visit Lea.

A few minutes later he stood opposite the senior physician.

"Yes, my dear Rosen," he said, "your wife is not well! I would even say that she is really in a bad way. This maltreatment has brought about many internal injuries, the extent of which we were not able to find out yet. We have to operate on your wife, but we just cannot do so at the moment because of her weakened condition."

Bernhard's head was whirling. From all these well chosen words he understood only that Lea's condition was very bad. That was too much for him. He collapsed in a fit of weakness and was quickly given an injection.

"So, soon you will feel better," said the physician and continued: "You have to be strong for your children! They are, by the way, visiting your wife. Come, I shall take you to them!"

The senior physician led Bernhard to Lea's sickbed, where the family embraced in tears.

"Bernhard, my love!" sobbed Lea. "They have let you go!"

She hugged him, lifting herself up a little and embracing his neck. Bernhard did not see that her face contorted with pain. He was too excited to see her again at last and to hold her in his arms. He was not ashamed of his tears. When he calmed down slightly he noticed, shocked, how thin his wife's body had become. He let her slide back onto the pillows and looked at her. One look into her consumed face, in which her beautiful dark eyes sunk deep in their sockets, was enough to confirm the diagnosis of the senior physician.

"Lea, Lea, Lea…!" stammered Bernhard and bent down over her. His lips roamed her face in wild desperation; he kissed her forehead, her eyes, her nose, cheeks and lips and then buried his face in the hollow of her neck.

Lea stroked his hair softly.

"Darling, look, the children." She then said silently, "You must take care of them!"

The two little ones stood terrified, close together at the foot of the bed.

"Promise me, Bernhard, that you will never leave them alone and will take care of them until they are big enough, yes?"

With these words Lea looked at Bernhard insistently.

"But Lea, dearest, what are you saying?" Bernhard asked gently. "At the most, in a week or two you are going to be well again!"

"Ach, Bernhard, my love, I don't have any illusions about my condition!" whispered Lea, and a coughing fit shook her so harshly that Bernhard became worried. "How gladly I would like to go on living by your side and see how our children grow up…! No, don't contradict me! I can feel how things are with me."

Lea breathed with difficulty and closed her eyes for a while.

"God will help you…and protect you…," she said quietly.

Deeply moved, Bernhard could not utter a word. He only kissed Lea's hand silently. Finally he left the hospital with his two children.

That night, Bernhard could not fall asleep. A new blow was added to the worry about his wife. According to an order given on 19 September 1941, all Jews had to fasten a yellow Star of David onto their clothes, easily visible by all.

With this act they had all been practically declared outlaws officially and were helplessly exposed to their persecutors. Many Jews thought that this was the end.

This was Bernhard's opinion too. He was convinced that after this new malicious campaign all the people wearing the Star would be struck down. The night seemed endless to him; his hopes began to dwindle. His thoughts were with Lea.

But the morning came and with it the sun, which was still shining for all – for the persecutors and for their victims.

With a heavy heart Bernhard sewed yellow stars onto their clothing. Meanwhile he went again and again to the window. Perhaps there were cries for help to be heard from the street…?

But everything remained quiet.

He prepared some slices of bread for the children for breakfast in the kindergarten, took hold of their little hands lovingly and brought them to the day-care center.

On the way, suddenly a man came out of an entrance gate and stood in Bernhard's way. He pulled a packet of cigarettes out of his pocket and put it quickly into Bernhard's jacket.

"Chin up!" he encouraged him quietly, pulled his hat lower over his forehead and vanished immediately.

After Bernhard relaxed from his surprise, he felt a little lighter at heart. Perhaps he had painted everything too black.

On his way to his new workplace, he went to the hospital for a short visit. Lea's condition was as bad as before.

Bernhard reached his workplace as last; all his colleagues were already present. Everyone, pale and serious, looked into the space in front of him.

"Has something happened?"

"Nothing…!" was the monotonous answer.

After all, it was a miracle that they all met together this morning, Bernhard, whom they had already thought of as lost, and the others who were still spared.

But, even now, most of the Berliners were not inflamed by the songs of hatred of the Nazi party. They behaved passively, because they feared for their own safety.

*

When Bernhard came home in the evening, the old neighbor greeted him in the hallway, breathing heavily, and said with her heavy Berliner dialect:

"Mister Rosen, Mister Rosen! Good that you are here at last! Have I been worried about you! You must go as quickly as possible to the hospital to your wife! I have just arrived from there. Take the little ones with you, Mister Rosen, and go quickly!"

Bernhard went pale. Without saying another word he took hold of Daniel's and Judith's hands and went by taxi to the hospital.

"Lea, Lea!" he called out to his beloved wife. "Lea, you must not leave me! I love you so much! Lea, don't you hear me? It's me, Bernhard!"

"My dearest," breathed Lea, "how wonderful…that you…have come…"

"Lea!" Bernhard covered her pale cheeks and forehead with kisses. Tears flowed down his cheeks. The children too began to cry.

"Mami, Mami…!" they sobbed and stroked their mother's hands.

"The children," whispered Lea, "the children are…here…?"

"Yes, Daniel and Judith are here."

Bernhard pushed the little ones nearer to Lea. With difficulty she stretched out her hand and caressed the children's faces. For a moment her eyes became clear. Frightened, she looked at Bernhard.

"The children are here? Bernhard, it's already dark outside! After eight o'clock we are not allowed to be in the streets! Take them home, Bernhard, take them home!"

Exhausted, she sank back onto the pillows. For one moment Bernhard thought that the worst had happened.

"Lea, Lea!" Bernhard called, frightened, and rubbed her bloodless cheeks. "Don't leave us alone, do you hear? We need you! What shall we do without you…?"

But Lea did not hear him any more. He had to bend down over her in order to understand what she said to him:

"Take care…of the…children…and take care…of…you!…I…love…you!"

Bernhard shook Lea by the shoulders, but she was already too weak. She could not speak any more. She opened her eyelids with difficulty, embraced Bernhard and the children with a long look, full of love, and fell back weakly into a deep coma from which she did not awake anymore.

She passed into a world where hate and sorrow no longer existed.

Bernhard and the children remained behind in silent shock. Bernhard grew stiff with his pain, unable to comfort Daniel and Judith.

He had no thoughts other than about his beloved wife who had always been a loving, giving companion to him and had now left him forever.

How would things go on for them now?

*

How could things go on now? What was going to happen to the children? Should he put them into a children's home? But the danger that children could be taken from there kept him from doing that. He had no other choice than to take their mother's place himself. He took care of them lovingly and tried not to let them feel that their mother was not there for them anymore. He washed and bathed them, cared for their clothing and prepared their food, he gave them his every free minute.

This new situation had one good aspect. It left him no time to brood, and it helped him to get over the loss of his beloved Lea more quickly.

Daniel was already seven and Judith three years old. As a Jew, Daniel was not entitled to go to school, but he was too big for the kindergarten. So he was left alone at home during the day, and sometimes, when his father had to work late, Daniel would bring his little sister home from the kindergarten.

One morning, as Bernhard was bringing little Judith to the kindergarten, the child said: "Papa, please buy me some ice cream!"

"All right," Bernhard agreed, and they crossed the street to the ice cream shop. He wanted to enter the shop when he noticed a big sign fastened on the inside of the glass door. On it was written: "Jews are not served here!"

Resigned, Bernhard shrugged his shoulder, turned around, raised his little daughter onto his arm and continued on his way.

Little Judith said indignantly: "But Papa! You wanted to buy me ice cream!"

"Yes, but you know," answered Bernhard sadly, "they wouldn't have sold us anything there."

"But why not?" she asked, astonished.

"Because we are Jews!"

"And why are we Jews?"

"Because God has created us as Jews."

"And what did the Jews do?"

"They created the Bible, in God's name."

"What is that, the 'Bible'?"

"They are the five law books of Moses."

The little girl thought about it deeply. "And because of that we are not allowed to eat ice cream?"

"No," answered Bernhard bitterly, "the reason is that people don't believe in God and the Bible anymore. Therefore they hate and persecute us. They don't believe in tolerance and brotherly love any more. Because of this there is also a war, and bombs are falling! And therefore," he added quietly, "they also don't sell us ice cream."

Meanwhile, they had arrived at the kindergarten. Bernhard left his little daughter there and hurried to his workplace.

At the factory, as he crossed the "Aryan Room," he smelled the smell of French cognac.

"It's the boss's birthday," whispered a colleague to him.

Reluctantly, Bernhard went over to the old man and congratulated him. "Go on to the 'Jews' shack'!" was the boss's response, but Bernhard knew that this was only meant as a joke. In honor of the occasion, the old man even sent over a few boxes of beer to the 'Jews' shack' so that the Jews could take part in the happy celebration too.

These Jewish men and women were already used to the permanently surrounding danger, to this constant dance on a thin swinging rope, from which so many suddenly lost their balance and fell down into the dark bottomless depth where nobody ever heard from them again…!

So it was comprehensible that they immediately took this opportunity to escape their worries for a few hours. One of them, the so-called "*Unter-bürgler*" (lower citizen), Alfred Baum, pulled a harmonica out of his pocket, and soon closely embracing couples swayed to the sound of dance music, kissing each other and forgetting the world around them for a short while. Like many Jews, most of these couples had married quickly in order not to be sent alone on a transport, if it would come to that.

Bernhard's best friend Alfried was among the dancers too, with his new wife Rebecca. This celebration was like a delayed wedding celebration for them.

Alfried and Rebecca were planning to flee to Switzerland in a short while, and from there to help Bernhard escape too.

The celebration ended, and everyday life took hold of them again.

*

One morning a few days later, when Bernhard arrived at the factory there was a big uproar all around. He asked, unsuspectingly: "What happened?"

"Haven't you heard what happened?" asked his colleagues agitatedly. "A fire broke out at the 'Soviet Paradise Exhibition,' and they have immediately placed the blame on us, the Jews!"

"Five-hundred Jews were straightaway arrested. They shot half of them on the spot, and the others were taken on a transport to KZ Sachsenhausen.

"And do you know whom they have also taken? – Your friend Alfried! Goldstein saw it."

"Yes, we were together on our way home. I saw the SS men right away and escaped into an entrance corridor. Alfried was not quick enough, and so they caught him and dragged him away!"

"My God!" groaned Bernhard, putting his hands over his face. "Why don't you let it be enough? Poor Rebecca!"

Bernhard could not calm down that whole day. His best friend's fate had shaken him deeply. How easily this could have happened to him. At that time, the transports were no longer well organized. Therefore, if there was still some space left in the trains, they just picked up Jews at random, from their apartments or the streets. At any time this stroke of fate could also hit him, Daniel or Judith, if he did not take some action against it immediately.

So Bernhard took his two children to Beelitz to one of his old friends, Anna Schaefer. Here, he knew, the little ones would be safe for the time being, and he could prepare their escape with more concentration.

The next day he went to a good friend and came back a short time later, equipped with "Aryan" papers and the name "Gerhard Baumann." With these papers and his looks, tall, blond and blue-eyed, no one could tell he was a Jew. Bernhard now felt safe enough to move about the city and to even visit his two children from time to time.

The small country house of Anna Schaefer in which Daniel and Judith had found shelter was situated several kilometers from Beelitz. On his visits, Bernhard slept in a little wooden garden shed in the big garden surrounding his friend's house. This little garden shed was just big enough for two wooden beds, set one above the other. Here he could be together with both his children, undisturbed and unnoticed by curious neighbors.

It was unusually hot this summer of 1942. The children ran around in bathing suits, romping about in the spacious garden or in the adjacent wood and seemed to feel quite content in the country.

Once, as they came out of the woods, a strange man followed them and thus met Bernhard who was there for a visit. Bernhard was startled when he saw the party badges on the stranger's jacket. He sent the children away quickly and called his hostess:

"Anna, Anna! A visitor for you!"

"Ach, this is only my cousin Franz," whispered Anna, coming in a hurry. "Don't fret, he is harmless."

She turned calmly to the fat stranger: "Hello, Franz! What are you doing here in this neighborhood? – This here is Mister Baumann, a distant relative of my late Willi. – Come, Franz, sit down. Meanwhile I am going to bring you something cold to drink!" With these words she disappeared, heading for the cellar. Cousin Franz, moaning, let his big body fall into a garden chair, causing the wood and the metal to let out a tormented shriek in protest, pulled out a huge handkerchief and wiped the beads of sweat from his red forehead.

He just wanted to begin a conversation with Bernhard when Anna came back and put an ice-cold lemonade in front of the unwelcome guest.

Bernhard felt miserable and would have liked very much to follow his children to the garden, if he had not been afraid to arouse more suspicion in that way. So he put on a cheerful and relaxed face and listened to the conversation between Cousin Franz and Anna.

"Ach, it's a pleasure to see you once again!" Anna was saying at that moment to her cousin. "But why didn't you bring your wife with you? Or doesn't it suit her to visit an old Social-Democrat like me?" she led the conversation skillfully into a less harmful direction.

"Ah, do stop reminding us of the old stories!" the cousin warded her off, "I was visiting a friend on the birthday of Horst Wessel, and I wanted to have an additional small drink at your place."

"Who is that, Horst Wessel?" asked Anna naively.

"What, you don't know that? And you want to be a German woman?"

Cousin Franz was furious, and his face became bluish-red from excitement.

"Oh, calm down!" Anna appeased him nonchalantly. "As it is, I don't know Horst Wessel. But I'm nevertheless a true German, just like you!"

That was too much for good cousin Franz. How could his cousin compare herself to him?

He jumped up so abruptly that the garden chair fell over, and the whole table would have been overturned also if Bernhard had not caught it quick-wittedly. And he did not even excuse himself. He just squeezed out: "…must go now! Shall come again! See you!" With these words he swung his heavy body around and trudged through the garden, hurrying away, and all the time still murmuring and cursing his 'backward cousin.'

"So, we got rid of this one, didn't we?" smiled Anna.

"You know, Bernhard, he must have thought that I had also turned into a fanatic Nazi, like his sister. She handed her own brother-in-law over to the Nazis, because he was a Jew. In return, she now has a good position at the headquarters' office in Paris. I only hope that one day I can look her in the face and say: 'I have rescued a whole Jewish family!' And about Horst Wessel, of course I know about him. He was a real miserable type. Another pimp shot him because of a woman, and the Nazis have turned him now into a national hero. And good-natured guys like Franz believe this immediately!"

Bernhard nodded his head in agreement, but actually he disliked this dispute. He was afraid that his children could become playthings for the hostile parties. But at the moment he did not have any choice but to leave Daniel and Judith there. It would have been too dangerous to remove the children from their hiding place now. So when it got darker, Bernhard returned to Berlin alone and worried.

However, the children did not remain much longer with the friendly Anna Schaefer in Beelitz, because one evening little Judith opened her mouth, and without thinking twice answered a neighbor's question of why her brother didn't go to school:

"But he cannot go to school. They closed the Jewish schools!"

The little girl immediately realized that she had said too much and asked the woman with tears in her eyes:

"Ach please, please don't tell anybody! Nobody must know that we are Jews, my brother and I. My Papa said that we would be dragged away then!"

The woman was so moved by the tragic fate of the children that she kept this secret to herself, for the time being. But the next day, after much hesitation, she made up her mind to speak to the woman who was taking care of the children.

"Listen, Mrs. Schaefer, I know about the children you have taken into your house. They are Jewish! Little Judith told me unintentionally. But don't be afraid, I shall not tell anybody. I only wanted to inform you that you had better be more careful and impress upon the little girl once more not to say anything!"

First, Anna feigned ignorance, but after the neighbor had finished, she thanked her and promised that she would take better care of the children from then on. However, when the friendly woman left the house, Anna hurried without delay to the post office and sent her brother-in-law a telegram:

"The children must be taken away from here at once!"

The next day, her sister came and took the children herself. Sotte Weinreb and her husband had known Bernhard for a long time. So they kept Daniel and Judith with them, for the time being. Their apartment was not far from Bernhard's, so that the children could be taken home to Bernhard for nights.

But after the long weeks of free unconstrained life in the country they did not fare well in the city, because they had to be kept in the apartment for long hours, for security.

Now Bernhard knew the children to be in safe hands during the day, but even so, their whereabouts were not secure enough in his eyes. He loved his children very much, and he had sleepless nights when he thought about losing them. He just had to do something. The present situation could only be temporary, anyway.

Therefore, in the coming days he called on all his friends and acquaintances in order to figure out the best possible way of escape. One of them told him that she would be visiting her sister in Konstanz. She promised him that she would gather information about the possibility of crossing the border to Switzerland illegally.

On his way home, on the same day, Bernhard met one more friend. "Fritz, Fritz Blum!" he called quietly and put his hand on the shoulder of the man walking in front of him. Fritz turned around frightened, but his face brightened up when he recognized Bernhard.

"Bernhard Rosen! So you have managed to remain unrecognized until now too?" he asked, happily surprised, and looked at Bernhard from head to toe.

"And you also don't wear our yellow identification sign?" he observed, grinning.

"No, not from the time my name changed to Gerhard Baumann. However, I haven't had an easy time until now either. I cannot tell you my whole story now. Only this: Lea is dead! She was arrested and maltreated in such a way, that she died in the hospital a short while after being released. Now I am on my own, alone with my two children. I had hidden them away for a while in Beelitz, but they attracted attention there, so now they are in Berlin again, with me. But, of course, this is not safe enough for long. Ach, I would escape with them immediately, if only I knew where to!"

"Why don't you go to France?" asked Fritz. "There you can find enough unoccupied land in which you can hide with your children. Look, give me your address and I will send somebody over to you. You will see, in a few weeks you are going to be safe in a little French village!"

Bernhard agreed right away and gave him his address.

*

On the following day, a French woman appeared at his home.

"*Guten Tag*, my name is Yvette. Fritz Blum has sent me to you. Listen, Bernhard, I can get you a French passport, but not free of charge. You understand…?"

"Yes," he answered reluctantly, "what price did you have in mind?"

"Well, approximately…two thousand Marks!" answered the French woman, with a furtive glance.

"For this sum I will accompany you and the children over the border!" she added quickly, as she noticed Bernhard's hesitation.

"Good," said Bernhard, moaning. He had roughly four thousand Marks left over. If he bought the passport for this sum, he would still have enough money to live on for a while.

"And when am I going to get the passport?" he asked now.

"Soon, tomorrow evening," answered the French woman, and quickly said good-bye.

Bernhard could hardly wait for the next evening. It seemed to him so unreal that his escape would happen so soon. Therefore he did not really think that the French woman would actually come back.

But she came! She handed the longed-for passport over to Bernhard and took from him the sum of money they had agreed upon. As a surprise, she also brought Bernhard a bottle of French cognac and told him that they could set out on their journey in three day's time.

They had to drink to that, of course. Since the children were already sleeping, Bernhard and Yvette were on their own. They touched glasses and wished each other success with their plan. The cognac went to their heads quickly and it made them forget all scruples.

Bernhard had not held a woman in his arms for so long that he could not resist the attraction of the young Yvette.

"It is so late already!" complained Yvette. "Where shall I go to, now?"

"Stay here," he answered, and looked at her with longing. "Here with me!"

"But surely I cannot!" said Yvette, pretending to be reluctant but already removing the shoes and getting nearer to Bernhard on the sofa. He pulled her towards him at once, and a long kiss let him forget that there was a war going on, that he was a Jew and was persecuted…

He thought only for a moment of the sleeping children and reached behind him to put out the lights, which brought him an astonished look from Yvette.

"It's only because of the children, my little French angel!" smiled Bernhard and pulled her towards him again. They loved each other passionately, again and again, and only with the first light of dawn did Yvette quietly sneak out of the house.

Bernhard lived through the next day as if in a dream. He already saw in his mind how, in a short time, all of them would arrive in France together, Daniel, Judith, he and, of course, Yvette, his little French angel, as he was still amorously calling her. He was sure that their meeting was more than just a chance acquaintance, and that a higher power had led Yvette to him in order to take care of him and his orphaned children.

Bernhard brought the children to the Weinrebs, collected them again in the evening, fed them, kissed and caressed them, but he did everything distractedly. In his mind, a little raven-haired person haunted him and did not let his turbulent thoughts settle down.

He had just put the children to bed when the doorbell rang.

Bernhard started.

Were these perhaps the Gestapo men, coming to take him away?

The bell rang a second time. He had to open the door.

If he had been by himself, he would have escaped by springing through the window into the backyard, but with the children it was impossible to flee in that way. He opened the door with a heavy heart and breathed a sigh of relief as he recognized Yvette.

"Yvette!" he called out, delighted. "My God, how you startled me! I thought the Gestapo had arrived to drag me away!"

"Yes, yes, all right," she put him off hastily and pushed herself past him into the apartment.

"Look, the man who was the owner of the passport has returned, and he wants it back now!"

"Yes, but…and the money…?" asked Bernhard, distraught.

Yvette changed in an uncanny way. She stared at Bernhard with screwed up, stinging eyes and her usually gentle voice hissed dangerously in her French accent:

"Should I go to the police, perhaps?"

While hissing these words, she made an unmistakable gesture, holding her hand before her face with her fingers apart.

The little angel had turned into a grown up devil…!

Bernhard was dumbfounded. Just a little while earlier, he had painted their mutual future in the most glowing colors, and what was going to happen now? Everything had been crushed in a few moments, collapsed like a house of cards. A cold rage took hold of him, but there was no way out. He had no choice but to hand back the passport. Yvette took hold of the precious passport and disappeared. Bernhard heard the irregular clatter of her heels as she ran quickly down the steps, then the sound of the entrance door closing, and everything went silent again.

Bernhard still stood in the corridor, without moving. What had actually happened? Looking at it, not much, only a dream had burst like a shimmering soap bubble.

Bernhard stroked his forehead tiredly. He felt humbled and deceived.

"No," he said to himself, "and if only for the children, I am not allowed to give up!"

He took his coat and went to the acquaintance, who had promised to tell him about the chances of escaping to Switzerland. But only the young woman's father was at home. The girl was not home yet, but had sent a postcard.

"Many greetings to B. Have not found out anything!" was written on the back.

So there was no other way but to wait on patiently.

Bernhard talked for a while with the father of his acquaintance, but his thoughts drifted in other directions.

Before his mind's eye he saw each land of the globe and considered the possibility of living there, but he immediately dismissed these ideas, because there was no way to get out of Germany. How big and at the same time how small the earth seemed to him. There was no place for him and his children to live on this earth.

He said good-bye and went on his way home in a gloomy mood. Like always, he looked up at the windows of his apartment and started. Somebody had turned the light on!

His first thought was again 'the Gestapo!' Who else could it be? The children had been sleeping soundly when he had left them.

He was choked with fear, as he crept up the stairs. He hardly dared to breathe. Bathed in sweat, he opened the door. A strange woman sat in the room…!

Flabbergasted, he stared at her. He was surprised and at the same time angry that this person had frightened him so much.

"What are you doing here? Who are you, anyway, and how did you get into my apartment?" he asked.

"I…I…, ach please, don't be so scared," begged the young woman, big tears rolling down her cheeks. "I, I," she sobbed then, "I escaped from the assembly point for the KZ-transports, from the Levetzow-Temple. Mister Takács gave me your address and said that you were his good friend, and that I could find shelter with you for a few days for sure. Your children opened the door for me."

"Well, all right," said Bernhard, embarrassed. He went over to her and passed her his handkerchief. "Try to calm down. I didn't mean to be so rough. It is only that in my situation, one always thinks of the worst…! When I saw the light from down there, I thought immediately that the Gestapo was waiting for me up here in order to drag us away with them. Well, anyway, what is your name?"

"Marianne."

"Tell me, Marianne," asked Bernhard suspiciously, "are you in fact a Jew…?"

"Yes, I am a full Jew!"

Bernhard was distressed. In order to change the subject, he asked: "So Mister Takács is back from Hungary?"

"Yes, he came back yesterday."

"Did he not say anything else?"

"I cannot remember anything else."

"Well," said Bernhard then, "let us think where to accommodate you."

It was already midnight. At this hour, one could not send a girl into the streets. So Bernhard let the young woman have his bed and made do with sleeping on the uncomfortable carpet. Marianne wanted to thank him exuberantly, but Bernhard curtly rejected this and sent her quickly to bed. The experience with Yvette was still too fresh in his mind; he did not want to lose his self-control once more.

*

The following morning, he visited Mr. Takács.

"Tell me, Takács, what were you thinking, just sending a strange person to me, and a young lady on top of that!" he asked straight away instead of offering a greeting.

"Well, you know, Bernhard," Mr. Takács said, short of words, "I was so sorry for her, and I also didn't know where to send her. You know my wife…! She would show me the door from the outside if she thought something was fishy. And, as we are such good friends, I thought…"

"Well, all right," Bernhard stopped him, "I shall find a place for her, don't fret. But tell me, Takács, how was it in Hungary? How are our people there?"

"I tell you, Bernhard," answered Takács, "only there are you Jews still safe, for the moment. It will surely not take much time before they persecute your fellow Jews there too, but at this point I would advise everybody to escape to Hungary."

"But how does one begin doing that?" asked Bernhard.

"What, you want to escape with your two little children?" Takács said doubtfully.

"Yes," said Bernhard, "I don't have any other alternative. The thought that something could happen to the children here almost drives me out of my mind. They are all that I have left. We just have to get away from here!"

"Well, if you really want to escape, I can help you, of course," said Takács. "There are many Hungarians here, living in their lodgings' center in Koepenick Street. I know some of them very well. Go there tomorrow afternoon, around five o'clock. I shall speak with my friends today and prepare them for your visit."

Bernhard thanked him warmly and hurried back home. He brought Marianne and the children to the Weinrebs and went quickly to his workplace.

The next day, precisely on time, he stood in front of the entrance to the lodgings' center of the Hungarians. There was a lively hustle and bustle, people were coming and going, but Bernhard did not dare to speak to anybody. He noticed two men who, on the opposite side of the entrance, loafed about and glanced at him furtively from time to time. Bernhard waited a while, and when nothing else happened, he went over to them.

The two were about to light a cigarette, and Bernhard gave them a light. He was also offered a cigarette. He lit it, breathed deeply, and said: "I love Hungary, especially Hungarian cigarettes."

"Is your name Bernhard?" asked one of the Hungarians doubtfully.

"Yes," he answered. "You know why I am here?"

"We have heard about it," was the evasive answer.

"Good," said Bernhard, "then let's go over there to the pub. One can talk better over a glass of wine, don't you agree?"

"Why not," smiled the two Hungarians.

Together, they entered the nearest pub, whose owner was one of

Bernhard's acquaintances. Inside, they ordered some wine and clinked their glasses together.

"To Hungary!" called out Bernhard.

"To Hungary!" answered the two young men happily.

Now Bernhard felt that the right moment for his request had come.

"You must have heard that I am a Jew?" he asked quietly, and the Hungarians answered in the affirmative. "Then you also know that I must flee! For that I need a passport and the necessary emigration papers."

"That could be arranged, but what are you offering for it?"

"Nu, what sum did you have in mind?"

"Well,…around one thousand Marks!"

"Agreed, one thousand Marks!" Bernhard breathed a sigh of relief.

"But what are you going to do if you are caught without a passport?" asked Bernhard.

"Oh," said the Hungarian, grinning, "I'll just report that I lost it."

"Yes, sure. That is a possibility. Well, here are one hundred Marks as a down payment. When do we meet again?"

"Let's say, tomorrow at the same time, here in the pub. By the way, my name is Csató Miklosh."

"Good, Miklosh," said Bernhard, "then we shall see each other tomorrow."

The following evening, they met again at the same place and at the same time.

"In three days you will get the passport, with a visa stamped in it, and the red certificate of employment. Give me your address and I shall bring everything to you myself."

Pleased, Bernhard wrote down his address and gave it to Miklosh. He trusted the Hungarian completely.

Meanwhile, Bernhard's acquaintance had returned from South Germany with the information that an escape through the Swiss border was impossible. Just a short while earlier, a Jewish woman had been caught crossing the border illegally, and she and her children had been shot down on the spot.

'My God,' thought Bernhard, 'what if the same thing happens to us at the Hungarian border?'

Horror crept over him just thinking about this possibility. Harassed by fears and doubts, he decided not to go ahead with his plan.

"It would be madness!" he gasped out. "We just cannot go. It's too dangerous!"

His little son Daniel snuggled up to him and said:

"Papa, if we stay here, we are certainly going to be carried off and killed, but if we manage to escape, we might stay alive, true?"

"Yes, that's true," answered Bernhard hesitantly, and looked at the boy, amazed. He stood up and walked restlessly about the room. Then, with a quick movement he put his hands on the tender shoulders of the little boy, whose early maturity had shaken him.

"Tell me, Daniel, shall we go? As you know, this decision is very important. It can be highly dangerous for us, do you understand?"

The boy nodded and said without a moment's hesitation: "Yes!"

"Well, my son!" Bernhard breathed a sigh of relief. "Perhaps God's voice has spoken to us through you. We are going to Hungary. May God protect us."

The next morning, Bernhard called his workplace on the telephone to report himself sick, and he visited the Weinreb couple. He told them about his planned escape and said a warm good-bye to Marianne, who had found refuge with the friendly couple of physicians.

At home, the necessary things were quickly packed. In any case, they could not take more than two suitcases with them.

Now they had only to wait for the Hungarian, Miklosh. Daniel sat by the window, on the lookout for him.

"Here he is! Look, Papa, isn't that Miklosh?"

Bernhard hurried to the window.

"Yes, that's him!"

When the doorbell rang a few minutes later, Bernhard was at the door in a second.

"Miklosh, come in. We are already prepared for our departure. These are Daniel and Judith, my two children."

Bernhard now took the dear passport with shaking hands and handed over the rest of the sum.

"You know," Miklosh said, looking at the children, "I think I had better buy the tickets. I will not be asked any unnecessary questions."

"You are a real friend!" answered Bernhard, moved. "I was not mistaken about you!"

Miklosh went out without delay and came back a short while later with the tickets. Meanwhile, Bernhard had replaced the picture in the passport with his own and had entered his date of birth below it.

Miklosh accompanied them to the Charlottenburg railway station. There he attached a Hungarian badge onto Bernhard's jacket, and then they parted warmly from each other.

"Good-bye, Uncle Miklosh!" called Daniel and Judith. Bernhard lifted the two children into the train carriage and climbed aboard himself. Miklosh handed the suitcases to him, together with Judith's teddy bear, which the child immediately pressed tightly to her body.

They found an empty compartment. Bernhard stowed the suitcases and then pulled down the window. In a flash, the silent compartment was filled with the hectic atmosphere of the station. The children pressed their noses excitedly against the window and watched the noisy hustle and bustle on the platforms, while Bernhard leaned far out of the window and shook hands with Miklosh for the last time.

A shrill whistle sounded, and the heavy steam locomotive started to move and drag the green train carriages out of the station.

Bernhard closed the window, sat down and stared at the passing rows of houses.

After a short while, the scenery changed. The train began to move more quickly, as they traveled through fields and meadows into an obscure future.

'Am I ever going to see Berlin again?'

He heard Judith saying: "You see, Teddy, now we are going into the big wide world, to Hungary!"

"Hush!" said Daniel rudely to his little sister.

The journey into the unknown had begun, and the only thing to do was to look ahead.

Their fate was now in God's hands only.

7.

YANKEL AND RACHEL had been living with the people of the woods for quite a while. They had settled in, even if it was not always easy. For Rachel it was particularly hard to learn how to shoot. But she was told that this knowledge was essential.

Other than Esther, Mayer and Mendel, with whom they had arrived, they became good friends with Leib, the commandant, and with Nikolai. The latter did not rest until they could move outside as safely as he did.

"Just think what would happen if they caught you! Now you are responsible not only for yourselves, but for the entire group! Through careless behavior, you endanger all of us!"

The friends understood this and tried as hard as they could to meet the demands of this harsh life, in exchange for which they had security and companionship.

The friends also honored the unwritten laws of the people of the woods. One of them was that a woman could not have love relations with more than one man at the same time. Lovers could appear before the commandant to give a vow of fidelity, after which they would be considered married and could live together as a married couple.

Any third person interfering in such a relationship and wishing to ruin that camp marriage had to justify himself before the court of the people of the woods. As a minimum punishment, he would have to "organize" food for a few days, or even weapons and ammunition from the surrounding villages.

The most severe punishment was reserverd for someone who raped a woman or threatened a comrade with a weapon. He would be bound and taken before the camp court, which could, in extreme cases, sentence him to death.

Generally, such severe punishments did not have to be given, as the people of the woods lived together in harmony and unanimity. Each of them had lived through too many horrors. Besides, they needed all their strength in order to survive. All the food had to be organized in the surrounding farms or villages at the risk of their lives. Nobody knew the outcome of such an "organizing mission" and if and how he would return from it. Nonetheless, there were always more volunteers than necessary for these missions.

The camp was situated in a clearing, surrounded by dense undergrowth and tall trees, and could only be reached by way of hidden paths. At any given time, someone was sitting among the tallest branches of the highest tree and keeping watch on the surroundings. This way, he was the first to notice the returning comrades and could quickly inform the whole group. Then everybody would gather from all around, out of the underground woodsheds, in order to greet their friends and hear all about their supply mission.

Usually, they did not have much free time for discussions. They spent their time carving wooden crosses, figurines and toys and also manufacturing small articles and pieces of household equipment in order to exchange them for food in the villages. Unfortunately, the farmers no longer had any use for these articles. The people of the woods were therefore left with no way to obtain their bare necessities other than by illegal means. Naturally, the police found out. They were on the suppliers' trail, and it often lead to bloody fights with the Ukrainian militia, sometimes ending in casualties.

One evening, a supply group returned to the camp. The comrades, among them Yankel, rushed over and heard some bad news from them.

"An SS patrol caught us just after we had removed two sacks of potatoes from a truck on the main street!" panted one of the men, hardly able to breathe. "They shot at us and we shot back. But we were very close to the street and escaped into the woods!"

Another man continued: "We only brought one sack of potatoes with us, the other…"

"The other one was carried by Yanosh, Rachel and Lena," finished his friend. "They were running behind us, but we haven't seen them for the last half hour…"

"Rachel!" groaned Yankel, his hands over his face.

"Pssst!" called Leib suddenly.

At once everybody stopped talking, and for a few long seconds a deathly hush ruled in the woods.

There, all of them heard it now!

Something was approaching the clearing with an uncanny, dragging noise, accompanied by the crackle of branches and twigs. The people of the woods took cover and held their breath. The cracking noises grew louder, and suddenly the brushes parted. A dark form stumbled onto the moonlit clearing, staggered to and fro and collapsed.

"It's Yanosh!" called one of the comrades.

Immediately everybody hurried over to the man lying on the ground.

"He is seriously injured!"

"Is he still alive?"

"Yes, he is still breathing! Don't you see that his chest is rising and sinking?"

"Somebody bring a light, so we can see!" These calls and others sounded from all sides. Leib knelt down beside the wounded man and Yankel followed him. Another friend shone a lamp onto the face of the bloodstained man.

"Yanosh, Yanosh!" Yankel called desperately to him. "Where are the girls? Where is Rachel? Tell me! Can you understand me?"

"Yes," breathed Yanosh, "I hear you." He stammered on, brokenly: "The SS caught us…were not quick enough…only I could escape…shot at me…took the girls with them…pain in the chest…blood, so much blood…with my last strength…dragged myself…the girls, save the girls!"

A few men examined Yanosh's wounds. One of them said, shaking his head: "It's too late, nothing more to do. There are too many bullet holes. It is a miracle that he managed to get here at all!"

The man was right. Yanosh died a few minutes later.

Yankel jumped up and ran frantically to his shed. He returned, holding his submachine gun. He had put a few hand-grenades into his pockets.

"I'll show them!" he cried out in a rage. "Who is coming with me?" Nikolai jumped up first, and almost all the others wanted to follow him.

"Stop, stop!" called out Leib. "Only twenty men may go! Yes, Vanda, you may go too, to free your friend Lena. Nikolai will be in command. Yankel in his present state of mind could be too careless and put you all in danger. The others stay here. Good luck!"

After arming themselves with guns and hand-grenades, the liberation party marched quickly to the edge of the village. Vanda was sent forward while the others waited under the cover of some bushes.

"Everything is quiet, not a soul can be seen in the streets!" reported Vanda a short while later.

"Good," whispered Nikolai. "Yankel and you three there, and of course Vanda, come with me. The others will cover us and secure our way back! Let's go, now!"

Quick as lightning, they entered the police station with drawn weapons.

"Hands up, don't move!" called out Nikolai. In spite of that, two SS men reached for their guns, but before they could shoot they fell off their chairs dead, expressions of astonishment on their faces. The other SS men surrendered without fighting.

To Yankel's brusque question: "Where are the girls you arrested today?" one of them answered straight away: "In the cellar!"

Yankel pushed the barrel of his gun against the man's ribs and ordered: "Get up and lead us there!"

The man jumped up at once and led Yankel and Vanda to a cell in the cellar where the girls were being kept, while Nikolai and his men kept the SS men covered.

In the cellar, the gendarme now unlocked a thick iron door and Yankel pushed him into the cell. Rachel and Lena lay helplessly on the floor, tied up. They were so surprised that at first they could not utter a single word.

"Take off their ropes!" Yankel ordered the SS man.

"Yankel, Yankel!" sobbed Rachel. "Now everything is all right! When we heard the noises from above, we thought that our last hour had come!"

"Did this man tie you up?" asked Yankel.

"Yes!" called out Lena.

"Then come, let's tie him up and leave him here!"

They tied the SS man and left him in the basement. Upstairs, the comrades had already gathered whatever could be useful for them later and bound and gagged the SS men as well.

"Now we can treat you just the way you treat us!" Nikolai said to the bound men. "You know, you would not have one more second to live if we were to return evil for evil. But we want to show you that we are human beings, and I hope you will also treat us as humans if one of us should fall into your hands one day. Perhaps you had better think if you are not taking the wrong side after all. You will have enough time to think about it now, because you certainly won't be freed before tomorrow morning!"

With these words, Nikolai turned around and the six left the police station quickly, with the freed girls.

"You gave them a splendid speech," said one of the men to Nikolai. "Too nice words for these butchers! They certainly didn't understand what you meant!"

"I don't know, but I have the feeling that they were rather impressed when we spared their lives," said Nikolai, smiling.

They reached the rest of the group and the freed girls were greeted joyfully. Together they sneaked out of the village unnoticed and at last reached the camp, where they were warmly welcomed.

That evening, they all sat together for a long time and told their stories. Each of the sixty people of the woods had a sometimes-bizarre escape to recall. They managed somehow to escape from the Hungarian and Ukrainian thugs, this way or that way. Rachel and Yankel sat together side by side holding hands and listened as Leib told his story:

"I come from Kolomeya," said Leib. "The gendarmes arrested some of us there, off the street, and added us to a transport that was going straight to the KZ. The wagons of this train had barred windows. But my friends and I were able to pry loose a few planks of the wagon and at the first turning point we jumped off the slowing train, one after another. Then we rolled down the embankment. One of us broke his leg and remained there on the ground, helpless. Unfortunately, we could not help him. We had to run for our lives! A few minutes later, we heard the guards shooting him. And then they kept catching more of us.

"Only Yossi and I managed to escape from those henchmen. After a long march full of privation we found shelter at last, here in the Carpathian woods. But Yossi had an even tougher experience than I, didn't you, Yossi?"

"Yes," sighed Yossi, "I was an engineer in Kolomeya and lived there peacefully with my children. Then I heard about the abductions and about the anguish and death that awaited us Jews. At first I could not believe that such things could be possible. I just could not imagine that people from a cultured nation could commit such crimes. But when the danger became obvious and more and more threatening, I tried to protect my family. I dug an underground shelter in the garden, camouflaged it well and hid my two little children in it. As for me, I tried not to be seen out in the streets more than was necessary.

"Meanwhile, the Nazis were already picking up Jews from the streets and taking them away. I too was caught one day when I went out for some food. A Ukrainian informer turned me over to the SS men who dragged me to a transport. Then, on the train I met Leib. How we managed to escape, he already told you…! Yes, that's how it was…," sighed Yossi.

"And the children?" asked Yankel, after some hesitation. "What happened to them? Have you heard anything about them?"

"A tale of horrors!" replied Yossi, with a shaking voice. "I was relatively safe here in the woods, but I just couldn't bear it anymore. I spoke with Leib and told him that I wanted to get through to Kolomeya somehow, to look for my children. Leib agreed and even permitted me to bring the children back with me here to our camp. So I went on my way and managed to reach Kolomeya unnoticed. There I heard about the terrible fate of my two children…"

Yossi swallowed and his eyes became wet, as he continued: "At that time, when I had been outside the cave too long, the children went to search for me. An SS patrol picked them up, identified them as Jews and dragged them away, into a dark basement. There they were shot…!"

Yossi let his head fall onto his hands; he could no longer speak. Only after a while could he end his tragic story: "Yes, my friend, you don't have any children, yet. So you have been spared this pain!"

Yankel answered bitterly: "It is incomprehensible, that so many innocent children are being murdered without bringing the guilty ones to account for it!"

"One day they will be punished!" Nikolai threw in.

In response to that, Leib remembered a story:

"Perhaps you have heard of the ruler who besieged Jerusalem with his army. As his army could not conquer the city, he wanted to force the inhabitants to surrender by force of starvation. Then, one day, passing a village near Jerusalem, the ruler met a little boy. The sovereign beckoned to him to come over and asked him:

'So, what have you learned at school today?'

The boy was said to have answered to that:

'Sir! We were taught that God punishes the Jews when they gravely sin. But then he punishes those who dare condemn them twice as hard.'

At first, the ruler was angry about the boy's candor, but then he began to think about it and at last he ordered his army to stop the siege of Jerusalem."

"He was wise!" said Yossi with an ironical smile. "I'm only afraid that the Nazis and their followers will not be as clever. They will surely not stop persecuting us until the cup of their sins is full!"

But Yossi seemed to be wrong for the time being, because after their mission to free the girls there was no retaliation. Everything remained quiet; only the arrival of an early harsh winter made life more difficult for the people of the woods.

During this cold winter, the spring water froze, although they had sheltered it from the frost. They were faced with an extreme water shortage. The water was distributed daily in small quantities and was used only for drinking.

Therefore, everybody greeted the first snow with a hearty welcome. At last, everyone could wash himself again thoroughly, from head to toe.

They melted the snow in a ditch, dug with difficulty. Fortunately, there was enough wood. Nobody had to suffer from the cold in the three bunkers. The women lived in the first bunker, the men in the second and the couples in the third one.

Rachel and Yankel did not live together yet as a couple. Rachel had recovered somewhat from the terrible experience. She was proud of her Yankel. But when the girls did not stop their continued praising of him, she became jealous and did not leave his side. One day she was looking over his shoulder during a game of chess. Yankel was playing against Nikolai and had lost.

"Yes, if one has such a beautiful companion by one's side he certainly loses," laughed Nikolai.

Rachel wanted to leave, embarrassed, in order not to disturb them, but Yankel seized her hand and pulled her back onto her seat.

"Play on with Leib, Nikolai, all right?" he said, and then turned to Rachel.

"I'm just playing to take my mind off things, to think of other matters, but if you are with me I can't wish for anything better."

He held her hand firmly in his and Rachel leaned her head against his shoulder. They sat like that silently together for a long time. They were both thinking about the terrible things they had suffered and survived together.

What else was going to happen to them? Nobody could foresee the end of the war, and when the Nazis would at last stop their persecution of the Jews. So they were both silent in order not to speak about the gloomy future.

"Ah," said Rachel with a sigh, "I thank God that at least we are together!"

Both had only one wish, to survive and to live together happily.

Yankel and Mendel had prepared a surprise for Rachel. They had worked tirelessly for many hours and had built a guitar. They had even managed to obtain some strings.

Now Yankel proudly handed her the guitar and said:

"Here, my darling. This present is for you, to remove that constant sad look from your pretty eyes!"

"How beautiful!" cried Rachel, embracing Yankel lovingly and taking the instrument carefully into her hands.

"Beautiful, not exactly, but one can draw a few sounds from it," said Mendel, "try it, Rachel."

And Rachel played the guitar and sang along to its sound. In a flash, all the other comrades surrounded her; everybody sang with her, some of them with tears in their eyes.

Rachel too lost her composure, which she had kept diligently for such a long time, and collapsed into Yankel's arms. Somebody brought a glass of water and Yankel gave Rachel a drink from it, looking at her worriedly. But Rachel recovered quickly and wanted to leave Yankel's arms in a hurry. She was ashamed that the others had seen her in a moment of weakness, but Yankel calmed her down.

*

The winter continued and brought with it long and furious snowstorms. The men built a few sleds and supplied the farmers with wood. In that way, they again had something to bargain with in exchange for food. They even managed to stock up a rather large supply of bread, which improved their mood considerably; they began to hope again and one was able to hear laughter and jokes.

Rachel was said to be the most beautiful girl at the camp, and even if everybody knew that she was Yankel's bride, some of the young men tried to make advances on her. But Rachel knew how to evade such approaches skillfully.

Once, Yankel appeared just as a comrade tried to kiss her. Rachel warded that young man off with a slap on his face. But when Yankel wanted to beat up the uncouth fellow, she stood in his way.

"Let him go, Yankel! I don't want a fight at the camp because of me!" she said. "And besides," she added self-confidently, "I can defend myself quite well!"

Yankel shook his head indignantly.

"But I belong to you alone!" declared Rachel, nestling against him and kissing him gently.

Yankel was half appeased, but not satisfied.

"You do not belong to me really," he whispered lovingly into her ear and continued in a shaking voice:

"Rachel, we do love each other, and with God's help we shall also marry later…!"

He pressed her to him and kissed her passionately.

Rachel did not understand what Yankel really wanted of her, as until now they had only kissed a little and held hands. She only knew that she loved her Yankel more than anything and that she felt safe in his arms.

"Let's marry now, here in this camp!" exclaimed Yankel decidedly. "Then nobody will be allowed to pester you! Rachel, my love, I beg you, please let's marry, please say yes! We do have more than ten Jewish men here, so we can put up the *Huppah* according to the old Jewish custom and marry under it!"

"But the year of mourning has not ended yet," objected Rachel.

"That is only a custom and not a rule!" answered Yankel. "But if it is your wish, I shall not touch you until the year of mourning is over. The main thing is that we be man and wife, and no other man shall ever come too close to you!"

"You are really jealous," smiled Rachel and snuggled up to him. "You know that I only belong to you, forever. Whenever you wish it, I shall be your wife!"

"Rachel, my darling!" called out Yankel, beside himself with happiness, and kissed her passionately. "Come, let us go to Leib and tell him the great news!" he said, and pulled Rachel with him.

"Leib, Rachel and I want to get married!" he said breathlessly.

"Well then, you have decided, at last?" asked Leib, with a smile.

"Why 'at last'?" asked Rachel, baffled.

"Well, look," grinned Leib, "for some time now, you have not left

Yankel's side, and he also guards each of your steps jealously. We have all been waiting for you two to become a couple!"

Rachel blushed, and Yankel was a little embarrassed too.

"We are real Jewish children and want to wed under the *Huppah!*" he said.

"*Mazel-Tov!*" congratulated Leib and Nikolai. Then they gathered all the people of the woods in order to tell them the good news.

"Listen, comrades!" called Leib. "Rachel and Yankel want to get married at last!"

"*Mazel-Tov!*" and "At long last!" could be heard from all sides. Everybody liked the two young people and so they did their best to make the young couple's wedding day as beautiful as possible. They even got hold of wine and Schnapps. One of the friends presented Yankel with a ring and one woman gave hers to Rachel.

The *Huppah* was put up outside the bunkers among the trees of the wood. The witnesses for the marriage ceremony, Leib, Mendel and two young women, led the happy couple to the *Huppah* and the ceremony began.

After the marriage ceremony, they all celebrated happily in Yankel's bunker.

Mendel had, as if by magic, conjured a violin and surprised the celebrating party with old Jewish songs. The violin laughed and cried under his fingers. The comrades listened, deeply touched. Then Rachel took the instrument and played the song of the people of the woods. Everybody joined in:

> The leaves on the trees in the wood
> Rustle in the wind, as they would;
> We sit together and it's spring,
> The birds above twitter and sing.
>
> They jump and fly from tree to tree,
> We wish we could also be free;
> But our hearts resound and sigh,
> As hour after hour passes by.
>
> Dusk is falling and then the night,
> Our limbs get heavy and tight;

We almost don't dare to breathe,
Although inside we rage and seethe.

So one to the other we cling,
Asking what the future will bring;
And promising the dead again,
That their death will not be in vain.

The chains of tyranny will break,
By us, all the partners of ache;
In this hour of need and night,
The name of our life is "Fight."

To strive for our freedom and land,
This is all of God's and our command.

After the singing, all of them were silent, moved. Suddenly, they heard
cries for help from outside. Everybody jumped up and hurried out.

The cries came from the bunker where two Ukrainians had remained.
These two had returned from 'organizing' and had held back some Schnapps
for themselves, with a high alcohol percentage. They had just opened the
bottle and were drinking it together, when one of the women of the camp
had found them out. The drunken men discovered her and fell upon her,
trying to rape her.

The woman defended herself vigorously and cried for help.

The comrades quickly came to her aid, freed her, overpowered the
drunken men and left them lying there tied up in order to let them sleep
off their drunken stupor. As punishment, they were sent away for a few
days to 'organize.'

Yankel and Rachel were given a few days off without any duties to carry
out. Even so, they helped everywhere that help was needed.

Mendel, in his free time, played his violin for them. He played some
Jewish-Hebrew and Hungarian songs. Under his fingers, the instrument
sang in the finest tones.

"Why does the violin cry only for you, and not for me too?" asked
Nikolai, the Russian.

"Did you see how your parents, brothers and sisters and so many children, women and old people were murdered, only because they were Jews? No! They persecute you for political reasons and you know that your relatives will survive, if they are not hit by a bomb during an air raid. But if we Jews are so lucky as to be spared by the war, this will not prove to be a guarantee for our lives in the future. You can flee from a bomb, but our biggest enemy, the Nazi regime, lies in wait for us everywhere and wants to eliminate us. We innocent Jews are being chased and hunted, deported and murdered! And this is why my violin cries!" said Mendel with a sigh, tucked the violin under his chin and played the song of the "*Yiddishe Mame*".

The comrades listened, very moved, and some of them cried.

At that moment, Leib returned from his usual daily rounds through the camp and its surroundings. He was concerned about the long absence of the two Ukrainians.

"Three days have passed already since they went away! Something must have happened," said Leib worriedly.

Nikolai said: "I don't trust those thugs. Perhaps they have betrayed us to the gendarmes!"

"It is possible," answered Leib, "we must be prepared for the worst!" He ordered an additional guard to the ones around the camp.

And indeed, on the following day, that guard and the man from the outlook on the tree reported that a rather large group of armed people was approaching the camp. The commandant himself climbed up the tree and, looking through the field glasses, affirmed that around fifty men were approaching the wood. A dog was running in front of them pointing the direction. Leib climbed off the tree. Everybody was awaiting his orders.

"Comrades," began Leib, "first of all we must keep calm and remain cool headed. We are lucky to have seen our enemies in time, so that we have time left to prepare our defense. All the weapons will be distributed. Then we take cover behind the trees. Nobody remains in the camp. The first line of defense will be a hundred meters from the camp and the second fifty meters from it. Let them approach up to around fifty meters. Upon my order, you open fire from all sides!"

The people of the woods hurried to carry out their commandant's orders.

Two men in the first line were ready to render the dog harmless, using an iron rod. All of them were waiting tensely in hiding places, well camouflaged with leaves and soil.

Then they heard the sound of the panting dog breaking through the bushes. A few seconds later, before it could warn the soldiers with its barks, the two men overpowered it.

Now the squad of armed men was approaching noisily, getting nearer and nearer.

When the uniformed men had gotten to about forty meters from them, Leib gave the order: "Fire!"

From all sides, the people of the woods began shooting at their attackers. After the first salvo, some of them fell down, wounded, while others escaped. They had not expected such a reception!

The partisans followed the retreating soldiers to the edge of the wood and immediately returned to camp. There, amongst the dead they recognized the two Ukrainians whom they had sent to 'organize.' So they had changed sides and joined the enemy! They must have thought that they would get a special position with the SS for this.

Yankel, who had fought in the first line, ran back in search of Rachel. He found her with a gun in her hand, looking aghast at the bodies of the dead enemies.

Yankel took her in his arms and carried her back to the camp.

Leib was waiting there by the time all of them had gathered. Then he spoke to them:

"God was on our side, therefore we have won this time! But we have to expect that our enemy will come back shortly with reinforcements. We have to vacate the camp and search for new shelter. Go and eat once more, and then take from your personal belongings and supplies as much as you can carry. We march in two hours!"

Dusk had already descended when they left their camp as planned. They found accessible paths and made good progress, for the freezing winter had already passed. The commandant and Mendel rode in front on their horses and scouted their way. If there was no evident danger, they let the others follow.

On the fourth day of their march, they met two strangers in the wood who attempted to run away as soon as they were spotted. But the people of the woods stopped them and discovered that they were two Polish Jews who were on their way to the next village, where they wanted to obtain some food. The two men knew their way around every place of the region and they advised Leib to set up camp on the west side of the city of Stryy, near the Hungarian border. They said that there was less danger of being discovered by the SS men there.

The refugees went on in that direction and after three days they found a location which seemed to be suitable for a new camp. Within two weeks they built a few wooden bunkers, one-and-a-half meters deep, which they covered with earth and then with branches and bushes, so that they looked like small mounds. Then they fitted out the underground dwellings for living.

Their only problem was how to obtain food. The inhabitants of the surroundings were so poor that they could not even exchange the valuables, which the people of the woods offered them, for bread or other food. The few prosperous farmers did not want to sell anything.

So the people of the woods again carved objects from wood and employed a girl from their group, Mariussa from the Ukraine, to get in touch with a distant village. Mariussa even found work as a waitress in an inn, and due to her pleasant ways the villagers soon trusted her.

She became a friend of the village baker, and so she could often send her friends, the partisans, back with horses fully packed with bread.

After a while, Mariussa became acquainted with some young people who worked in a central storage camp in which the crops for delivery to the Germans were stored. In addition, there were other supplies stored there for the occupying power. Mariussa received information from these young people, which she immediately passed on to her friends in the camp in the wood. One night, after careful preparation, the partisans cleared out most of the supply camp and set the rest on fire.

The next day, the authorities began an in-depth search, which was unsuccessful for the time being. The excitement rose even more after a second attack was carried out shortly afterwards. The railway bridge on the stretch between Stryy–Lemberg, which passed the village, had been blown up! The SS searched zealously for the persons responsible and spread their agents out everywhere.

Mariussa was aware of her dangerous position, and therefore she kept her eyes and ears open attentively. One day, two SS men entered the restaurant. Mariussa was acquainted with the two already, but she had never revealed to them that she could speak German. So the two talked in their mother tongue quite freely, and Mariussa listened. Startled, she learned that they suspected her and her friends to be the thieves. To her dismay, they called her to their table and invited her for a drink in order to sound her out.

"Hey, Mariussa, how about a drink? Come, keep us company for a while!" one of them said and pulled her down onto the wooden bench near him. Turning to his comrade, he said in German: "This is a real cunning one, with her we have to be careful!"

Mariussa gathered all her strength in order to appear entirely natural. She joked with the two and served them as attentively as the other guests. But inside her, she had only one thought: 'How do I get out of here?!'

Help came by pure chance, when the landlord approached the table of the two SS men and greeted them:

"Good day and 'Heil Hitler,' gentlemen! So, do you already have an idea who the assailants could have been? Or are you still groping in the dark?"

"Well, yes, we have found out a few things already," said one of the SS men with a smile. "As you know, we have our ears and eyes everywhere! But let's not speak about such things now!"

Turning to Mariussa, he went on: "Come, Mariussa, tell us a little about your life!"

At these words, he winked at his comrade eloquently and said to the landlord: "I love the Hungarian language and like to listen when somebody speaks in that language!"

"With pleasure," she answered, "but let me go out for a few minutes first. I have to breathe some fresh air! I have a splitting headache!"

"Go then, go, Mariussa," said the landlord, and turned again to the SS men.

Mariussa didn't need to be told this a second time. She disappeared into her room quickly, put on a pair of solid shoes, wrapped herself into a big woolen shawl, took the gun from its hiding place and left the house unnoticed. She escaped from the village in the darkness and reached the camp of the partisans after a long march, in the early hours of the morning. Exhausted and breathless, she reported to her comrades:

"They are on to us! Two SS men were at the inn today. They wanted to sound me out, but fortunately I understand their German and so I had ample warning. Under the pretext that I had a headache, I went out and escaped here during the night unnoticed! I tell you, the village is much too dangerous for me at the moment. I cannot go back there, and you too should not be seen there, for the time being."

This was a heavy blow for the people of the woods because they had only a little food left, which was now quickly dwindling away. Sixty hungry people were constantly being given smaller and smaller rations. Finally, Yankel, Mendel and two other comrades were sent across the nearby border to Hungary. Their mission was to try and find some food there.

Without being noticed, the group reached a little farm over the Hungarian border. There lived an elderly couple with two grown daughters.

The partisans were received there kindly and were soon invited to take part in the farmers' meal.

"May we, perhaps, stay with you overnight?" asked Yankel after they had eaten. "We have already been walking today for many hours!"

Shaking her head, the elderly farmer's wife answered: "We only have two beds, in one of them I sleep with my husband and my two girls sleep in the other. So you see, there is no place for you, gentlemen."

"But we are no gentlemen!" said Yankel. "We also don't need a soft bed. We would gladly put up with the floor. The main thing is that we should have a roof over our heads and wouldn't have to sleep in the open air." Smiling, he added: "You also don't need to be afraid for your daughters. We are not barbarians, but tired migrant workers. Besides, I am already married." The daughters giggled and the farmer's wife agreed. "Well, you can sleep here tonight."

"Actually, where do you come from?" asked the farmer now.

To Yankel, the farmers seemed trustworthy and so he declared openly: "We are Jews and are hiding on the other side of the border, in the woods."

Suddenly the farmer's attitude changed. He said openly: "You are refugees? Don't be afraid, you are safe here. We Ruthenes don't like the Magyars! The bloody war has taken our two sons away from us!"

Sighing, he stroked his forehead with his workworn hand and continued: "And so I must in my old age still do all the work alone…!"

Deep in thought, the old man stared in front of him.

"This must be sad for you," said Yankel, "but you still have two daughters who will surely bring a son-in-law into your house. Then you can retire."

Yankel looked at the two girls and noticed that Marie, the youngest, was particularly interested in Mendel. She really devoured him with her eyes, and Mendel also seemed to look at the girl with some affection.

Yankel smiled, but was immediately serious again.

"Do the gendarmes come to you often?" he asked the farmer.

The old man reassured him: "No, it's been a long time since the border police or the gendarmes from the village have come to our farm. You don't have to fear anything in our home. If somebody should come, our dog will bark loudly."

Nevertheless, every once in awhile Yankel sent Mendel out to be on the lookout for possible enemies.

The farmer's wife gave them some pillows and blankets and showed them where to sleep. Satisfied, all the comrades lay down. A long time had passed since they had had an opportunity to sleep in a house. Marie came and brought Mendel an extra blanket, so that he could lie more comfortably.

"You are well in with that one!" Yankel teased Mendel.

"Ah, nonsense!" grumbled Mendel, put out, wrapping the blanket around himself and turning to the wall.

The elderly farmer's wife bolted the door, made an additional round through the house and also lay down to sleep.

*

After a few hours, the dog began to bark.

At once all of them were awake. Mendel looked out of the window into the darkness, but he could not see anyone approaching the house.

As a precaution, the four comrades erased any traces of their presence and climbed up to the attic. Marie would tell them if somebody came to the house.

Then somebody knocked sharply on the door.

"Open up at once!" ordered a man in a powerful voice.

Shaking, Marie opened the door and two gendarmes entered, pushing in front of them two bound men.

"Lie down on the floor!" one of the gendarmes ordered the men and pushed them down. The unfortunates obeyed, unresisting.

"Ah, beautiful child," said one of the gendarmes to Marie and patted her cheek. "I didn't know what a beauty was hidden here in the wasteland! Now bring us something to eat!"

"Marie!" called the old farmer's wife in order to bring the girl to her. "You remain here! I'll deal with this."

She sent Marie out and prepared an omelet for the uninvited guests, adding some milk, bread and butter to it. She turned around to feed the bound men too, when one of the gendarmes shouted:

"Stop! These Jew-pigs don't get anything!"

Then he lay down to sleep, after commanding the other gendarme to stay awake and keep guard carefully.

Meanwhile Marie crept up to the attic to tell the comrades what was happening. Mendel asked her to give a sign when the gendarmes were both asleep. They agreed that Marie would give two short coughs.

Marie went down again and the partisans waited tensely for the sign.

At last the time came when they heard Marie cough. The comrades breathed a sigh of relief and crept down carefully. Opening the door in one quick movement, they caught hold of the guns of the gendarmes, who tried to jump up immediately and rush towards them. But Yankel and Mendel held the loaded guns to their chests before they had a chance to move.

"There is no sense in that! Give yourselves up!" called Mendel.

Quickly, the gendarmes were disarmed and the bound people freed. "Who are you?" asked the two Jews.

"We are Jews and persecuted like you," was Yankel's answer. "You can come with us, if you want to!"

"Yes, yes!" cried the two, pleased.

"Good," said Yankel, "but before we can return home we have to carry out some tasks. In the meantime, you can tie the gendarmes up and guard them, until we get back."

"Agreed!" answered the two and began their task.

"We had better go without delay!" said Yankel to his comrades. They went on their way and returned at dawn with two horses, two bulls and one cow.

Without wasting time, Mendel drove the animals with the help of the two new comrades towards the border. Yankel stayed behind with the others. He wanted to give Mendel a head-start. They planned to meet again on the other side of the border. At the agreed time, Yankel and his comrades swung themselves into the saddles and rode after Mendel.

Mendel's group had meanwhile almost reached the border. Suddenly an old Jew with sidelocks and a well-groomed beard walked towards them. They stared at him, surprised; he looked to them like some ethereal apparition.

The man stopped hesitantly, as he did not recognize them right away as Jews.

"Come nearer, good uncle!" called Mendel to him. "We are fellow Jews!"

Then they pressed the old man with questions:

"How is it that you can simply walk around here? Aren't you afraid of the gendarmes or the SS? Do more Jews, who are not persecuted, live here?"

"Oy, it is not easy for us either," said the old man. "They have taken all Jewish men, up to the age of forty-five years, to the so-called work-brigades and sent them to the Ukraine. We have not heard from them since!"

"And the older Jews and women and children, are they left in peace?" asked Mendel.

"No," answered the old man. "We are guarded all the time and have to expect house searches every day. We also cannot hide anybody, because our neighbors are so untrustworthy that they reveal everything."

Then the man pointed to the cow and asked: "Tell me, where do you have this animal from? She looks like our cow!"

Mendel scratched his head in embarrassment.

"Well, you know, we are a large group out there, hiding in the woods. We don't have money to buy food, so…"

"I understand that, but you must leave our cow here," said the man. "We really need her!"

"All right, take her back," answered Mendel.

Satisfied, the old man said good-bye, took his cow and led her back to the village.

A short while later, Yankel's and Mendel's groups met and they made their way back to the camp.

*

Meanwhile, back at the partisans' camp, the comrades were becoming anxious. They were worried about the fate of the supply group they had sent out. Rachel feared that the worst had happened to her Yankel and asked Leib to send off a search party.

The commandant declined resolutely.

"You don't even know which direction they took. Be patient, Rachel! If they don't arrive by tomorrow, we will all have to leave the camp and flee."

But Rachel would not listen to Leib. She took her machine gun and a few hand grenades in order to carry out some plan of her own.

Leib stood in her way.

"Stop!" he called. "Stay here!"

But when Rachel continued to oppose him strongly, he finally gave in. He chose some comrades to accompany her and, with a heavy heart, let her go.

The group walked stealthfully through the wood. Rachel led, and the others followed her, one after the other, a short distance between each of them. They had not been going for long when Rachel gave a signal of warning.

Before them, at the edge of the wood, two SS men, heavily armed with machine guns, were standing with their back turned to the comrades. Fortunately, the SS men did not have a dog with them.

Rachel guessed correctly that they were searching for the partisans' camp. But they seemed to have discovered something else, because they stared attentively in a certain direction.

"My God, what if it's Yankel they are waiting for?" said Rachel in a tight voice.

"Hold your weapons ready!" she ordered the men, whispering.

Now they could hear the patter of hooves, and from a distance Rachel recognized Yankel and his friends on their horses.

The SS men raised their guns.

"Fire!" cried Rachel.

The salvo cracked out, and the two uniformed men fell down, before they could shoot even one shot. Rachel and her comrades jumped up and ran over to the two SS men. Both were dead.

"Yankel, Yankel!" called Rachel, excitedly, because Yankel had stopped his group immediately upon hearing the shots. He started when he heard Rachel's voice, as he thought she was in mortal danger. He dug his spurs in the horse's flanks and rode headlong through the bushes to the edge of the wood. He stopped his horse in front of Rachel, jumped down and hurried to his young wife.

"Rachel, darling! Are you wounded? What happened here?" cried Yankel as he pulled Rachel to him, worried.

Then, with one look he thought he grasped the situation. He pointed to the two bodies, which still had their guns ready in their hands and uttered: "My God, have these been in wait for you?"

"For us?" said Rachel seriously. "They were waiting for you!"

"What, they were laying in wait for us?" asked Mendel, who had followed Yankel with the group. "We would have fallen into the trap unsuspectingly!"

"How fortunate that you happened to be here by chance!" said Yankel, and kissed Rachel warmly.

"By chance?" grinned one of Rachel's companions. "You should have heard Rachel and Leib! They were really shouting at each other! Like market women! Rachel was determined to go and search for you, and Leib wanted to wait one more day and then evacuate the camp. Neither of the two wanted to give way! But then Leib gave in and sent us in search of you."

"Then you have saved my life!" said Yankel, his face beaming with joy, and he pressed Rachel to him until she protested.

"Stop, do you want to kill me out of gratitude?"

Actually, this treatment was not so unpleasant to her at all.

"I suggest that we get away from here quickly!" said Mendel from behind.

They all agreed. They quickly dragged the bodies into the bushes, after taking their weapons, and the group hurried back to the camp.

At the camp they had heard the shots too. The comrades were running around frightened. They had already packed their belongings for an escape.

When they saw the whole group of friends returning to the camp, they approached quickly and asked: "What happened? Why did you shoot? Is Rachel wounded?"

"No, no!" answered Yankel. "Nobody among us is wounded. Two SS men were waiting in ambush for my group, but Rachel's group shot them, and they were dead before they could make use of their guns."

"Forgive me, Rachel," said Leib, embarrassed. "I should not have hesitated to allow you to leave the camp. It must have been the voice of God which called you to go!"

"Don't think about it, Leib," smiled Rachel. "Let's forget the incident."

She kissed Leib's cheek and went on: "For me, the most important thing is that I have my Yankel with me again!"

The rest of the partisans gathered and all of them cheered her.

Then the returning search party reported everything that had happened in detail, and Yankel and Mendel told them about the situation in Hungary. Right after that, the people of the camp talked about whether after the dangerous incident with the SS men they should stay on at the camp or move on immediately.

"You know," said Nikolai, "I think the two men were on patrol, therefore nobody will miss them straightaway. But soon they will send out a bigger search patrol. In the meantime I think this will leave us enough time to decide what to do."

Most of the members agreed with Nikolai's assessment, and so it was decided to stay for the time being and just to fortify the guards. With this decision they made a grave error, which was to lead to serious consequences.

That night passed calmly, but it was the calm before the storm.

Early in the morning, the guards were startled to hear dogs barking from far away. They reported this at once to the commandant. Leib climbed up to the lookout. He stared frightened at a procession of soldiers which was approaching the camp with a few dogs. In no time at all, he climbed down from the tree and gave the alarm.

"Prepare for a fight, people, arm yourselves now! It's going to be a fight for life or death. A whole procession of soldiers is on its way here. We must try to break through and get to Hungary. Those who want to come with me can join us!"

"We can divide ourselves into two groups," suggested Nikolai. "You with your group flee to the west and I with the other one to the south."

The partisans agreed with him. They hurried feverishly to take their weapons and few belongings and divided into two groups. They took cover behind the trees and waited tensely for the attack.

The SS men noticed that something was happening in the partisans' camp, so they shot a few MG-salvo into that direction. Leib sent out ten volunteers to delay the soldiers. Out of the ten, only six came back. Nothing remained but to flee quickly.

In two groups, led by Leib and Nikolai respectively, the partisans moved forward and tried to reach the edge of the wood.

Suddenly the soldiers' dogs attacked them from behind. A few well-aimed shots removed this danger. Much worse though was the merciless barrage with which the SS unit hit them.

Yankel and Rachel fought side by side. Murderous gunfire closed upon them when they crossed an open field with their group in order to reach the other part of the wood.

"Down!" ordered Yankel, and immediately all of them threw themselves on the ground. For a while, there was no pause as the bullets flew around them.

When the firing eased off slightly, they decided to attack. After a hard battle, they finally succeeded in destroying a nest of machine gunners and thus forced their way to freedom.

But what a price they had paid for their path of escape! From their group, only Yankel, Rachel, Mendel and two other comrades remained. All the others, among them Leib the commandant, were left behind, lying dead on the ground in the clearing of the woods.

*

The other group, led by Nikolai, had not fought with them in the clearing, but had tried during the general confusion to take off to the south. Little Esther was with them. The girl had wanted to join Rachel at first. But when she saw how some men were hit and fell to the ground, she cried out loudly in panic and just stood still, shaking, with her fists held tightly over her eyes.

Nikolai saw the child standing still in the clearing, while around her shots hit the earth. He ran to her quickly, took hold of the shaking girl, carried her into the bushes and took her with him when his group tried to break through the enemy line.

*

Meanwhile, Yankel and his comrades ran for their lives. They had reached the wood, but the soldiers continued to pursue them. So, from time to time they had to take cover and shoot back.

Suddenly Rachel stumbled and fell into a deep hollow.

"Rachel, darling! What happened to you? Are you injured?" called Yankel, startled, and jumped down to her into the hollow.

"No, no, I have only stumbled," she reassured him. "But I cannot get up. My foot! I don't think I can run anymore!"

Rachel tried several times to stand up but doubled over with a cry of pain each time. Making a quick decision, Yankel and Mendel picked her up and carried her together. At the same time, the other two comrades fought the soldiers for a while and delayed them in order to let the three friends gain some ground. Then they hurried on too. After a short while they reached Yankel, Rachel and Mendel and they ran on together until they all were exhausted and had to rest.

There they lay in the grass: five survivors out of more than twenty people! They looked at each other, depressed.

"Oh, Yankel," moaned Rachel and put her head on his chest. "What do you think has happened to Esther and Nikolai and the others? Do you think they have managed to break through?"

"I don't know," answered Yankel, wretchedly. "I didn't have time to check up on Nikolai."

"But he took Esther with him! She cried so pitifully and just stood there. So Nikolai took her with him. But I should have taken care of her," sobbed Rachel. "And I just ran away and let her down! For that, God has punished me now! Because of that I cannot walk on now…!"

Rachel cried unceasingly.

"Let me lie here and you save yourselves! Then at least you will have a chance to get out alive through all this!"

"But Rachel, how can you say such a thing? Calm down, little one! We are going to get through this!" said Yankel, and caressed her gently.

"Yes," said Mendel, "but where should we really escape to?"

"We can only flee to Hungary," answered Yankel. "Nobody knows us there. Perhaps we could find shelter at the farm of our friendly hosts!"

"What do you think of that?" Mendel asked the comrade nearest to him. "Shall we go to Hungary?"

"Why not," both comrades answered, "we cannot stay here. The Nazis would quickly track us down and shoot us."

Meanwhile, no more shots could be heard. It seemed as if the soldiers had given up their pursuit for the time being. Nonetheless, the friends soon set out on their way.

After a laborious march of four days, they at last arrived at the small farm. Yankel carried Rachel over the threshold.

"This is my wife!" he said to the farmers.

"Is she injured?" asked the old farmer's wife with pity.

"What is the matter with her?"

"She fell down during our escape and twisted her ankle, or perhaps even broke it!" explained Yankel.

"Then bring her over here quickly and lay her down," said the farmer's wife. She examined Rachel's ankle and then said:

"Fortunately nothing is broken!"

She put cold compresses around the swollen limb, and the swelling went down gradually.

Meanwhile, the farmer greeted the other comrades and asked them about the partisans.

"Yes," Mendel was just relating what had happened to them, "…and we are the rest of our group. We are the only ones who managed to flee into the woods. The others lost their lives there at the fight in the clearing."

"But there were more people in your camp, weren't there?" asked Marie. She was sitting opposite Mendel and did not take her eyes off him.

"That's right," he answered. "We divided ourselves into two groups. The others wanted to flee to the south. We lost sight of them during the fight, and so we don't know what happened to them."

"So sad," said Marie, with a sigh. "And what is going to happen now? Where do you want to escape to?"

"At the moment," said Yankel, "we cannot flee anywhere, as Rachel cannot walk."

Turning to the farmers, he went on: "Therefore I wanted to ask you to let us stay here for a few days. We will take care of ourselves and take on all your work!"

"Look!" called Mendel. "We are strong men, farmer! As long as we stay here, we will do all your work and you can rest!"

"Well, as far as I am concerned you can stay with us for a while," said the farmer, and his wife nodded approvingly.

"Tell me," asked Marie, "your name is Mendel, right?"

"Yes," answered Mendel with a smile, "why?"

"You are Jewish too?"

Mendel nodded. "Why shouldn't I be a Jew?"

"You don't look like a Jew at all!"

"How do Jews look, then?" asked Mendel, grinning.

"Well, yes, they are just…well, it's all the same to me if you are a Jew or not," said Marie, embarrassed. "But here Mendel is 'Martin,' and I shall call you so, all right?"

"It's all right with me!" laughed Mendel. "Call me Martin if you want. Anyway, I still remain the same Mendel."

Yankel cut in: "Yes, from now on his name is Martin!"

Laughing, they all called him by his new name until 'Martin' indignantly warded them off.

"By the way, what happened to the two gendarmes we left here?"

"Ah," said Marie, contemptuously, "they asked us if we knew you. Naturally we said no. I told them that you had entered through the unlocked door. But both of them were suspicious and didn't seem to be entirely convinced. Then I said to one of them: 'If your friend, the blockhead, had not slept, this wouldn't have happened!'"

"You are quite courageous, aren't you!" said Mendel with an appreciative look.

Blushing, Marie then continued:

"And then we untied them. Before they left we had to promise them to tell no one what happened here."

Marie giggled.

"The whole thing must have been rather embarrassing for them!"

"And since then you haven't heard anything from them?" asked Yankel.

"Well, yes," answered Marie. "They came back once and searched the house and the garden. When they didn't find anything they left, and since then they haven't shown their faces again."

"Actually, why didn't you shoot the gendarmes?" asked the farmer.

"How could we shoot them if we were not in mortal danger?" answered Yankel. "If somebody points a gun at me to kill me, I shoot him first without a second's hesitation. But I would never kill a defenseless person standing before me with his hands up. None of us would do that!"

The comrades nodded. "We are against unnecessary bloodshed!" declared Mendel.

This attitude pleased the farmer and his family, and so they got along with their guests. And between 'Martin' and his Marie, a special bond grew.

Marie obtained a smart local farmer's costume for Martin and walked around with him boldly through the whole village; she even took him to church with her. After that they often visited people in the village. They also went to the old Jew who had taken back his stolen cow from Mendel the last time.

"Do you remember me, dear uncle?" Mendel asked him.

"How could I not remember you, when I had so much trouble afterwards because of you!" answered the man, outraged.

"My wife ran through the whole village and told everybody that our cow had been stolen and we would starve to death! And half the people of the village gathered around her, and all of them wept because of our sad fate. And suddenly I came, walking through the village with the cow, pulling her with a rope fastened around her neck. I had to explain and explain again until they believed that it was not I who had stolen all the animals!"

"I am so sorry that you had this trouble because of us," said Mendel and told the old man what had happened to him and his comrades in the interim.

The old Jew listened, shaken, tugging at his long white beard and in the end he wiped his moist eyes. "And what plans do you have now?"

"For the time being we are safe here," said Mendel. "What we shall do if we cannot stay any longer in our present hiding place, we don't know yet."

"Can I do anything for you?" asked the old man. "I cannot offer you shelter as we are under inspection all the time, but perhaps you need something?"

"Well, yes," said Mendel, embarrassed, "we need some bread urgently!"

"Good," said the old Jew. "Wait here until I come back!"

With these words he set out on his way and left Mendel with his wife and son.

"Don't lose your confidence!" the old Jewish woman consoled Mendel. "God will not let you down!"

"How can you be so confident, with everything that is happening around you?" asked Mendel, astonished.

"I believe in God, in the goodness of the people and in justice. God will not destroy the people of Israel. He will send us the Messiah, and then there will be an end to all the sufferings," said the old woman. "They have taken away my eldest daughter. Nevertheless, I haven't lost my faith in God. He will surely protect her!"

"I hope so!" interrupted her son now.

"How can you say such a thing!" said his mother, angrily.

"Up to now, have they left you in peace?" asked Mendel in order to prevent a quarrel between mother and son.

"I'm not living here anymore. I'm working with a carpenter in Budapest, and now I'm only visiting my parents!" explained the young man.

"What is happening to our fellow Jews in Budapest?" asked Mendel, interested.

"In Budapest it is just the same as here," said the man. "They have deported all Jewish men under forty-five years of age who were not in hiding. Almost daily, there are Jewish refugees arriving, most of them with fake papers. They are living in the city, hiding somewhere. But there are more and more raids, so that life is getting unbearable for the illegal refugees. If they get caught, they are deported and put into internment camps."

"Oh, if only all this would pass and we could live somewhere in peace," said Mendel with a sigh.

Meanwhile, the old Jew had returned with some loaves of bread. "Here, Mendel," he said, "take this! I cannot give you more, I'm sorry. We are all poor and have only the barest necessities for our survival."

Mendel thanked him warmly and said good-bye to the kind people.

"Go with God!" said the old Jew to him when they parted. "I shall pray for you!"

Mendel and Marie went back to the farm and told the comrades about the situation in Budapest. Afterwards they all were silent for a while. They sat gazing into the space in front them, despondent.

"What shall we do now?" asked Rachel in despair and looked at them, one by one. "Say something!"

"Yes, what shall we do?" said Yankel at last. "In my opinion, we should stay here for as long as we can. After all, you see that it is dangerous for us everywhere!"

The others agreed to stay as long as their friendly hosts allowed them to. They made themselves useful in any way they could.

Marie obtained a violin and a guitar, as she had heard that Rachel and Martin could play these instruments. So the young girl brought a little zest for life into the little group, despite their fears and worries. In the evenings, they sat pleasantly together, and sometimes they sang and danced.

The old farmer's wife was the only one who was not entirely happy with the situation. She regarded her daughter Marie and 'Martin' with suspicion.

The two young people showed their love quite openly; they did not see any sense in hiding their feelings. One evening they danced together and kissed each other, entirely thoughtlessly, in the presence of all the others in the living room. They did not notice that the farmer's wife left the room angrily.

The following Sunday, when Marie was at church, the farmer's wife approached the friends and said to them: "You cannot stay here as our guests any longer!"

"Did we offend you somehow?" asked Yankel, alarmed.

The old woman shook her head.

"No," she said, "you are all dear people and I don't hold anything against you, but I think that everybody should stay within his own religion!"

Turning to Martin, she continued: "Marie has confessed to me that you want to marry! But I shall not allow this! My daughter shall not marry an unbeliever! I must forbid her to do so! I am a believing Christian!"

The friends looked at each other, confused. Martin's face was as white as a sheet, and he could hardly maintain his composure as he said to the farmer's wife:

"I thank you for your openness and respect your opinion. I shall leave at once, but please don't let my friends suffer because of my mistakes! Let them stay, I beg you…!"

The old woman let herself be moved.

"Well," she said to Yankel and Rachel, "all the others can stay. But Martin has to leave immediately, before Marie returns from church!"

Mendel packed his belongings straight away and said good-bye to his friends.

"Where will you go now?" asked Rachel, with tears in her eyes.

"Probably to Budapest!" said Mendel sadly. "Anyhow, I'll inform you of what happens to me. I have a favor to ask you. Tell Marie why I have left her. Tell her that I love her more than anything, but I don't want her to fight with her parents on account of me. One day I shall return and take her with me. Good-bye!"

Mendel embraced the friends once more, very emotionally, took a satchel with food which the farmer's wife had prepared for him, and left the small, peaceful house. He walked away with quick steps, without looking back.

As he passed the house of the old Jew, he stopped and knocked on the door, but nobody answered.

He found out from a neighbor that only a few days earlier all the Jews had been ordered to leave this border village.

He had wanted to ask the old man for the address of his son in Budapest in order to have some starting point in the strange city. Sad over the fate of the old people, he went on his way to the small railway station.

Nobody guessed that Mendel was a Jew. He was dressed like a farmer and had fake papers, which Marie had arranged for him. So Mendel felt safe. Arriving at the station, he immediately asked about the train to Budapest.

Meanwhile, Marie had returned home. She looked with surprise at the depressed faces of the friends.

"What has happened here?" she asked, confused. "Where is Martin?"

When she did not get any answer, she guessed that something terrible had occurred here.

"Where is Martin? Where is he?" she screamed loudly at the old woman while bursting into the kitchen. "Did you send him away?"

"He…went…away…!" answered her mother hesitantly.

"You! You have sent him away, say it!"

"It is better for you!" said the old woman, shaking all over. "You will thank me for it one day!"

"Do you know what you have done?" Marie shouted, her voice cracking. "You have destroyed my life! Why did you send him away? Did he eat up all your bread? They will catch him and shoot him!" she sobbed. "You have driven him to his death and me too!"

Without letting her mother hinder her, Marie took the letter Mendel had left for her and ran frantically to the railway station. There she was told that the train to Budapest had left a few minutes earlier. In despair, she ran into the wood. With a cry of pain, she fell onto the moss and cried her heart out. Gradually she calmed down and the tears stopped. Only then did she remember the letter. She opened it and read the words which Martin had written to her. He had written that he would come and take her away with him, if he should survive the time of horror.

After carefully thinking it over, Marie came to the conclusion that Mendel had acted sensibly. It would be easier for him to manage alone than with her. She could only wait patiently now. She went home sadly.

Everybody breathed a sigh of relief when she returned. They had been worried about her. All of them tried to console Marie and make her happy, but she was deaf to every word that was meant to cheer her up. She did her chores quietly and gloomily, until at last the longed-for letter from Mendel arrived. He wrote that he had found work at a greengrocer's in Budapest, but had not yet found permanent accommodation. He advised Marie to stay with her parents for the time being. As soon as he would have some lodgings he would let his beloved Marie come to him.

Suddenly the sun was shining again in the little farmers' house. Marie moved through the house, singing and laughing, and in the evenings they again sat pleasantly together.

Yankel held Rachel tightly in his arms and she cuddled up to him.

"Don't squeeze us so much!" said Rachel with a smile.

"Why 'us'?" asked Yankel, surprised.

"Can't you guess?" Rachel whispered into his ear. "You heard correctly!"

"Rachel, my love! Is this really true?" Yankel kissed his wife, overjoyed. But then a shadow passed over his face. How would they manage with this new responsibility? Rachel looked at her husband with an inquiring glance. She felt the kind of thoughts passing through his mind.

"Don't fret, little one!" reassured her Yankel. "We shall find a solution. I think I have an idea! We are going to write to Khust and find out who of our relatives is still alive. Let's think of Aunt Hanna; she was already over seventy years old. I hardly think that they would deport her. Surely she will take you in."

"And you, Yankel," asked Rachel quietly. "Are you not going to stay with me?"

"If it is possible, of course I shall stay with you, but we shouldn't worry too much now. First, let's wait and see if we get an answer to our letter."

So Yankel wrote a letter to his Aunt Hanna in Khust. As a return address, he used the house of the farmers. And indeed, after a week they received a reply from the old aunt. She wrote that she was overjoyed to receive a sign of life from a member of the family, and that she would gladly take Rachel into her home to be with her.

Marie organized fake papers for both of them, and a few days later Yankel and Rachel set out on their journey to Khust, the starting point of their odyssey.

As they got off the train at the small railway station in Khust, Yankel held Rachel's hand tightly in his own. He knew what she was feeling now. He also saw in his mind's eye the terrible pictures, of how they had all been pushed and crammed together into the wagons, here at this station. But now they must not let their faces betray any of those feelings.

"Come, little one!" he said lovingly, and led Rachel out of the station and through the town, to Aunt Hanna's house.

"Oh, there you are, my children!" cried Aunt Hanna, full of joy, and embraced Rachel and Yankel. The old woman burst into tears when she heard that Rachel was expecting a baby.

"You can both stay here, as long as you want!" She assured them, sobbing. "Oy, this is wonderful, to have somebody staying with me. My son, his wife and the two children were taken away at the same time as you, and I still haven't heard from them. You don't know anything about them, do you?"

"No," answered Yankel quickly, "we jumped off the train and we don't know where they were taken."

Rachel and Yankel had decided not to tell the old woman about the horrible massacre at the river Dnjestr.

"Oy," moaned the aunt, "I myself escaped only by chance. I was just visiting my sister in another city. When I came back, all of you were already gone!"

Rachel consoled the old woman: "Now I shall stay with you, Aunt Hanna, and Yankel, my husband, will take care of us."

But it was not so simple. Yankel soon discovered that he could not remain in Khust. Almost everybody knew that he was a Jew, so there was the danger that he would be taken away to work at forced labor. And with his papers, which showed him to be a Ruthenian, he could be picked up to serve in the army, at any time. So Yankel had to part from Rachel. With a heavy heart, Rachel let her husband go.

Yankel traveled by train to Budapest, hoping to find some shelter there. Right after his arrival, he went to see Mendel.

"Yankel, how are you?" called Mendel, delighted. "Has Rachel come with you too?"

"No, Rachel has remained with our Aunt Hanna in Khust," answered Yankel, and they shook hands warmly. "I would have stayed there too, but there are too many people in Khust who know me. So I came here. Tell me, what are the chances of finding work and accommodation here? I would like to bring Rachel here. You know, she is pregnant and I would like to be together with her until the birth of our baby!"

"Oh, this is a surprise! *Mazel-Tov* to you both! I wish it were like that for Marie and me too," said Mendel with a sigh. "If only she was here already! But let's not talk about this now! Back to your question, Yankel. I was incredibly lucky when I was looking for work. Normally, one cannot find such a position as mine so easily. There are so many refugees here who want to work!"

"Don't you think that I will be able to find something?" asked Yankel, worried.

"Well, yes! I think I have something for you already. Now and again I meet up with some Jews who live nearby. Last time, I was asked if I wouldn't like to work at the so-called 'Palestine office.' There they deal with applications from Jews who want to emigrate to Palestine. I would advise you to simply go there and ask for work. Surely they will have some position for you!"

Yankel followed Mendel's advice and indeed he found employment at the Palestine office. They even arranged a room for him, which he lovingly prepared for himself and his young wife. Now Rachel could come and join him, at last. Yankel wrote the good news to her, and a few days later he was once again holding her in his arms.

Rachel too found employment at the Palestine office. This office was actually rather ineffective, as only rarely did the authorities issue an exit visa to Palestine. And if the Hungarian authorities did finally authorize an emigration, everything failed mostly at the Turkish authorities' end. They delayed the issuing of a transit visa, which was essential for traveling to Israel through Turkey, for an unbearably long time. At that time, the chances to emigrate to Palestine were better for children.

Yankel and Rachel tried to help their fellow sufferers and encourage them a little through their work and through lectures.

*

At the farmers' home in the little village at the Hungarian border life went on as usual after Yankel and Rachel's departure. Whenever some unwanted guest came to the house, the two remaining refugees would hide in the attic.

But suddenly a letter arrived from Marie's brother-in-law, the husband of her elder sister, in which he informed them about his imminent arrival. Until then he was reported to have been missing.

This unexpected news forced the refugees to decide to leave the house of the farmers that very day.

Without further ado, Marie also packed her belongings and wrote her parents a good-bye letter, in which she wrote to them that together with the two refugees she was going to Martin in Budapest. She would inform them of her new address as soon as possible.

At dawn, the three went on their way to the railway station, and long before the parents awoke the travelers were sitting aboard the train to Budapest. When they arrived in Budapest they found a place to hide, for the time being, with Mendel who had found a room by then.

The two young men registered as Polish citizens of Aryan descent, and so they were quickly able to find accommodation and work.

Marie managed to find work at the greengrocer's where Martin was working as well. She and Martin had the room to themselves now and were happy and satisfied.

8.

BUDAPEST was in those days a city overflowing with refugees. Those Jewish inhabitants who were still spared deportation were watched all the time and therefore were of little help to the homeless people. They themselves often fought for their own survival, and because of their own distress they had gradually become insensitive to the misery and suffering of others.

This was the situation that Bernhard discovered when he arrived in Budapest, after a long, dangerous trip with his two children, Daniel and Judith. For days he had to keep the two little children quiet in the tiny train compartment in order to escape being noticed by anybody. At the border, they had to hide behind some coats, which he had hung up on both sides of the window for that purpose.

Bernhard's knees still trembled when he thought of the scary moments when the border police officers had been in his compartment. Cold sweat had covered his forehead as he handed over his passport and papers with a friendly smile. 'Please let them keep quiet and not make a sound, or move!' he had prayed silently. 'My God, please give me the power to smile!' And everything had been all right. Without much ado, the officers had given him back the papers, had said good-bye, tapping their caps lightly with their hands, and had left the compartment.

Continuing their journey, Bernhard's heartbeat had then stopped each time he saw a man in uniform. But they had reached their destination, Budapest, unmolested.

Bernhard and the children were tired to death, but that could not dim their feeling of joy at the success of their escape. But later, after unsuc-cessfully roaming the streets for hours in order to find some place to stay, Bernhard suddenly asked himself why they had burdened themselves with the hardships of the escape at all.

The situation there was just as bad as in Berlin. Only, in Berlin he had friends while in Budapest he did not know anyone who could offer him shelter. Desperate and disappointed, he was told everywhere that as a foreign Jew he had to register immediately at the police station. The people he turned to for help sent him with the two children from one place to another, until he arrived at last at the Jewish Relief Organization.

This organization was situated in a large building, where there were about one hundred offices. The corridors were crowded with the persecuted, people in need of protection and help.

Bernhard was given a number and had to wait until he was called. He spent two agonizing hours waiting with the tired children in an unheated corridor, in the middle of a huge number of exhausted people.

At last he was called in. Expectantly, he entered the office with his children.

An overworked young woman sat at a desk in the middle of the room.

"Yes, what do you want, please…?"

"My name is Bernhard Rosen. I have escaped from Berlin with my children and have arrived here today, and now I am looking for a place to stay."

"And why have you left Germany?" asked the young woman coldly.

This took Bernhard's breath away. He opened his mouth but could not utter a word.

The woman did not take notice of him and went on: "I have read in the papers that the Jews in Germany are being paid well, same as the German workers!"

Bernard regained his breath and could speak again:

"I did not flee from Germany because they made me work hard at forced labor or because I was hungry! We Jews in Germany would have worked without grumbling and without sufficient food at the hardest of jobs, if only they would let us live!"

He continued agitatedly in a raised voice: "Don't you know that the Nazis deport the Jews into so-called 'concentration camps' and kill them there? I have lost almost all my relatives, my parents and my friends this way. I have managed to escape here with my children only with the help of some understanding Hungarians. At the border checkpoint, the children had to hide; we could only save ourselves in that way…! And you ask me, why did I flee!"

The woman answered icily: "I am sorry, but I cannot help you. We are subject to the laws of this land, and therefore we have to list you as a foreigner. Then you and your children will be put into a camp! I am sorry, but I cannot help you!"

When Bernhard heard the word "camp," he quickly took his children by their hands and, startled, left the office. In the corridor he bumped into an old bearded Jew, who looked at Bernhard and the children with pity in his eyes.

"Where do you come from?" he asked Bernhard.

"From Berlin!" answered Bernhard, dejected. He was still shocked from the recent conversation.

"And you don't know where to go now?" continued the stranger. "Go to the Ship Lane! There you will meet many fellow sufferers whom you can ask for advice. They will help you somehow. I cannot help you more, I'm sorry!"

Bernhard thanked him and set out on his way. The two suitcases seemed to weigh tons; it seemed to Bernhard as if his arms were getting longer all the time. In addition, Judith and Daniel were clinging to him. They held on desperately to the edges of his jacket and let themselves be pulled forward by him.

Walking on, they met a fellow Jew who immediately understood what Bernhard was looking for and sent him to the synagogue.

In the main hall of the synagogue, he met only two elderly synagogue attendants who showed them the way to the courtyard, where they found a few refugees from Slovakia already gathered there. Those people advised Bernhard to first obtain the necessary papers. Then he could rent a room for himself and find a place for the children.

"But now?" asked Bernhard. "Where can I go now with the children? They are dead tired!"

The refugees shrugged their shoulders at this question. "We don't know ourselves where to put our tired heads!" they said regretfully. "We live in permanent fear of being arrested by the police, with our fake papers!"

We too don't have a roof over our heads and have to search for a different accommodation each night. During the day we work for our existence. However, our earnings are hardly sufficient to buy enough food!"

So Bernhard left the synagogue and let himself be driven onward into the unknown. He did not know where to turn. Nobody could or would take them in, and the night was beginning to descend upon them.

Judith was crying from exhaustion and hunger and Daniel was walking bravely alongside his father, even though his little legs could barely carry him. Bernhard prayed silently within his soul: 'My God, You have given us freedom, please do not let us die here now!'

He picked Judith up into his arms and tried to comfort her.

Suddenly, from behind he heard the sound of a woman's voice, speaking in German: "Why is the child crying?"

"She is tired and hungry!" said Bernhard. "We have just now arrived from Berlin!"

"Ach, from Berlin?" asked the woman. "I lived in Berlin until a few years ago!"

They began to talk and walked on together. Bernhard found out that the woman was a Jew. Soon they reached her apartment. The two children immediately sank down together onto the sofa and fell soundly asleep.

Bernhard and the woman recalled some memories of Berlin. It turned out that the lady remembered his shop and had even known his wife. Now she listened, distressed, as Bernhard told her about how his wife had died.

At that moment, the doorbell rang.

"Oh my God!" exclaimed the woman, jumping up and hurrying to the door. "These must be my daughters and I haven't prepared dinner yet…!"

Two young ladies entered. They were very friendly at first, but when they saw the children on the sofa they said: "But Mother! You do know the law regarding the foreigners!"

"Ach," said the mother, "nobody will notice these two children sleeping one night at our place!"

Bernhard felt as if a load has been lifted off his shoulders! The accommodation of his children had always been his biggest worry.

"How can I thank you?" he asked, moved, and shook the woman's hand.

"But of course the children can sleep here with us tonight!" said the woman. "Only we cannot accommodate you, I'm sorry."

"That doesn't matter," smiled Bernhard. "I shall find a place somewhere!"

He wanted to say good-bye immediately, but the women held him back.

"You must be hungry!" said the woman. "Come and eat with us!"

The daughters quickly set the table. Bernhard felt poorly when he smelt the food. He could hardly swallow a mouthful. The children slept so deeply that they could not be woken up. Soon Bernhard said good-bye. They gave him the address of an acquaintance and assured him that this man would surely help him.

It had become rather late. It was a windy autumn evening. The air was cold and it was drizzling. Discouraged, Bernhard set out to find the man whose address he had been given. The city lay in darkness before him and it was difficult to find the street. But at last he arrived there and was let in. Curiously, it seemed as if the man did not find it exceptional that a visitor was coming at such a late hour.

Bernhard told him his story and asked him for help. The man listened attentively and sympathetically. He seemed to be well informed politically and they soon began a lively discussion. But Bernhard's silent hopes that they would let him sleep there turned out to be deceptive. The man's wife appeared and reminded them of the late hour. She warned them that he had to depart soon. When Bernhard got up to go, the man offered to accompany him and arrange some sort of accommodation for him. They were unlucky. Everywhere they went Bernhard had to tell his story one more time, but nobody offered him a bed for the night.

So Bernhard said good-bye to the friendly man and went on to the synagogue. He intended to sleep on one of the benches. There were already some refugees settled down for the night in the side room of the synagogue. These were some young men from Czechoslovakia who wanted to emigrate from Hungary to Israel. They told him that they had already registered themselves at the Palestine office and that they were only waiting for the emigration documents. One of the young men gave Bernhard the address of the Palestine office and told him that the best chance of getting the necessary papers and documents in those days was at that office.

While they were talking, they suddenly heard a loud knock at the entrance door.

"Open up! Police!" called someone in a loud, gruff voice.

All of them jumped up frightened and escaped through a window into the courtyard, for, even if most of them had passports, they were afraid of being sent on a transport. Through a second courtyard, they then ran along a narrow lane, up to one of the main streets. From there everybody hurried on alone.

Hour after hour, Bernhard wandered aimlessly through the dark streets. It seemed to him as if the houses had solidified into high rocky stones, impossible to get around.

'Are the people who live here as unapproachable as their houses?' he asked himself. And again he thought about his children. 'At least they have a roof over their heads!'

In a flash, he remembered the words of his wife:

"Go home, Bernhard! The children are waiting! They need you, you cannot save me anymore!"

All of a sudden, Bernhard felt the hopelessness of his situation. Only the thought of Daniel and Judith pushed him on, while tears ran down his face and mixed with the rain, which had already soaked him thoroughly.

He met only a few people in the streets.

Frightened, he pressed himself into a house entrance or into the corner of some entrance gate whenever he saw a policeman doing his rounds. He knew that he would be arrested at once if he could not identify himself sufficiently.

Therefore, Bernhard started when somebody suddenly touched his arm. He breathed a sigh of relief when he saw that it was a woman's hand, which had slipped through his arm unabashedly.

"Yoy, am I cold!" he heard a silky voice. "Aren't you cold too? Come with me! I live not far from here. We can warm ourselves up together, yes?"

"I'm sorry, but I don't have any money," said Bernhard regretfully. "You had better search for a paying client!"

But the girl urged him: "But I don't want money from you! I only want someone to warm me up! It is such a miserable night. I don't want to be alone on such a night. Come on! You don't have anywhere to stay, for sure!"

With these words she pulled Bernhard with her. Even now he would not have been prepared to go with her, but he saw a police officer approaching, so that he accepted her invitation quickly.

"You are not a Hungarian! Are you a Daitscher?" she asked in broken language.

"You guessed it!" answered Bernhard.

They walked silently through the streets. Bernhard felt uneasy about the whole thing, but he was pleasantly surprised when they arrived at the girl's apartment. The room was furnished very comfortably. Bernhard felt right away more at ease there. Everything was arranged comfortably for meetings of a delicate nature.

"I shall prepare some hot coffee for us," said the girl. "Meanwhile, you can get out of your wet things. There, go into the bathroom. You can also wash yourself a little, yes?"

Bernhard gladly agreed. He disappeared into the bathroom, got rid of his wet garments and washed himself from head to toe. It was a great comfort, as he had not been able to clean himself like this on the train.

The girl laughed out loud when Bernhard came out of the bathroom wearing a bathrobe with a red floral print.

Jokingly, he wagged his finger at her.

The young girl pulled him down next to her on the sofa and poured fresh-smelling coffee into his cup. Bernhard only now saw how pretty she was, slim, black-haired, with dark, silky skin and smoldering brown eyes.

This sight shook him out of his apathy and brought him back to life. He drank his coffee without letting the girl out of his sight. Then he put down his cup and took the girl's face in both his hands.

"What is your name?" he asked in a shaking voice.

"Mitzi…!" answered the girl.

"Mitzi!" whispered Bernhard.

She pulled aside the blankets. "Come!" she said, invitingly. "Come, lie down here!"

Bernhard let himself sink onto the bed, and Mitzi cuddled near him and put the blankets over them. Bernhard now felt how tired and washed out he was. He could, on the spot, fall into a death-like sleep.

But there was the girl…!

Bernhard lay there without moving. He dared not breathe. His excitement grew. Then he suddenly felt a small hand caressing him tenderly on his forehead. He thought that it was only a hallucination, but then he heard Mitzi whispering enticingly: "Nu, come on…!" Bernhard forgot all the hardships he had gone through. His tiredness vanished, as he pulled the girl into his arms with a groan. A wave of passion engulfed them…!

The next morning, the alarm clock dragged them out of their sweet slumber, without pity. Mitzi had a good stretch and then kissed Bernhard until he was fully awake.

"Yoy, have I slept well!" she said, with a smile.

Bernhard would have preferred to stay with her, but he could not waste any more time. Somehow, he had to obtain some documents of identification urgently.

"Wait!" called Mitzi. "Before you go, I want to see your future in the cards!"

She brought the cards and spread them out before her.

"You are a Jew, right?" she said in an undertone, without looking up. "I see that you have had many sufferings. Bad people wanted to harm you. Perhaps they even wanted to kill you, because you are a Jew. But I can see that you will be saved. In the end, everything will be all right again! So, now I am relieved," said Mitzi with a sigh, and gathered her cards.

"The cards don't lie!"

Smiling, Bernhard bent down to her and kissed her good-bye.

"Oh, you poor devil!" called Mitzi after him. "If you don't know where to go again, come to me again!"

However, Bernhard did not hear these words, since he was already on his way to his children. As he looked in a windowpane, he was startled by his own appearance. His stubble had already thickened into a real beard and his hair stuck out tangled on his head.

"With this appearance, it is no wonder that nobody wanted to let me sleep at his place!" he murmured to himself. He entered the next barbershop and asked for a shave and a haircut. Then he hurried to his children. He gave the good woman some German money and a ring, as a 'thank you' gift.

"Ach, this is not necessary!" the woman pushed him off, embarrassed, but took the presents with pleasure.

"Leave the children here for a while until you arrange your documents," she then offered.

Bernhard gladly agreed and set out for the Palestine office. He entered the building discouraged, because it was already crowded at the entrance.

Only after standing in line for a long hour had he advanced to a point from which he could see the doors of the offices from afar. One of the doors opened and a man came out and walked along the corridor towards Bernhard, his eyes all the time looking carefully at each of the people standing there in line, as if searching for someone he would know. The man was looking at Bernhard as if he recognized him. He must have met him somewhere. The man stopped in front of Bernhard.

"Don't we know each other?" he asked. "Yes, I remember now! You are Bernhard, Bernhard Rosen from Berlin!"

Suddenly, Bernhard felt as if a curtain had been lifted and it came all back to him…Khust, David and Sara, Hershel's Kibbutz, his visit to Mother Golda's…!

"Yankel!" he called out excitedly, and embraced his friend warmly. "I almost did not recognize you!"

"I almost didn't recognize you as well!" smiled Yankel. "You have changed quite a lot."

He could hardly believe that this thin emaciated man could be the businessman from Berlin, whom he remembered as an imposing and well-fed figure.

"Come with me to Rachel!" said Yankel after a moment, putting his arm around Bernard's shoulders and showing him the way. "She is here too and will be so happy to see you!"

"So, do you still know me?" asked Bernhard, as he stood in front of her.

Rachel looked at him with a frown and thought frantically. Then her face shone all over.

"Bernhard Rosen!" she called out, happily surprised. "How did you get here?" Rachel embraced Bernhard and let him kiss her on her forehead.

"That is a long story," Bernhard sighed. "Lea is dead. I was persecuted and it became more and more dangerous for us there. So I escaped here with my two children Daniel and Judith!"

"My God!" said Rachel, shaken. "And where are the children now?"

"With a woman who used to live in Berlin. I met her yesterday in the street," answered Bernhard. "We were roaming through the streets, homeless."

"How awful! You can come and stay with us, of course, until you find a room. Isn't that right, Yankel? They can stay with us, can't they?"

"But of course they are going to stay with us," said Yankel.

"Tell me, Bernhard, how old is your boy?"

"He is eight years old," answered Bernhard.

"Then we are going to take his particulars right away and send him with the next *Aliya* to Israel! What do you say, do you agree, Bernhard?" asked Yankel.

"Yes, sure, but I wish I could also go with him!" agreed Bernhard, gladly.

"Listen, Bernhard," said Rachel, "actually, the place where they take care of children the best is a children's home. We have a very good Jewish home here. You are going to look for work, and Yankel and I work the whole day too. So who will take care of the two children in the meantime?"

"Well, I think it's a good idea!" said Bernhard.

"So come on, let's go then. Let's take the children and go home first. There we will think about all the next steps," said Yankel, and they set off on their way to the children.

The children hugged their father happily and then the nice aunt and the uncle, who fished a few candies out of his pocket. Judith took one at once, but Daniel stared unbelievingly, first at the sweets and then at his father.

"You can take one!" said Bernhard, encouraging him, and Daniel helped himself.

Then they all went to Yankel's apartment, where Yankel and Rachel told Bernhard their story in detail, from the time he had visited Khust. When Bernhard heard that almost all the Jews from Khust had been deported, he asked: "And David and Sara...and Hershel and Hanna?"

"Nobody has heard anything about them since then...!" said Yankel sadly. "They must have been killed at the massacre at the Dnjestr!"

Bernhard stared at them, confused. "What massacre?" he asked.

Yankel then repeated the whole terrible story in more detail, finishing with his and Rachel's arrival in Budapest.

Shaken to the core, Bernhard listened to them. "My God, how fortunate we have been in our misfortune!"

The three sat there silent and dejected, reliving the horror in their minds.

Then there was a knock at the door, and Marie and 'Martin' entered. After greetings, full of short exclamations, the mood changed for the better. Bernhard spoke about his escape again, for the umpteenth time, but afterwards they talked about different matters.

"Tell me, Bernhard, do you have any documents at all?" asked Mendel.

"I had a passport, but it was taken away from me at the Hungarian border," answered Bernhard, depressed.

"It doesn't matter," said Marie, "I am going to arrange everything for you! I have my sources…!"

Everybody grinned. "Oh, you are bad!" called Marie, pretending to be angry. "I am loyal to my Martin!"

"Don't get excited, they only want to annoy you!" laughed Mendel.

"I know!" answered Marie, amused, and snuggled up to him. Laughing and joking, the friends sat together late into that evening.

The next morning, the children were brought to the children's home. A load fell from his shoulders, as Bernhard saw how well Daniel and Judith were accommodated there. Now he only had to find some work. He knew that Rachel and Yankel would have taken him in gladly, but he saw that Rachel was expecting a child. He did not want to become a burden on the two dear friends.

He was fortunate. Through Martin he found a position in a textile factory and was therefore soon able to rent a room with a Jewish family. He rather liked living with this family, even though they argued a lot. The religious landlord did not like it that his two daughters went out of the house nearly every evening. In his eyes, this was reprehensible. But the young girls only wanted to enjoy what was left of their youth, as long as they still could.

A few weeks later, Bernhard got news from the Palestine office that his son could emigrate to Israel in a few days' time. The emigration permits were granted only to twelve children. Almost all of them were children of refugees from different countries occupied by Germany.

Bernhard parted from his little son with conflicting feelings. It was hard for him to let the boy go, but he was sure that this was the best thing for Daniel. At least one of them should be saved!

"Take care of yourself and don't forget us, Daniel!" Bernhard kissed his son good-bye and lifted him onto the train.

Daniel had a lump in his throat upon parting from his father. He swallowed his tears bravely and even forced himself to show a small smile on his earnest young face. "Good-bye, Papa, see you again! Give my best to Judith. I shall write a letter to you after arriving in Israel! See you again!" He waved to Bernhard.

The train began to move slowly, gaining speed and rolling away, beyond the sight of the people remaining behind. Tired, Bernhard turned around and walked to the exit. "Come soon after me!" the boy had cried to him at the last minute. "Yes, we shall come soon!" he had answered. But he knew very well that this could be good-bye forever. Who knew what the future would bring?

Bernhard started. A piercing pain passed through his chest. With difficulty he dragged himself home. On his way, he had to stop often, as he had become quite dizzy. At last he reached the house where he lived and pulled himself upstairs by the banisters. In front of the door to his apartment he collapsed.

"Oy!" called the landlady, as she, her attention drawn by the banging noise in the staircase, opened the door and saw Bernhard lying there, motionless. She called her daughters and together they managed to move Bernhard into his room.

Quickly they called a doctor, who admitted him to a hospital. There they ascertained that Bernhard's heart had been severely weakened. The forced labor, lasting for years, and all the excitement of the past had injured his health and weakened his heart considerably. The physician advised him now to avoid any physical effort and any excitement. But how could one avoid effort and excitement in such times? Bernhard had to work and earn enough for his existence.

He was soon discharged from the hospital and returned to work. During this time, his condition worsened.

A few weeks later, a telegram arrived suddenly for Bernhard. It was sent from *Eretz Israel*. "Have arrived okay, Daniel!" it read.

Bernhard got so excited over the good news that he again suffered a severe heart attack. The doctor had to be called. He gave Bernhard an injection and massaged his heart. After a few days of bedrest Bernhard was able to get up again. He went with little Judith and the landlord's daughters on trips to some of the surrounding parks. But they saw SS men everywhere.

Bernhard's landlord had an idea. He gave him the address of some good friends in a small Slovakian village.

"There, there are almost only Slovaks!" he said.

Bernhard thanked him and traveled there by train with Judith.

The people there received him warmly, the food was good and the countryside was beautiful. Bernhard went for long strolls and began to feel much better. The young girls working in the fields surrounded him and showered him with questions. Each one of them would have gladly gone out with him, as most of the men were at war. The girls flirted with Bernhard and waved to him merrily upon parting.

One day, though, everything suddenly changed. Bernhard had just returned from a walk when his landlady received him with the following words: "A gendarme was here and asked about you. You have to go to the police station at once!"

"What do they want from me?" asked Bernhard, astonished. Nobody there even knew that he was a Jew.

Bernhard went to the police station. He planned in his mind how to behave there. 'I have a medical certificate with me,' he thought, 'so I can prove that I came here to recover.' He entered the police station.

"Good day. You wanted to see me?"

"Yes, what are you doing in our village?"

"I am here to recover. Here is a letter from my doctor, in which he recommends a stay in the country!"

"This is a lie!" shouted the gendarme now. "You are carrying out Bolshevist propaganda here!"

Bernhard denied these accusations strongly.

A man in civilian clothing came out of the adjoining room and looked at Bernhard.

"Listen," he said, "I can only advise you to just disappear from this village! You are surely intelligent enough to follow my advice! So leave at once, if you don't want to get into trouble!"

Sadly Bernhard packed their belongings and returned to Budapest with Judith. But the landlord thought of another place where Bernhard could rest. He sent Bernhard to his cousin who was living in the small town Nyir-Balkány, about one hundred and fifty kilometers away from Budapest.

"Why didn't I think of this before!" he called out and clapped himself on his forehead. "I shall call her immediately!"

Mrs. Kornfeld met Bernhard at the station in a horse drawn carriage. Judith cried out with pleasure when she saw the little horses. Then they rode for two hours until they reached Nyir-Balkány. The small town lay in the middle of vineyards and cornfields. Bernhard liked his landlord's cousins, Mr. and Mrs. Kornfeld, very much. They lived with two daughters in a beautiful house surrounded by a big garden. Mr. Kornfeld had a shop in which he sold clothes, and the men had plenty to talk about. But most of the time, Bernhard sat in the garden under the trees and watched Judith playing. He gradually recovered in this comfortable atmosphere. But this place too afforded him only a few days of peace.

One day, a gendarme appeared at the Kornfelds' house and asked about 'a man from Berlin with a little girl'!

Startled, Bernard jumped up and ran into the house.

But the Kornfelds had already sent the gendarme away with the words: "We? We don't know of any man from Berlin!"

Even so, Bernhard no longer felt safe at the friendly people's place. He was afraid that Judith may have chatted to the neighbors and unintentionally told them something. So Bernhard packed his suitcase again, thanked the Kornfelds warmly and went back to Budapest.

There he began to work again. As often as possible, he took Judith from the children's home and they talked much about their wonderful vacation.

9.

I N BUDAPEST the situation was growing more and more aggravated. The *Aliya* to Israel had been stopped entirely. The German Nazi regime gradually increased its pressure on Hungary, and the laws regarding Jews became more severe. Each day the numbers of arrested Jews increased; raids were carried out daily, and the Jews arrested were sent to concentration camps. Fear and horror spread among the Jews of Budapest.

"You know, Rachel," said Yankel one day, worried, "I'll bring you to Aunt Hanna in Khust! Here, the situation is too dangerous for you."

Rachel was almost due and Yankel was worried about her. He brought her to Khust and returned to Budapest.

There was not much work left at the Palestine office. Many Jews still listed themselves, but no emigration authorizations were being granted anymore. Thereupon, Yankel, Martin, Bernhard and some friends gathered and provided their unfortunate fellow Jews with fake papers which they manufactured in their own workshop.

One afternoon, Yankel was sitting in his room 'working' on a passport. Two weeks had already passed since he had taken Rachel to Khust. He stopped working and looked thoughtfully out of the window. 'Is she feeling well?' he thought, 'I hope everything will be all right, when the child comes!' Yankel shook his head and continued to work.

That evening, the doorbell rang suddenly and Yankel received a telegram. "You have a boy! Hanna Mandelbaum." Yankel ran euphorically to his friends Mendel and Bernhard. "I have a boy! Just imagine, a boy!"

"And how is Rachel?" the friends asked.

"I, I don't know!" Yankel was stupefied. Indeed, old Aunt Hanna did not mention how Rachel had come through the birth of their son! Well, he would see how Rachel was, because he was already on his way there in order to embrace his wife and son.

The train trip seemed exceptionally long to Yankel. He could not wait to see Rachel and the baby.

And then, at last, he stood beside his wife's bed. Rachel lay exhausted upon her pillows and slumbered. Near her, Bernhard saw a small bundle, out of which a small raven-haired head and two tiny fists showed.

'This is my son!' thought Yankel, in a wave of emotion, and tears appeared in his eyes from sheer joy. With his forefinger he carefully touched the delicate small fingers of the little one.

"Well, how do you like your son?" Rachel asked, awakening. "Yankel, my love!"

Yankel took her into his arms and stammered: "I thank you! I thank you for our son, my darling!" He kissed Rachel dearly. In the following days, they spent most of their time together.

"What name shall we give our son?" asked Yankel once.

"I would like to name him Haim!" said Rachel with shining eyes.

"*Haim*, life!" Yankel agreed, liking the name. It was like a symbol for him. The boy was born and would go on living, even if the future lay in darkness!

Yankel remained inside the house his whole time in Khust, as he did not wish to endanger himself unnecessarily. On the eighth day of his life, little Haim was circumcised, and right after that Yankel returned to Budapest.

Rachel needed to rest and was to stay on in Khust, for the time being. Yankel thought that this was safer. He went back to his work. Rachel was not bored, as little Haim kept her occupied all day long. When she sat beside his bed, she often asked herself how little Esther had come through the battle in the woods.

*

The second group of partisans had had a hard battle. Nikolai fought desperately to break through the enemy, but only four people of his group survived: Esther, Mariussa, another comrade and himself. They ran for their lives for two hours. Then, suddenly, the other comrade collapsed and died. He had been severely wounded from a shot during the fight and had lost too much blood during their flight.

Only Esther, Nikolai and Mariussa remained. They hid in the woods for some time and ate the food which they 'organized' from the surrounding villages, as they used to. But Nikolai did not feel safe enough. He thought it would be safer to reach the Rumanian side of the border.

So the three of them left their hiding place and a week later reached a region, well known to Mariussa. In fact, it was a place very close to Mariussa's home village. In the darkness of the night, the girl sneaked to the house of a good friend who lived at the entrance of the village. Mariussa was received with open arms and decided to stay and live there again. She wanted Esther to stay there with her, but Nikolai did not agree to this. He thought that it would be better for Esther to go to Czernovitz and live there with a Jewish family. So Esther parted sadly from Mariussa and went with Nikolai, on their way to Czernovitz. After a while, they found a place between some trees where it seemed safe to have a rest and eat.

Suddenly two shepherd dogs attacked them, barking furiously. Nikolai pointed his machine gun and shot them. The situation worsened when two men in uniform appeared under the trees and immediately opened fire.

Although Nikolai and Esther were armed, they preferred to flee. However, Esther was so exhausted that she could hardly stand on her feet. So after a few steps she stumbled out of weakness and fell down. Nikolai turned around and shot at the pursuers in order to hold them back. Then he lifted Esther into his arms and ran as quickly as he could. But, a few steps later he was hit by a bullet and fell. Desperately, Esther raised her gun and shot at the attackers. One of the uniformed men gripped his chest and fell to the ground with a cry, and the other fled.

Immediately, Esther took care of Nikolai. He was unconscious and bleeding heavily from a wound in his shoulder. Esther bandaged the wound as well as she could and then sat down next to Nikolai until he at last regained consciousness. With her help, Nikolai managed to rise. He then hobbled on, his face contorted with pain, leaning on Esther's shoulder. They advanced very slowly, as both were exhausted and often had to stop to rest and breathe.

After several hours it began getting dark. Esther and Nikolai crept into some bushes and stayed there all night.

The next morning Nikolai could hardly move. But, gritting his teeth, he pulled himself up. He dragged himself along, pushed by his worry about the girl. Nikolai's hand, which clung to hers, felt feverishly hot and he staggered from one side to the other.

With their last ounce of strength, they reached Czernovitz that evening. They wandered through the streets for almost an hour, until they found shelter in a Jewish woman's house.

Nikolai had managed to keep himself upright until they had arrived there, but finally he could not take it any more and collapsed. His fever rose and he hallucinated. In his feverish delirium, he suddenly jumped up and ran out into the street. Esther, who had meanwhile fallen asleep out of sheer exhaustion, did not notice him leave.

Passers-by spotted Nikolai staggering through the street and brought him to the hospital. In his delirium, he called out again and again: "Esther! Esther!" Thus the physician presumed that this patient was a Jew, and he placed the wounded man in the Jewish ward. There, they did not have the time to check his identity, because they had to take him directly to the operating theater, where they removed the leaden bullet from his shoulder.

Esther too was admitted to the same hospital. Her blood circulation had grown so weak due to the recent hardships that she had to be treated urgently. When she was carried into the hospital on a stretcher, she suddenly saw in the corridor two well-known friends from home approaching her. There were Haim and Feigele. She cried out from sheer joy and grasped Feigele's arm.

Feigele did not recognize Esther, but she pitied the little frail person.

"What is the matter, little one?" she asked sympathetically and bent over Esther. "Everything will be all right!"

"Oy," sobbed Esther, "Feigele, don't you recognize me? I am Esther, the daughter of the locksmith Lazar!"

"Esther!" cried out Feigele, surprised. Then she took Esther into her arms and kissed the child, with tears in her eyes. Feigele and Haim accompanied Esther to her room and listened as the girl told them the terrible story of her rescue.

"Yes, and then we divided into two groups," Esther was telling them. "One group wanted to go to Hungary. I escaped with the other group and we fought our way out through the attacking soldiers, in a southerly direction. But from our group only three managed to get through, Nikolai, Mariussa and I. We fled on. Mariussa went back to her village. She wanted to take me with her, but Nikolai wouldn't allow it."

"And how did you get here, then?" asked Haim, astonished. "Did you come by yourself?"

"No, I came together with Nikolai, but on our way here we were attacked by two gendarmes and they shot Nikolai. Then I shot back at them. One fell onto the ground and the other ran away."

"You poor child!" called out Feigele, shaken, "and where is your companion now?"

"I don't know! We dragged ourselves here with the last of our strength and an old woman took us into her house. Nikolai had a high fever and collapsed. Suddenly he jumped up and ran out into the street. Since then I haven't heard anything about him!" Esther sobbed.

"I hope he was not arrested and taken away!"

"Wait a minute," said Haim, thoughtfully, "yesterday they brought a man to the hospital who didn't have any papers on him. He was wounded by a shot and was repeating a name over and over again!"

"Yes, yes," said Feigele excitedly, "of course! He said 'Esther' all the time! That must be your Nikolai, Esther!"

"Nikolai is here?" asked Esther, and her tired features began to shine. "How is he?"

"He is still unconscious. They have removed the bullet from his shoulder, and he hasn't regained consciousness yet. But he has a good chance of recovering. As soon as you feel better, I'll take you to him."

Esther recuperated quickly under the loving care of Feigele. She visited Nikolai as often as she could. She sat next to his bed and kept watch over him. At last the moment came; Nikolai's eyelids trembled, he moved his hands restlessly to and fro, and then he opened his eyes slowly. He looked around, confused.

"Nikolai!" Esther called out happily.

He raised his head and spotted Esther. His face beamed all over.

"Esther, where am I? What happened?"

"You are here, in the Jewish hospital in Czernovitz!" said Esther happily. "We have made it, Nikolai! We are safe!"

Nikolai recovered slowly. Esther made herself useful and helped Feigele care for the sick. They grew fond of her quickly.

One evening, two security officers entered the hospital and asked about the wounded stranger. The director of the hospital was not in the building, so the men were led to Haim. "What is the name of the wounded man who was admitted here?"

"I cannot tell you yet who he is or where he comes from, as he has still not regained consciousness."

"Take us to him! We want to go and see for ourselves!" Haim led the men to Nikolai's room, opened the door slightly and said loudly:

"The unidentified man is lying here in this room. You will see, dear sirs, that he is still lying in a coma!"

Nikolai heard this and immediately understood the situation. When the men entered the room, Nikolai lay there without moving and did not react when spoken to.

The officers left the room unsatisfied.

"You take responsibility for this man! Don't let him escape under any circumstances!" they said before they left the hospital.

Haim immediately told Feigele about the incident. Together with Nikolai, they thought about the best way the danger could be averted.

"Of course we are not going to hand you over to the SS men!" said Haim. "Listen, we are going to rent a room and move you into it already this evening. And Feigele and I are going to take care of you medically, all right?"

Nikolai agreed to that.

Haim informed the senior physician. At first he was a little skeptical. However, out of respect for Haim he at last agreed. Straightaway, a room was rented and in the evening Nikolai was taken there.

Two days later, the same two officers reappeared and demanded to see the patient. When they were told that the patient had left secretly, they took the senior physician to the headquarters. The commanding officer asked the senior physician: "Was the patient, who was not identified and who sneaked away a Jew?" The senior physician did not want to endanger all his patients. So he answered: "Yes!"

"You are lucky that they didn't bring you to another officer but to me. You may leave, I'm setting you free!" said the commanding officer. "But in the future, take care, if you don't want to get into trouble!"

The senior physician thanked him and went out quickly.

He could hardly believe that he had been given back his freedom. He told Haim and Feigele about the interrogation at the headquarters, and the two decided to wait for a while, until the dust settled over the incident, before returning to work again at the hospital.

But at the hospital, Haim and Feigele were sorely missed, as they were irreplaceable. Three days later, the two were already back at work.

One Friday morning, Feigele said to Haim before they parted: "Please don't come home too late. The Sabbath begins shortly after six o'clock. Today Nikolai is coming to visit us and I want it to be particularly festive!"

"I shall run all the way home," said Haim, with a smile, and kissed Feigele gently.

The day passed. Feigele was the first to arrive home. Quickly she set the table and prepared everything with care. Every now and then, she hurried to the window and looked out for Haim. Outside, it was already dark. Sadly she lit the Sabbath candles as Nikolai watched her. Feigele loved the Sabbath. For her, it was really the most beautiful day of the week. She honored the old customs as these were, for Feigele, the only things that the enemy could not take away.

Hours passed, but Haim still did not show up. Feigele was very worried about him. What could have delayed him? She took her coat and went out to search for him.

Nikolai and the landlady could not restrain her from going. The landlady shook her head and said to Nikolai: "These youngsters today, they don't have anything in their heads but love!" Nikolai could understand Feigele's fear better. He knew what they had gone through…

Feigele hurried to the hospital. The physician on duty told her that Haim had left three hours earlier. The senior physician also did not know anything about Haim's whereabouts. He too was worried and offered to help Feigele search for him. They went off together and asked every acquaintance they met if they had seen Haim. Finally they heard that late in the afternoon several Jews had been arrested and dragged away.

"Two SS men arrested a Jewish man on the street. He defended himself, but it didn't help him. They took him with them! I saw it clearly!" said a little boy, "I know the man from the hospital!"

Feigele's face became ashen. She was frightened to death, and so was the senior physician. He supported Feigele and brought her home. In front of the door to her apartment, she fainted. Nikolai heard the muffled impact of her fall and opened the door.

"She is unconscious! Come, let's take her to bed!" called the senior physician. Then he told Nikolai what they had found out about Haim.

Feigele had a high fever when she awoke. In her despair, she called out again and again for her Haim. Nikolai thought it was a delusion when three days later the door suddenly opened and Haim stumbled over the threshold and sank exhausted onto the sofa.

"Haim, Haim!" called Nikolai, surprised. "We thought they had taken you away!"

"Yes, they had!" panted Haim. "I was not careful enough when I left the hospital on Friday. I didn't look around, so I didn't see the two officers who came after me. They had waited for me in order to ask about the stranger who disappeared. 'You encouraged that creature to escape!' they shouted at me. 'No, it's not true!' I shouted back. They would not listen to me but grabbed me, dragged me away to the railway station and pushed me into a waiting transport train. I've already jumped off a running train once; now I tried it again. With the help of a few other abducted people I broke open the door. It took hours of effort, but then we managed to jump off the moving train. Then I kept running for three whole days, almost without any rest on the way, until now. But what has happened to Feigele?"

"Feigele fainted when she heard that they had taken you away!" said Nikolai.

"Feigele, darling! I am back with you again!" Haim bent down over Feigele and kissed her. As if by a miracle, she opened her eyes and looked at him unbelievingly.

"Haim! Where did you come from?" Feigele cried out of happiness. Then she fell asleep again, exhausted.

The following day, both Haim and Feigele were quite recovered and decided to invite their friends to have a joyful evening together with them. They sat together, happily and satisfied, with Esther, Nikolai and the senior physician. They all raised their glasses to Haim, who had returned safe and sound, and his bride Feigele.

The senior physician gave them one week of leisure, so that they could recover properly. The young couple enjoyed that time together.

10.

B
Y THAT TIME, the whole eastern front of the German Wehrmacht was already in retreat, pushed back by the Red Army. The Germans were being driven out of cities and villages. Former Jewish refugees and volunteers reported to the Red Army.

Beryl and Levi signed up as well and joined the Polish army, which was assembled in the Soviet Union. After a short training, they were sent straight to the front line. Everybody knew only one direction: forward!

"Forward!" they cried when they attacked, in order to spur themselves on, because most of them were young people and they were loathe to kill, but knew that against the Nazi regime they must use force. Here they had to fight for freedom and, if necessary, pay with their blood or even their lives.

Meanwhile, the Polish-Russian units had already reached Polish regions. Beryl fought in the front line. It had been raining for days, and so the ground in the woods was muddy and slippery. A thick fog obstructed vision in the area of the fighting, making it difficult to distinguish between friend and foe.

Suddenly, Beryl and two comrades ran into a German military news unit in uniform, three soldiers and one girl, probably a reporter. The two enemy units were standing so close to each other that nobody had time to pull out his gun.

They all held their breath, and Beryl and the girl looked into each other's eyes. They looked at each other with a faraway look, until the girl suddenly started to laugh. The soldiers, too, began to laugh. They all decided to retreat to their own lines.

Then they turned around and left the place, each group in the direction of its unit. Beryl and the girl even waved at each other before parting.

The comrades found the way back to their unit. For a long time afterward, they would talk about this curious incident, and Beryl just could not forget the girl's eyes, which had looked into his so intensely.

In the following nights they had to fight tough battles, over and over again. The Nazi Wehrmacht tried grimly to hold its position. Beryl's unit suffered many casualties. Nevertheless, they were quickly advancing and just short of Warsaw they started to slow down.

Then came the day when the Polish people greeted the liberation army with a big 'Welcome,' waving small flags and shouting with joy. But the mood changed quickly when the liberators confiscated the peoples' meager food for their own needs. On top of that the Polish people quickly realized that most of the soldiers of the liberation army were Jews and neither Polish nor Russian, as they had originally assumed. So the Jews were still hated, and the Jewish soldiers were often attacked and viciously murdered.

Gradually, Jews who had miraculously survived the concentration camps or who had hidden in the woods began coming back. Each one hoped to find some member of his family. Most often, those homecomers were greeted with the words: "What, you are still alive? Why didn't they kill you? Go to Palestine! We don't need you here!"

Polish people were already living in the former apartments of the Jews, and they did not want to return everything and move out now. They threw the former landlords out and even cursed them loudly. But the Jews only wanted a roof over their heads. They only wanted to live in the old homeland, where the souls of their late family members were alive, where they could live in the past and console themselves about the present that held no compassion.

*

Elsewhere, the Jews were still being hunted down, dragged away and tortured, despite the German loss of territories. Such was the situation in Budapest then. The Jews there were also finally forced to wear the yellow Star of David, and they too were no longer allowed to change their location. The Nazis set up ghettos into which they crammed the Jews. From there, they could transport the Jews more easily to the concentration camps. In the provincial cities too they set up ghettos and rounded up all the Jews from the surrounding villages, who had up to then evaded the transports.

It was in May 1944 when Yankel heard of this imminent danger, and, he immediately issued Aryan papers for his family and went to Khust by train in order to save Rachel and little Haim and flee with them.

But he came too late!

Just before Yankel's train arrived in Khust, the gendarmes had driven all the Jews they could find to the railway station and packed them into cattle wagons.

Yankel ran to Aunt Hanna's house, but found the doors open and the house empty! In despair, he hurried back to the railway station and ran alongside the train, hoping to somehow find his family and save them.

Many onlookers were standing around there. One could see faces full of pity, stunned, but also expressions of rejoicing, which became intoxicated by the disaster of those unfortunates.

Yankel aroused the curiosity of the onlookers, and suddenly one of them called out to a gendarme: "Hey, that one is a Jew too! Yakob is his name!"

This man who had informed on Yankel was a former Ruthenian neighbor. When the gendarmes heard his call, they seized Yankel immediately.

"Well, are you looking for somebody?" "There!" They pushed him into the wagon where Yankel had just spotted Rachel. "There! In you go! When you arrive at the destination, you will surely find the one you have been searching for!" the gendarmes laughed and slammed the door.

In the semi-darkness, Yankel squeezed himself through to Rachel and took her in his arms. His eyes filled with tears of rage, as he heard his little son Haim crying pitifully.

"Don't cry," he comforted Rachel and his little son. "God will protect us! He will not give up on us. He has saved us already once, he will let us escape once more!"

Yankel did not really believe what he said, and as they rode on and on in the dark, narrow, stifling wagon, he realized that this time it was impossible for them to escape.

The train left Hungary. At the border, the gendarmes handed the transport over to the SS men. They traveled for a week, until one morning they reached Auschwitz.

The SS men drove them out of the wagons and separated the men from the women, as they had to stay in separate barracks. Some thought that they were saved: they were brought here to a labor camp. But, to their horror, when they passed the crematoria, they came to understand the contrary.

Rachel cried, because they had separated her from Yankel; little did she know that something much worse was going to happen to her.

When she reached the delousing shack, she observed something strange. The women had to give up everything they held in their hands; even children were taken from them. Unable to suffer this, some women went crazy and grew wild. Their motherly instincts told them that they would never see their little ones again.

Rachel also went wild and shrieked loudly. She fought like a lioness for her little Haim.

"No, I'll never give away my child! Let me go! I don't want this! No!"

But all the resistance did not help her. Haim was so very small, he could not hold onto her. It was easy for the so-called 'nurses' to tear the bundle out of her hands.

So little Haim ended his young life in the gas chamber.

11.

THE FRONT MOVED nearer to Czernovitz too, in the late summer of 1944. An SS commando had to defend the city. But these men were too busy confiscating food and semi-luxury items from the population and persecuting Jews to properly defend the city.

So the Jews of Czernovitz managed to barricade their apartments and houses and defend themselves as best as they could.

Nikolai had rented a room with a Ukrainian lady farmer and beseeched Haim and Feigele to seek shelter with him. "We must stay together. That's the only way we can help each other!"

Haim and Feigele agreed and brought with them a supply of food. Nikolai was living in a house with a large surrounding garden. The lady farmer had a small farm with one cow and a lot of chickens and geese. She treated the three friends very courteously. She was pleased to have other people in the house, so that she would not have to confront the SS men alone.

Feigele and the lady farmer slept in one room, Haim and Nikolai in the other. They got along well. However, nobody actually slept at night, as the booming of the guns from the nearby front increased. So they often sat together playing cards.

One evening, while they were sitting together absorbed in their game, they suddenly heard some noises from the outside, followed by a loud bang. Somebody cursed dreadfully and then ordered in a brusque voice: "Open up! Open up at once!"

The friends jumped up, startled. "This can only be the SS," whispered Nikolai. "Come on, we have to get away!"

He opened the window quickly, and they jumped out into the court-yard and hid in the garden behind the trees.

In the meantime, the lady farmer opened the door. She shuffled along and approached the door slowly, calling: "Yes, yes! I'm coming!"

She acted as if she had just awoken.

The SS men stormed in and searched the house. They found the three disheveled beds of the friends.

"Who sleeps here? Answer me!"

The woman did not utter a word. Then the uniformed men saw that the window to the garden was wide open. They jumped out and searched the garden with drawn guns, using the light of their flashlights.

"They are coming exactly in our direction!" Haim took hold of Feigele's hand. "Come on, let's go!"

Bending down, they ran to the fence and climbed over it as fast as they could. Nikolai followed them. The SS men ran after them and shot at them from behind.

Suddenly Feigele started and fell to the ground. Haim wanted to pick her up and carry her, but Nikolai grabbed his arm and pulled him behind a bush. He gave Haim a loaded gun and whispered: "Let them come nearer, up to twenty meters, and then we'll shoot them!"

Within minutes, the two SS men appeared out of the darkness. They thought they had already shot down their victims, so they moved carelessly through the grounds.

"You take the right one and I'll take the left!" ordered Nikolai then. The shots whipped through the night, and both SS men sank to the ground, dead.

In a flash, Haim jumped up and ran over to Feigele. Together, he and Nikolai carried the panting girl into the house. The lady farmer was still trembling with fear.

"You don't have to be frightened! They cannot harm you anymore!" Nikolai calmed the woman. "We have shot them down!"

"Jesus! What is the matter with her? Is she wounded?" called out the woman, as she saw Feigele.

"I don't know. She has to be examined first!" Haim cleaned the wound on her thigh and dressed it with a makeshift bandage, but the bleeding did not stop.

It startled him to see that Feigele was becoming weaker.

"I'm taking her to a doctor! The bullet has to be taken out, or she'll bleed to death!" Haim uttered and began readying Feigele to take her away.

Nikolai held him back forcibly.

"Do you want both of you to get killed? In the stream of bullets outside, you couldn't move even ten steps without being hit!"

And sure enough, the thunder of the cannons became stronger and stronger.

"Wait until tomorrow," said Nikolai, "by then the Red Army will have marched in, for sure!"

'What shall I do now?' thought Haim desperately. '*Until tomorrow will be too late!*'

Making a sudden decision, he turned to the lady farmer: "Prepare plenty of hot water and give me a sharp knife!"

Startled, Nikolai asked: "What do you intend to do? You don't mean you want to…?"

"Yes, I shall take out the bullet!"

Haim turned to the door.

"I cannot allow you to kill her!" shouted Nikolai and tried to block Haim. They struggled with each other, until Haim finally knocked his friend out with a blow to his jaw and sent him to dreamland for a while.

Haim regretted the fight with his friend, but he did not have anytime to lose. He left it to the lady farmer to wake Nikolai up with a bucket of cold water. In the meantime, Haim crept out to the two dead soldiers in the garden and searched their pockets. He found bandages, but not what he was looking for, namely alcohol.

'Then it will have to be without alcohol!' he said to himself, but this made him feel rather queasy. He crept back carefully and began to prepare the inevitable operation. He laid Feigele on the kitchen table and sterilized the knife by heating it. Nikolai came to his senses and realized that he could not dissuade Haim from carrying out his plan. So he decided to help him.

"We are going to tie you to the table, darling! Unfortunately, we don't have anything to anesthetize you with! You must be very brave now!"

"You don't need to tie me down, Haim! I shall not move!" said Feigele, and looked at Haim confidently. Haim asked the woman for some spirits and she brought him a full bottle.

Fortunately, Haim's medical studies in the past and his work as a nurse at the hospital in Czernovitz served him well then, yet there is a difference between observing something and doing it by yourself. Haim had to urge himself to begin. With the sterilized knife he carefully enlarged the wound and searched for the bullet. But the piece of lead was lodged so deeply within the thigh muscle that he had to enlarge the incision further.

Up to then, Feigele had not made a single sound, but all of a sudden she uttered a cry of pain and twisted her face into a grimace. Groaning, she clenched her teeth and clung to Nikolai's hand. Her face went deathly pale and big drops of perspiration appeared upon her forehead.

At last Haim managed to get hold of the lead and pick it out. A thick bloodstream gushed out with it. Haim closed the wound as well as he could and put a pressure bandage on it. It took a long time for the bleeding to stop. Haim sat beside Feigele's bed and anxiously checked her pulse and breathing, which gradually returned to normal.

Haim's strength finally left him and he had to lie down. Immediately, he fell into a deep, trance-like sleep.

*

Two days later, the Red Army marched into Czernovitz.

Feigele still had a high fever and was very weak. Haim could finally take her to the hospital.

There, the senior physician was just about to sit down for a few minutes with his colleagues in order to celebrate the liberation. He and his assistants looked bleary-eyed. They had not slept much during the last days, because the wounded were being brought in from everywhere and they had been on constant duty. All wounded, whether friend or foe, were taken care of equally.

The old senior physician now looked at Feigele, startled. He examined the wound and immediately sent her to the operating theatre.

"You have done well, Haim, but the wound is infected. We have to reopen the wound and take out the point of infection."

Haim was allowed to observe the operation. Later, he sat for hours next to Feigele's bed. Her fever went down, but the girl was still very weak. The physician decided that she needed a blood transfusion. Haim and Nikolai both wanted to be donors and both had the suitable blood group, so she could be helped. After the blood transfusion, Feigele's condition improved quite quickly. Haim and Esther took turns nursing her until she was back on her feet again.

Finally they could allow themselves to start making plans.

Nikolai asked Haim and Feigele: "What are you going to do? Do you want to stay here?"

"We are going to marry, right, Feigele?" Haim caressed Feigele's hand. "And then we are going to Israel. Here, there is nobody from our families left alive. What would we do here? We are going to build us a new homeland in the land of our ancestors!"

"And Esther is going to come with us too!" Feigele stroked the girl's hair. "You will stay with us, yes?"

"Do you really want to take me with you?" Esther embraced the young couple, overjoyed. "Of course I'll go with you!"

"Well, if you are going to take care of Esther, I can leave too," said Nikolai relieved. "I am going to join the Red Army. I want to help and break the Nazi regime!"

After a while, the friends parted.

Nikolai went and joined the Red Army, and Haim, Feigele and Esther prepared themselves for the long journey, first to Bucharest and from there onward to Israel.

12.

I T WAS 1944. In Budapest, the Nazis still ruled. The Jews felt their hatred more than ever.

Bernhard, Martin and several other young men continued to manufacture fake documents and distribute them among the people residing illegally in Budapest. But, since Yankel had left the group, the documents were not as professional as before. Yankel had been the expert and had carried the major load of the work. Nevertheless, the friends did not want to give up after Yankel left; they carried on grimly and supplied their unfortunate fellow Jews with fake papers.

In any case, those fake documents did not offer real promise to the refugees. They were worthless and even dangerous, especially when checked by the authorities or the police. Thus, the people who had fake papers in their possession lived in constant fear of being discovered. They changed their location almost daily and had to search for another place to stay every night. Often it was the prostitutes who saved them from their misery.

The Jewish inhabitants of Budapest, nearly all of them living by then in the ghetto, were taken on transports to the concentration camps, one by one. So, Martin went to the ghetto almost daily to distribute fake documents, so that at least some of them would get the chance to flee.

One day, when he again entered the ghetto, he was caught by the SS men. They arrested him and questioned him for hours.

"Who are your accomplices? You are not doing this alone! Where is your workshop? What, you don't want to answer? You just wait! We are going to make you talk!"

Martin was kicked and beaten; they denied him food and water and did not let him sleep. He held himself erect for three days, withstanding hunger, thirst, sleeplessness and threats. Then, physically and psychologically worn down, he could take it no longer. They finally tricked him into speaking out.

"Today we arrested a girl who said she knew you. Her name is Marie…!"

"My God!" moaned Martin. "How on earth could she have fallen into your hands?"

"We caught her inside the ghetto. She went to search for you there!" This sounded credible enough. Therefore Mendel was convinced that only he could save the beloved girl. "Let her go!" he cried. "I shall tell you everything, but let her go!"

"Good. We are setting her free. But you must give us the names and addresses of all your accomplices!"

Mendel gave them these facts only after they showed him a paper confirming Marie's release. After this they locked him into a cell and seemed to forget about him, because for days nobody came for him, except the guard who appeared once each day and brought him his ration of bread and water.

The reason was that the Gestapo could not catch any of his friends. All of them had already escaped. The officers gave up the search angrily. They had worked so hard in order to make Mendel speak, and everything had been in vain. In fact, they did not have the faintest idea who Marie was and what her relation to Mendel was. They had found a picture of her in Mendel's pocket, a picture, on the back of which was written: 'Your Marie!' And with this they had crushed Mendel's spirit!

But they were no longer interested in him. They gave the order to add him to a transport of Jews. A week later, Mendel was pulled out of his cell without any explanation and brought to an assembly point. From there he was driven to the Austrian border, together with Jews from the ghetto and arrested escapees. They had to trudge on a long march. On the way, the official cars full of SS men rammed the prisoners, who dragged themselves on with difficulty. The unfortunates were even shot at with machine guns, to speed them on. Panic broke out upon hearing the shots cutting through the air. Everybody ran helplessly to and fro. A few of them – among them Mendel – succeeded to escape during the chaos.

They escaped into the woods. But hunger drove them into the villages. There, they found some decent farmers who were willing to shelter the homeless. But others were confirmed Nazis their or followers who caught the desperate people and handed them back to their tormentors, afraid of reprisals.

Mendel was lucky. He successfully crossed the border into Austria and found shelter in the house of a farmer. That farmer had served under the Kaiser and had many Jewish friends among his comrades. At first Mendel told him he was Hungarian, but he was unable to convince the farmer of this. So he revealed his true identity to the farmer and told him his story. The farmer listened to him, very upset, and after Mendel finished his story, he remained silent for a while.

"I knew that you Jews were persecuted," he then said. "Yes, there are Nazis living here in the village too, and the Jews who lived here were taken away. But we thought that they were settled in some other place!"

The farmer sighed. "How could I even have imagined that such terrible things were going on?"

Lost in thought, the old man stared straight ahead.

"But here you are safe! What did you say your name was?"

"Martin!"

"Well, Martin, come with me into the house. I'll show you your room!"

The old farmer took hold of Mendel's arm and led him into the house.

"Ah, here is my daughter! Come here, Annerl. This is Martin. He'll stay with us for a while. Go and show him the workers' room. He'll stay there!"

"*Grüss Gott*! You are Martin? I am Annerl! Actually, my name is Annemarie, but Father and Mother and, well, everybody call me Annerl!"

The girl walked in front of him and led Martin to his new lodgings. "You are not exactly talkative! What is the matter with you?" asked the girl, looking at Mendel inquiringly.

"I'm just a little tired. I've walked so much today." Mendel passed his hand over his eyes.

"Well, then lie down a little. I'll call you for the meal."

The girl went out. With a loud groan, Mendel let himself sink down on the bed and hid his face among the pillows.

'Why did I betray them? I am a swine! All of them, I have betrayed all of them! What a coward I am! After all I did to my friends, I earned the fate those Nazi pigs intended for me! But I fled and now I am safe! My God, you should have let me die instead of them!'

Mendel's body shook with dry sobs. When the girl had said her full name, he heard only the second part of her name "…marie." And this name removed the numbness he had been feeling until now, and had raised the memory of his deed. Because he had – so he thought – betrayed his friends, Bernhard and all the others, whom they had probably killed in the meantime…! And all this, in order to save his beloved Marie!

'My God, why did I have to do that…?' Mendel asked himself in deep despair.

*

Mendel tormented himself in vain, for all his friends managed to escape.

Marie had waited for him for hours. As it became dark and he still did not return, she went to their friends to discuss the possible ways of finding him. She knew where he had gone. They went together to the ghetto, and there they were informed that on that day a man had been arrested there, giving out fake papers.

Marie broke down upon hearing this news. The friends had to support her. Quickly they left the ghetto, not returning to their apartments but sending an acquaintance over, under some pretext, to bring them some of their most essential belongings.

Marie was inconsolable. She did not want to flee. She did not want to understand that it was impossible to save her 'Martin.'

"Listen, Marie! If the Gestapo has captured him, we are not going to see him ever again! He will not want to betray us. So they will torture him. For how long they are going to do it depends on him, on his power of endurance! And as I know Mendel, he will keep silent for a long time!" Bernhard pulled Marie to him.

"I have to take care of my child, of Judith. I cannot help you find another safe place now, but I'll take you to the railway station and put you on the train. Go home, Marie! You cannot help Mendel any more!"

Marie gave in and let herself be taken to the station. Bernhard fulfilled his promise and waited until the train came. He helped Marie on board and waved to her when the train left the station.

Marie wept. But by the time the last houses of Budapest passed by the window, her tears had already dried. She sat there stiffly and looked straight into the space in front of her with burning eyes, without any feeling. She had to leave her heart in Budapest.

*

Bernhard left the railway station quickly and hurried to the children's home where Judith was staying. By that time the home already belonged to the ghetto compound. Bernhard had, in fact, to steal his own child from there. Packing a few clothes for the child, he impressed on little Judith: "Listen, little one. We have to get away from here. The police are searching for us. They want to put us away. So we have to flee. From now on your name is 'Rosi'! You must not tell anyone that your name is Judith, do you understand me? So what do you say if somebody asks for your name?"

"Rosi!"

"Good! And now come along! We are taking the train to a small town. You will surely like it there, Rosi!"

They managed to leave the ghetto unnoticed. Bernhard spoke to the child frequently and addressed her with her new name. He wanted them both to get used to it. On their way to the railway station, he stopped at the shop of a junk dealer and exchanged his attire for some simple working clothes.

The shopkeeper did not understand the world anymore. Here comes a man and exchanges his good suit for old patched rags! How was he supposed to know his way around, with customers like this? Shaking his head, he looked after Bernhard and Rosi, who turned into a smaller street. If he had seen what Bernhard did around the next corner, he would have doubted his sanity, for Bernhard bent down and rubbed his face with dirt from the street. Rosi's face too received some dirt stains. Now Bernhard felt safer. He had Hungarian papers, but from his previous appearance he had looked more like a German gentleman.

They reached the small town of Pásztó safely.

In this little town lived a couple of acquaintances, whom he had known long ago in Berlin. They had lived near his shop and had moved to Hungary around ten years earlier. Bernhard hoped that they were still living there. He was fortunate. He did not need to ask around much. A butcher gave him the address of his acquaintances who also owned a shop in Pásztó and were well known.

A short while later, Bernhard knocked on the door of the house in which the family lived. An elderly woman opened the door.

"Who are you and what do you want?"

"My name is Bernhard Rosen from Berlin! I know you, you used to live near my shop!"

"Rosen! Rosen…! Yes, now I remember! Didn't you have a textile shop? Come in, please!"

Bernhard followed the woman, feeling relieved.

"Look, Ilona, this is a gentleman from Berlin! Do you remember the textile shop of Mr. Rosen? You were quite young when we left Berlin, just twelve years old, but actually, I think you should still remember it!"

"Yes, I even remember you, Mr. Rosen!"

Ilona bent down to Judith. "What is your name, little one?"

"My name?" With a quick look at her father, Judith continued: "My name is Rosemarie!"

"Go a little into the garden with the child, all right?"

Ilona agreed and went out into the garden with Rosi.

Now Mrs. Mühlen said to Bernhard: "Please sit down, Mr. Rosen! Coffee?" She poured a full cup before Bernhard could answer. "So, now tell me, what has brought you to us?" The woman looked at Bernhard's face inquisitively.

"I fled from Berlin with my two children, because my wife was killed by the maltreatment of Gestapo men, and the children and I were being persecuted. Until now, I have managed to hide in Budapest with my daughter Rosi, but there it has become too dangerous for the little one. I wanted to ask you if the child could stay with you for a while. Of course, I would pay for it!"

"Yes, yes, we don't want to disappoint you! Of course the child can stay with us!" The woman named a large sum, which Bernhard had to pay for Rosi's monthly accommodation, food and care. Without batting an eyelid, Bernhard took out his wallet and counted the money onto the table. He paid for ten months in advance.

Mrs. Mühlen's eyes shone as she counted the banknotes. Bernhard was happy that his little Judith was going to be taken care of so well. 'I hope she'll not tell anybody that she is Jewish!' he thought. 'Well, God will protect us.'

Bernhard liked being in the house of the Mühlens. Ilona cared lovingly for little 'Rosi', and the child felt comfortable with her right away. Bernhard once again impressed on the child: "Don't forget, you must not tell anybody that you come from Berlin and that we are Jews, and you must not forget that your name is now 'Rosi'!"

They offered Bernhard a bed for the night and he accepted gratefully. In the evening, he had a long talk with Ilona and her father. Franz Mühlen was almost seventy years old, but still sprightly. He told Bernhard that Frieda Mühlen was his third wife. "Ach, if only I had not married this woman! She turns my old days into a living hell. She scrimps and saves and even begrudges me a good cigar and a glass of wine! But I have a business, which goes quite well."

"So why did you marry the woman?" asked Bernhard, astonished.

"My second wife died giving birth to Ilona. At that time, Frieda was working in our shop in Berlin. I didn't know how to take care of the child by myself, so I married her. She took care of us quite well for a long time. Only now, in the last years, has she changed and become stingy." The old man sighed. "Well, everybody has to bear his cross, isn't it so? *Prost*, Mr. Rosen! I wish you would also stay here with us!"

'I wish I could too!' thought Bernhard. Aloud he said: "*Prost*, Mr. Mühlen." The wine had already gone to his head, as he had not drunk alcohol for a long time. So he said good-night and went to sleep.

The next morning, he prepared for his departure. At breakfast, Frieda Mühlen suddenly said: "Tell me, Mr. Rosen, don't you want to stay with us too?" She looked at Bernhard with a furtive glance. "There is enough room, and you can pay the same amount for your accommodation and food as for your daughter's. That way, the child doesn't have to be parted from her father. You can care for her yourself. We can put an extra bed in the room; there is room enough for both of you. So, what do you say?"

Overwhelmed, Bernhard looked at her. "I, I, – but yes! Of course I accept! I didn't dare ask for it! I'll stay here with pleasure!"

"Good!" Frieda Mühlen patted Rosi's cheek, satisfied.

"So, everything is clear! Franz, you and Mr. Rosen go and bring the bed from the attic!" she ordered, "and you, Ilona, you brush the old mattress and put covers over the pillows. I am going to open the shop. And you," continued Frieda, "you go out to the garden, Rosi. Play nicely!" Then Frieda got up and disappeared behind the door which led to the shop.

The others looked at each other in silence.

"You do have a fresh wind blowing here, don't you?" asked Bernhard, grinning.

"What did I tell you?" Franz shrugged his shoulder.

"Should I argue with her all the time? I'd better do what she wants and have my peace!"

"I cannot say anything bad about her," said Bernhard, "after all, she has accepted me and Rosi here. This cannot be weighed in gold, and I shall never forget that!"

Franz Mühlen used his wife's absence to drink a glass of wine with Bernhard and to raise a toast for a good life together. "You know, Mr. Rosen, we could actually speak informally from now on, do you agree?" Bernhard agreed to that.

"And with me too! Please call me Ilona," demanded the girl.

"But only if you call me Bernhard!"

In the course of the conversation, Bernhard learned that Ilona had been engaged to a Hungarian. But just before Bernhard arrived, she had found out that she was not to be the only bride of that young man. He had a fiancée in almost every surrounding village or town, and each one, including Ilona, had handed over a large sum of money to him, for his alleged blooming business. After that, the swindler disappeared, never to be seen again. Because of this incident, Ilona's parents had great financial difficulties.

'Perhaps this is the reason they have taken us in so quickly!' thought Bernhard.

Anyway, Bernhard's payment in advance was a welcome help and even a partial compensation for the loss they had suffered, in a way.

In the following days, Bernhard and his hosts got to know each other. They got along well. Bernhard had long talks with Ilona and the landlord, and he often sat in the garden with his little daughter. There, they were hidden from curious looks of the neighbors. But, joyful children's laughter could be heard from the surrounding houses and gardens, and Judith asked again and again:

"When can I play with the other children?"

"Soon you will be able to play with them!" said Bernhard to Judith, caressing the little child's shoulder.

*

He was not feeling very well. He had a slight fever, his limbs hurt, and the dragging pain in the small of his back caused him the most pain. Bernhard did not want to visit a local doctor, as he was afraid of exposing his identity. So he took the train to Budapest to search for a physician in the ghetto.

When he arrived there, he marched straight to the entrance of the ghetto and, to his great horror, he saw a guard standing there.

What now?

It was too late to turn around and walk away. Decidedly, Bernhard went on, greeted the man with a brash "Heil Hitler!" and crossed the entrance, entering the ghetto. He reached the physician's waiting room with trembling knees. Everybody let him go in first, as they thought Bernhard was a German. The physician too thought he was a Nazi, as Bernhard did not wear a Star of David.

"You…without…?" asked the physician, but Bernhard did not let him finish his sentence. "My name is Benko. Please treat me. I cannot come again!" said Bernhard.

The physician examined Bernhard thoroughly, gave him an injection and sufficient medicine to take care of the infection. "Good luck!" he added when he said good-bye to him.

Bernhard thanked him and went on his way back to Pásztó.

Inside the railway station he pushed unintentionally against a person in an SS uniform. Quickly, he excused himself. The stranger looked at him and hesitated suddenly. "Don't you recognize me? But I'm Neumann, Neumann from Berlin!"

Bernhard looked at him more closely. 'Neumann, Neumann,' he thought. 'Yes, right! I once knew a Jewish boy by the name of Neumann in Berlin!'

In fact, it was the same boy! He had fled to Budapest and had somehow obtained an SS officer's uniform. Wearing this, he could live in the city without being discovered. He invited Bernhard: "Come with me to my landlady. You look bad. But take my advice: speak German, and talk much about the wonders of German weapons. This will impress my landlady, and she will not ask where and when I met you, etc.!"

Bernhard was glad that there was a bed waiting where he could lie down, for he was feeling rather awful. After walking for a short while, they reached their destination. Bernhard acted according to Neumann's advice and immediately earned the confidence of the landlady. The pleasant woman even took care of him during the following days.

When he was able to get up again, he visited some of his former friends. Together with Neumann, they made contact with the Swedish Red Cross and were able, with their support, to help many illegal refugees who lived in the city.

*

Now Bernhard had already been in Budapest for some weeks, and he was becoming restless. He thought more and more about Pásztó. He was worried about his little daughter and so he returned to the little town. It was the middle of the night when he arrived there. It was pitch dark and he was paralyzed with fear. What had happened there in the meantime? He did not dare imagine all the terrible things that could have happened to his child. He hastened until he stood in front of the house. He knocked very quietly on the front door. Then he heard steps; somebody was coming to the door.

"Who is it?" asked Ilona.

"It's me, Bernhard!"

Ilona opened the door, pulled Bernhard into the corridor and embraced him. "You are alive! My God, you are alive! I'm so happy!" stammered Ilona with tears in her eyes and caressed his face with both her hands.

It was as if scales fell from Bernhard's eyes, the girl loved him! He looked at Ilona and read the confirmation of it in her eyes.

"Ilona, dearest!" He kissed the girl tenderly and went with her into the living room. Bernhard told her about what he had been doing in Budapest, and she informed him about what had meanwhile happened in Pásztó. Afterwards, Bernhard looked in on his sleeping little daughter and then lay down to sleep, exhausted.

The following morning Bernhard woke up, feeling someone's breath on his face. It was little Judith.

"Papa, Papa, are you awake at last? How wonderful that you are here again. I was so worried about you!"

"Come here, you little crawly froggie!" Bernhard pulled her into his arms, and the child squealed with delight.

"What did you do all the time I was away?" asked Bernhard with a smile.

"Ooh, quite a lot! Once, I saw a real frog in the garden! But then the dog came and chased it away. Yes, and then I often played with Ilona. She even took me with her to the church. I can also tell stories from the Bible and do the sign of the cross, you see, so and so and so!"

Bernhard felt that this was not right. The child should not forget that she was Jewish!

Therefore, he said: "Come, let us pray!" Judith seized his hand and repeated after him, word for word: "*Sh'ma Israel Adonai Elohenu Adonai Ehad* (Hear oh Israel, the Lord our God, the Lord is One). I thank You, dear God, that you have helped us until now and beg of You to hold Your hand further over us to protect us. Let Your people Israel, the foundation on which You have built mankind, not perish. The sufferings and sacrifices of Your people are too hard to bear. Lead Your people who have survived back to the land of our ancestors! There they will renew Your teachings! Give Your people Israel peace, and let all the people of the world take part in it! Amen!"

"Does God help if one prays to him? Does He really listen?" asked Judith curiously.

"Yes, God hears each prayer directed towards him, and if He decides it is right, then He helps; sometimes he helps quickly, though mostly one has to wait longer. But there is always some point in time when the wicked get their punishment and the believer in God is raised!"

The child was satisfied with this explanation.

*

Over the next days, Bernhard noticed with growing alarm that Ilona showed him more than just friendly affection, and that she had become more than just a good friend in his eyes too. Ilona busied herself so much with his child that she soon neglected her housekeeping duties and was reprimanded for it by Frieda Mühlen, who kept constant watch over her daughter's actions. She saw that Ilona was fond of Bernhard, but she did not know if he felt the same way about the girl.

Ilona herself did not know this for sure, for Bernhard behaved in a very reserved way towards her. He did so as he was sure that Frieda Mühlen would not agree to have him as a son-in-law. In order not to endanger the safety of his child, he kept out of Ilona's way whenever he could.

But one day it happened that the two of them were left in the house on their own. Franz Mühlen had gone for a long stroll with his wife, and little Judith was playing in the garden. Bernhard was just selecting a new book when Ilona unexpectedly entered the room.

Bernhard heard the sound and turned around. The view took his breath away: Ilona's graceful slender figure in the light of the setting sun. He tried to maintain his composure, but his eyes betrayed him. Ilona came closer to him. "How do you like my new dress, Bernhard?" She swayed her hips coquettishly.

Bernhard could not take his eyes off her. Her closeness and the delicate scent coming from her body made him feel dizzy. He could not utter a word.

"Well, don't you like me?" Ilona demanded.

"Well, yes!" gasped out Bernhard quickly, "but…!"

"But what?" Ilona came closer to him. Warding her off, Bernhard stretched out his hands, but Ilona had already snuggled into his arms. She had read the truth in his eyes.

"Kiss me!" she whispered with closed eyes and held her face towards him. Bernhard lost his self-control. Impetuously, he pulled her into his arms and kissed her passionately.

Both were so lost in their feelings that they did not notice that Judith had entered the room. Only when the child called: "Papa, imagine, in the courtyard I saw two little birds playing with each other!" Bernhard and Ilona jumped apart, as if they had done something bad.

"So, and what happened with the two little birds?" asked Bernhard.

"One was Aryan and the other was Jewish!"

"How do you know that? I don't quite understand this!"

"One little bird had a yellow patch on its chest. That was the Jewish one!" said the little girl. "How fortunate that the bad people didn't see it. They would have certainly killed it immediately!"

With these words the little girl ran out again. Ilona and Bernhard looked at each other, embarrassed. But they quickly forgot all about it; the outside world didn't exist for them again, and they embraced and kissed lovingly.

They started when suddenly the door was pulled open and Ilona's mother stood in the doorway. The two jumped apart.

"Ilona! What are you doing here alone with Bernhard? Why have you sent the child out? You must have wanted to be alone with him, right?" Frieda grabbed her daughter's arm angrily and pulled her out of the room.

"We didn't do anything wrong or indecent!" Ilona said indignantly. "Rosi, come here and tell my mother if we sent you out of the room!"

"No, I wanted to look at the birds in the courtyard, but someone startled them and now they have flown away!" chattered the child.

"This is sad, but perhaps you'll find them again. Go out and look for them, Rosi!" Ilona turned again to her mother: "Now you see that your suspicions about Bernhard and me are unjust. He is a gentleman and would not touch me!"

"But you do like him, yes?"

"Yes, I love him!" admitted Ilona without shame.

"Don't you associate with the Jew!" exploded Frieda, red with anger, "otherwise there will be big trouble in this house! I shall throw him and the brat out if you start anything with him! I don't need the money so badly that I throw you into the jaws of a heathen. Just remember that!" raged the mother.

Ilona was silent in order to calm the woman. She did not want her mother to throw out Bernhard and his child. She knew that the woman would probably carry out her threats. Ilona waited for the next opportunity to meet Bernhard alone and tell him about the argument with her mother.

"I could find work in some other place and even rent a room there!" said Ilona to Bernhard. "We could live there together, all three of us!"

Bernhard shook his head. "No! Look, dearest, we are safe here! The war will soon end, and then the whole world will be open to us. Let's stay here now and not endanger Rosi unnecessarily, all right?"

Ilona gave in with a sigh.

In the evening, the mother seemed to have forgotten the dispute. "Come on, eat all the food from your plate!" she urged Judith and stroked the child's hair.

"I have to go to Budapest for a few days, to buy some supplies for the shop!" she declared to the others. "What shall I bring you, Rosi?"

"Two little birds I can set free!" answered the little girl.

"What nonsense!" said Frieda, outraged. "The child is totally confused! Take care that Rosi doesn't go out into the street, and that you don't do anything foolish!" With these words, Frieda gave Bernhard a threatening look, but he looked at her calmly. But Franz looked sideways at his wife, anxiously. He had been married to this woman for over twenty years now, but still could not get used to her shrill voice.

'Nagging old hag!' he thought, and continued to eat, bent over his plate.

But Bernhard turned to Frieda and said: "I understand what you want to say. I assure you nothing you don't approve of will happen in your absence. I don't want to upset you. On the contrary! I hope that one day you will be repaid a thousand times for the kindness you have shown my child and me!"

Frieda caressed Judith's cheek, flattered by these words.

"I'm doing this gladly, isn't it so, my child?"

The next morning, Frieda departed for Budapest. It was as if they all had woken up from a bad dream. Ilona went about the house singing and dancing, cooking delicious meals without scrimping and saving, like her mother always did. Now she could spare more time for Bernhard and his child, and Franz could work in his shop the way he liked to. In the evenings they sat together pleasantly, drank wine and talked. Bernhard and Ilona often danced to the sounds of the old gramophone, their minds wandering to faraway places, while Franz slept peacefully in the armchair.

But their fortune did not last long. On the evening of the third day, loud knocking on the front door announced the return of the landlady. While Ilona opened the door, Bernhard ran quickly into his room and took a book from the table; Franz put away the bottle of wine and the glasses, and waved about the room with a white handkerchief to get rid of the smell of his good cigar.

Then Frieda entered the room. With a frown on her face, she looked around suspiciously. But she could not find anything unusual or reproachable. The next day, she seized the reins tightly in her hands again. She noticed angrily that the others had somehow banded together against her. A strained, hostile relationship grew between her and Ilona. She did not spare Bernhard her angry looks, when she noticed the loving glances and touches that Bernhard and Ilona exchanged between themselves, thinking they were unobserved.

*

It was 1945, and by this time the Hungarian and Slovakian resistance fighters bravely started taking more and more risks. They carried out bomb attacks and set fire to official buildings. As a result, the Gestapo and the Hungarian militia joined forces and carried out sudden street raids and searches in houses.

Once, the house of the Mühlens was also searched. Bernhard quickly climbed up into the attic and hid behind some barrels. The sun burned onto the bricks of the roof, but Bernhard was perspiring out of fear as he waited for the gendarmes to search the attic. Upon hearing steps, he stopped breathing. But then, to his immense relief, he heard Ilona's voice.

"You can come out of your hiding place, Bernhard! The gendarmes have left!" she called quietly.

Bernhard came out from behind the barrels. He saw, startled, that Ilona was crying.

"What is it? Don't cry, little one! The danger has passed! Or is it something else? Have you perhaps had a row with your mother again?"

"Yes!" Ilona sobbed. "My God, I cannot take it any more! She demanded that I forget you! So I threatened her that I would leave the house or even kill myself!"

"But Ilona! You have to think of the child! You do love us, don't you?"

Ilona nodded.

"You see, then you must not say such things. Wait a little while longer. I'm certain the war will be over soon. Until then do what your mother demands. Don't come into my room. Go and meet with your friends now and again. And don't be so sad, do you hear?"

"Yes, I'll do everything as you wish, my dearest!" Ilona sniffled and gave Bernhard a kiss, before she left.

And indeed, it did not take long until at last the war came to an end.

It began with the German units arriving in Pásztó. They were in retreat, as the Red Army drove them back into the Reich. Several German officers were put up with the Mühlens, who introduced Bernhard as a distant relative not fit for the army.

The officers admitted openly that for Germany the war was already lost. They enjoyed themselves, played cards, drank and waited for relief.

"We don't feel like risking our lives further for Hitler's crazy delusions!" they said to Bernhard in confidence, before they disappeared in the dead of the night.

After them, some SS men moved into the small house and Bernhard hid in the cellar. The Mühlens dug a hideaway for him there, and they supplied him daily with everything he needed. The hours which Bernhard passed down there seemed neverending, and the nights especially seemed like years.

In addition to that, there was the constant fear that little Judith would talk too much and unwillingly draw the SS men's attention to him. But it could have been worse for Bernhard. At least he remained undiscovered in the cellar. He remained there, hidden in darkness, for some days. But at long last the SS men finally left. The Red Army had surrounded the town. The Mühlen's house was situated exactly in the center of the artillery fire, so they all had to evacuate the house.

Bernhard took Judith in his arms and ran to one of the neighbors, who had a well-built shelter in his cellar. He did not stop to look for Ilona in his hurry.

"Who are you?" asked the man in a brusque voice. Bernhard explained to him that he had moved to this neighborhood only a short time ago, but could not identify himself, since he had forgotten his documents at home in the hurry. But this did not satisfy the man, who was a hotheaded Nazi.

"Then go and get your papers!" he snapped at Bernhard. "You can leave the child here in the meantime!"

Just then, Ilona rushed in. "Bernhard! Thank God that you are here! Come quickly! I have been searching for you everywhere!" She pulled Bernhard from the cellar and confided to him outside: "That man, the owner of this house, is a fanatic Nazi! He would shoot you immediately if he knew you to be a Jew!"

They ran home, where they were still safer than in a place where people blatantly discriminated against other people, even at a time of such great danger.

Ilona, Bernhard and Judith had just reached the house when a grenade hit the building!

'My God! Is this going to be our end?' thought Bernhard in despair, as he threw Judith and Ilona to the ground and fell over them in order to shelter them with his body.

Stonework caved in, lime crumbled from the walls down onto them. Judith whimpered, and Ilona, too, sobbed quietly to herself. For awhile, the crashing continued outside, as the Mühlen's house was hit many times. The last blow tore off the roof and the house collapsed. Bernhard was still sheltering Ilona and Judith. Now, countless stones and beams clattered down upon them. He lost consciousness when one of the stones grazed his head. Ilona felt the dead weight of his body on her.

"Bernhard, Bernhard!" she cried out frightened, thinking he was probably wounded. But Bernhard did not answer.

Outside, it was suddenly deathly silent. The gunfire and the cannons were quiet; no more grenades came howling through the air.

Ilona managed to struggle out from under Bernhard and to free Judith. Except for some minor scratches, she and the child were not hurt. They turned Bernhard onto his back and wiped the blood off his face.

"You stay here, Rosi, I'm going to bring some water!" Ilona groped through the rubble of stones to the outside. There was a well in the garden and she wanted to draw some water from it, as the water taps inside the house were all covered with debris. Ilona crept out at last, with difficulty.

She stared horrified at the picture she saw. Most of the neighboring houses were destroyed, and some of them were ablaze. There were deep craters and many holes on the street; pieces of walls, stones and rubble lay everywhere.

Ilona tore herself away forcibly from this sight and rushed to the garden, or what had once been a garden. She found the well almost intact. Relieved, she drew water out of it and hurried back to Bernhard. After climbing carefully through the rubble, she reached him and gave him some water to drink. She cleaned the wound and put a makeshift bandage on it. Then she sat there, with Judith enclosed in her arms, waiting for Bernhard to regain conciousness.

After a while, she heard frightened cries. She recognized her parents' voices. "Ilona, Ilona!" The two called again and again.

"Here, I'm here!" Ilona answered.

She could hear that stones and whole parts of rubble were being cleared away, outside. Then her parents rushed in and took their daughter into their arms, overjoyed.

"How wonderful that you are alive!" they called again and again.

Bernhard came to. He was relieved to see that they were all still alive. He felt rather weak, but he was able to get up and help bring some order into the area of the house and also tidy up as much as he could.

The next morning, the news spread like wildfire through the little town:

"The Russians are coming!"

Bernhard went out in order to welcome the liberators.

At first, a drunken bandy-legged Mongolian, with a fur hat on his head, staggered across the street. A rifle dangled in front of his chest. In one hand he held a big demijohn, from which he now and again gulped deeply, and in the other hand and under his arm he held a loaf of bread and a big piece of ham. Belching, he called: "*Nemez-nintch*?" (No Germans?)

He was followed by a group of five Red Army soldiers, who waved their hands to Bernhard amicably. He would have liked to stand outside longer, but his head was aching. So he went in and lay down.

Little Judith could no longer be restrained. She had to go out into the streets! Bernhard took her by the hand and walked with her through Pásztó. They could again hear the noises of cannons and gunshots, but the noises moved further and further away from Pásztó.

Judith asked happily: "Papa, am I now allowed to say that I'm a Jew?"

Bernhard almost said "Yes," but the words got stuck in his throat, because a Russian officer walked towards them and shouted: "*Bey jedy spassei russia!*" (Hit the Jews, save Russia!) Startled, Bernhard made way for the Russian.

"No, you must not say anything for the time being. Once we are really safe, you can tell everybody fearlessly that we are Jews."

This small incident made it clear to Bernhard that he was still not safe. The new rulers hated the Jews just as much as the old ones. His decision was definite. He wanted to take Judith and go to Israel. After all, Daniel was waiting for them there.

They had just returned to the Mühlens when Ilona walked towards him. "Bernhard, you mustn't leave me alone!" she sobbed. "Soldiers keep coming and pestering me all the time! They even follow me into the house!"

Bernhard calmed her down and told her of his incident with the Russian.

"…and because of that I cannot stay here! I'll emigrate with Rosi to Israel. We still have to build the land, and we will all have to work hard, but then, we Jews will be free people in our own land."

"And I?" Ilona looked at Bernhard, thunderstruck.

"You could never be happy there, in a strange land and without your family. This would sooner or later have destroyed our happiness. Believe me, I love you too much for that. I feel very obligated to you, and I promise to help you financially, if I'm ever in a position to do so. Your house is destroyed, and with it the shop too; your entire basis of livelihood is gone! We, Rosi and I, would only be a burden to you at the moment. Therefore we are going to set out on our way early tomorrow."

Ilona swayed and would have fallen to the ground, if Bernhard had not caught her in time.

Frieda Mühlen joined them and scrutinized Bernhard suspiciously, but as he told her of his travel plans he saw the glimmer in her eyes.

"Well, what a coincidence!" she said astonished. "Just now, a friend of Ilona's has returned, the son of a neighbor who has survived the war as a soldier!"

"How convenient, then she will not be alone," answered Bernhard pleasantly, but in his innermost being, he went wild with jealousy.

"Come, Rosi!" He pulled the child with him into the garden.

"Are you happy that you'll see your brother Daniel soon?"

"Yes, of course! But tell me, Papa, we are going to take Auntie Ilona with us, right?"

"We cannot do that, unfortunately. We cannot separate her from her parents. Would you like to stay here alone, if I went to Israel?"

"No, never!"

"So, you see, because of that, Ilona also cannot come with us."

Later, Bernhard went to the railway station and asked at the information counter about the next scheduled departure. He was informed that the next day there was a Red Cross train going to Bucharest.

'Bucharest!' thought Bernhard. 'Why not? This is rather convenient for us.' He hurried back to the house of the Mühlens and prepared everything for their departure.

The following day, Ilona and her father waved sadly to the departing friends. Frieda Mühlen had found some pretext to say good-bye to Bernhard at home, earlier. She was barely able to conceal her pleasure at seeing Bernhard and Rosi leave.

On board the train, Bernhard left the window only after the station was out of his sight. He was not ashamed of his tears. Once again, he was leaving behind another chapter of his life.

*

Twenty-four hours later, the train arrived in Bucharest. Bernhard and Judith had not slept at all on the way, so they felt dead tired and exhausted. Nevertheless, before anything else, they went to the Palestine office, where they were both put on the list for emigration to Israel. The friendly clerk even arranged a room for them for their stay until they were to leave. The landlady was an elderly woman, who took good care of them. She put Judith straight to bed and then she told Bernhard how Bucharest had fared throughout the end of the war.

The city was not damaged at all, as it had been spared the war. Life went on as usual. Bernhard went through the streets, stunned, and admired the display in the shop windows and the well-dressed people. Refugees could be recognized right away by their emaciated faces, as most of the people of Bucharest were well fed. Bernhard walked along, deep in his thoughts.

Suddenly he ran into an elegantly dressed woman.

"Oh, forgive me! I'm sorry!" called out Bernhard in German and bent down to pick up the handbag that had fallen from the lady's hands. By doing so, he again bumped into her, because she too bent down at the same moment.

The woman laughed out loud. Bernhard looked into her face and was dazed with surprise.

"Excuse me, don't we know each other?" he asked, searching his memory. "Were you born in Bucharest?"

"No, I come from a small town called Khust," answered the woman quietly. "Oh, it is a sad story!"

"Khust!" called out Bernhard excitedly. "I knew that I recognized you from somewhere! My name is Bernhard Rosen from Berlin! I'm certain that I met you at the farm of Hershel Gutmann!"

"You are Bernhard?" stammered the woman. "I'm Feigele! My husband Haim was also a friend of Hershel!"

The two embraced in the middle of the street. Then Feigele dragged Bernhard home with her to Haim and Esther. They lived in a big house, together with Dr. Bernstein, the senior physician from the hospital of Czernovitz.

How had they all come to be living together? When Haim, Feigele and Esther had prepared for their journey to Bucharest, the old doctor did not want to be left behind. So he made a quick decision, appointed one of the physicians to his senior position and left with the friends.

Now they began to tell Bernhard what had happened to them over the years, and he told them the story of his escape.

"Do you want to earn some money?" asked Haim. "We have found some friends here, who have taken us in as their partners, and now we are co-owners of a well functioning textile shop and earning some money for a new beginning in Israel."

Bernhard agreed straightaway to work with them. They agreed that Feigele would take care of Judith while he worked.

Time passed, and one day the friends received news from the Palestine office. In a few days' time, they were to begin their long journey.

Now began the feverish packing of suitcases. All of them were happy at the thought that they would soon be in their land, *Eretz Israel*. Only Bernhard became more and more silent, from day to day. Then he plucked up the courage to speak his mind.

"I...I cannot come with you to Israel now! First I must go back to Berlin. Perhaps there is somebody still alive, somebody from my family or my friends...!"

"Are you out of your mind? You want to go back to Germany? There, where they tortured you and killed your wife?"

The friends were horrified. They could not understand Bernhard's decision. Nevertheless, they honored his wish. He promised to follow them as soon as possible. For the time being, they undertook to visit Daniel and tell him of his father's imminent arrival.

And then came the day when Haim and Feigele, Esther and Dr. Bernstein left on their big journey.

Bernhard and Judith waved farewell to them until the train was out of sight. They had wanted to take the child with them to Israel, but Judith was not willing to part from her father.

On that same day, the two set out on their way back to Berlin.

*

Martin had settled down well at the Austrian farm, for the farmer and his wife treated him like a son. But then, Martin did take most of the farm work off the farmer's hand. After all, he had grown up on a farm and knew well how to work on a farm.

Only one matter disturbed Mendel. Annerl, the farmer's pretty daughter, followed him everywhere. She did not make any secret of the fact that she liked him. And Martin realized that he thought less and less about Marie. He had thought that Marie's face would be deeply rooted in his heart, but the memory of her paled from day to day. Martin felt like a scoundrel and was therefore unusually reserved with Annerl.

It grew difficult for them to work together. Then one day, while Martin and Annerl were cutting grass on a meadow far away, a storm began brewing in the distance. It would have taken them too long to reach the house. So they took shelter on the hayrack and pulled the tarpaulin over themselves.

The nearness of Annerl confused him. He tried to move away from her a little, when he suddenly felt her groping hands on his chest. He grabbed them.

"Annerl!"

"Martin!"

Annerl was with him in a quick movement, wrapping her arms around him and nestling her cheek against his breast. Then she raised her face. "I love you so much!" she whispered, and as Martin still did not move, she added: "Why don't you want me? Don't you love me?"

Her eyes filled with tears.

"But yes, in fact I love you very much, but, but...first I must tell you something!"

Martin freed himself from her arms and moved himself away. Then he took a deep breath to calm his feelings, which were in turmoil, and he began to speak. He told her his whole story, including the story of Marie.

"And...do you still love this Marie?" asked Annerl hesitantly, when Martin had finished telling her his story.

"But that's it! I had believed firmly that I would love Marie until the end of my life, but now, after knowing you, I'm not so sure any more…! I could even say that I have banished her out of my thoughts!"

"Martin!" rejoiced Annerl, and pulled Martin over to her. This time, Martin did not push her away. Martin took the girl into his arms, and both succumbed to their feelings.

Much later, they returned home and did not try to hide their feelings for each other. The parents did not have any objection to Martin becoming their son-in-law.

But their happiness did not last for long. One evening the mayor of the village arrived unexpectedly and asked for Martin.

"Is your worker a deserter or a Jew?" he asked the farmer openly.

Annerl changed the subject cleverly. "Come on! We wouldn't take in a Jew at our place! What do you think, dear mayor? You've known us long enough!"

The mayor let himself be convinced, but the next day, a messenger brought an official letter, in which Martin was asked to report the following day at the Gestapo to present his documents.

"No, you mustn't go there! We shall hide you!" Annerl was beside herself with excitement. "Wait! I have an entirely different idea! We are going to travel to my uncle and aunt in Germany. They will take us in right away!"

"That's right!" said the farmer. "My brother is not a Nazi! You will be safe there!"

Annerl and Martin quickly packed a few things and Annerl dressed Martin up as an old woman. Even in their serious situation, they had to laugh. Martin looked so funny in the wide black dress and the veiled hat. He really could not be recognized.

At the light of dawn, the two crept to the railway station and caught the first train to Germany. People were standing and sitting closely, packed in the compartments and even in the corridors. Everybody was concentrating on finding a good place, so nobody took notice of the two 'women.'

More and more people pushed in as they got nearer to the border: wounded who came from the front and soldiers with less serious wounds, in worn-out uniforms and dirty, worn-out shoes. The gray faces revealed the hardships borne, the bent backs the deprivations and humiliations of retreat.

Martin felt compassion for the men, even if he could not forget that they had caused him so much suffering.

'What has happened to the proud German soldiers? Four years of war in the east has been enough to destroy their fighting spirit. The ghost of defeat has passed amongst them and broken their morale.'

Many of the soldiers deserted and were caught by the so-called "Chaindogs" (field police behind the front lines) and immediately shot dead or hung. One could see in their broken forms the misery of their defeat.

Annerl interrupted his chain of thought. She handed him an apple. They were not far from the border now.

A short while later, the train stopped, and German officers came aboard the train, accompanied by two gendarmes. Annerl and Martin waited tensely for passport control. The officers entered their compartment and arrested two soldiers who allegedly did not have adequate identity documents. The other passengers, mostly Austrian women, protested loudly. During the general excitement, the officers only glanced at the passports of Annerl and Martin.

One of the officers asked the old woman: "Are you Margaret Moser?" He only glanced fleetingly at her and handed back the passports. The two young people felt as if a heavy load had been lifted off their shoulders.

It took them a whole day of travel to reach, at last, the uncle's small village. It was already dark, and the ongoing drizzle soaked them to the bone. They trudged with difficulty against the wind. At last they reached the uncle's house. A dog ran back and forth behind the hedge, whining. He did not bark, for he recognized Annerl.

"Onkel! Onkel Heinrich!" called Annerl, holding back.

A moment later, the front door opened.

"Oh, what a surprise! Annerl! Where have you come from all of a sudden? And whom have you brought with you?"

The uncle embraced Annerl happily and greeted the "aunt." How astonished he was when Martin took off the hat, once inside the house, and turned out to be a young man!

"*Jo Sakra*! It's a young lad!"

"Yes, this is Martin!" answered Annerl and revealed to her uncle and aunt the whole true story. "And because of all that, we have come here. Perhaps we can stay here with you, until the danger has passed?"

"But of course you can stay!" The uncle was, in fact, rather glad that there would be a little more liveliness in the house. Besides, they could use an additional pair of hands at work. Martin did not show himself outside the farm, but at the farm and in the courtyard, he did all the tasks he could handle for the farmer.

One day, the farmer broke the news to them that he had just heard in the village. The Russians were advancing towards Vienna! Budapest had already fallen.

"What shall I do now? I promised my parents that if there were battles in their region, I would be with them!" Annerl was desperate.

"The war will soon be over. Nothing will happen to your parents. And when everything is over, we will go there together, all right?" Martin calmed Annerl down, but he himself was not entirely sure of the truthfulness of his words.

Who knew how the soldiers of the Red Army, drunken with victory, would behave?

13.

THE GERMAN MILITARY news reporter, Ruth, could not forget the incident with the Polish soldiers. Often, when she had a few minutes time for herself, she thought of the scene in the glade in the wood. Now and then, that pair of brown eyes seemed to be looking at her.

Ruth hated the war, and her being a part of it depressed her.

"Isn't it madness to wage war against the whole world? One should stop it and cease all acts of war! Why should more and more innocent people die?"

When Ruth said this to a comrade, he informed against her. The captain ordered Ruth to be brought before him, and as punishment he transferred her to serve in a so-called concentration camp.

Ruth resigned herself without a word. It was all the same to her, where they sent her. Her father, an active officer of a conservative mind, had already given his life for *"Führer, Volk und Vaterland"* (the leader, the people and the homeland), written so 'nicely' in the telegram which they had sent her mother. When they received that, Ruth finally woke up and came to her senses.

Until then, she had been a fanatic follower of the Nazi regime. No wonder, as she was raised from early childhood in that spirit. And right after her graduation, she had volunteered to the Wehrmacht.

But upon her father's death, she began to think about many things and observe her environment more critically. She learned to distinguish between ideals and reality. She saw how the Nazi officers lived extravagantly during the war, while the common soldiers at the front, who believed in their officers and the Führer, died by thousands in fighting.

And then, one day, Ruth began her service. She did not have to guard the prisoners, but was assigned, together with several comrades, to prepare their retreat. That meant that she had to guard the dismantling of the factories in the surroundings of the concentration camps. In those final days, everything went helter skelter. Everybody packed and prepared himself for the flight 'home to the Reich.'

Horrified and shaken, Ruth took the dreadful pictures, which she saw in the concentration camps, into her soul. She could not hide her aversion.

"This is inhuman, what is happening here! How can one treat people like this, worse than animals?" She was outraged.

"Keep quiet! You are risking your neck!" her friends admonished her.

"Cowards!" answered Ruth, and she decided to flee.

A few days later, on her way home with a few comrades, something that resembled a human form staggered towards them out of the wood. They did not realize at first that it was a terribly emaciated woman because she had a bald head. When this unfortunate woman saw the car, she tried to escape, but she collapsed, exhausted.

"My God! She must have escaped from the labor camp! Look at her appearance!" tears came to Ruth's eyes. "What shall we do with her?" asked one of the comrades.

"I'm going to take her home with me! And don't you dare report even one word of this incident!"

Ruth's eyes flared up upon these words. Nobody dared to oppose her.

They gave the woman some Schnapps to drink and tried to feed her a piece of toast, but her body could not take in any food. She only opened her eyes for a moment. When she saw the German soldiers, she closed her eyelids again. She did not want to hear or see anything.

"Listen, we only want to help you," said Ruth desperately to the woman. "We are not going to do anything bad to you!"

Hearing that, the woman opened her eyes and looked at Ruth, inspecting her. Then she seized Ruth's hand. They wrapped her quickly into a blanket and brought her to Ruth's apartment. Ruth lived in the house of a Polish family. How the landlady started when she saw the living human skeleton!

Ruth explained that this woman was an escaped prisoner.

"Can she stay here? I'll take care of her!"

The landlady agreed. Together they bathed the stranger, dressed her in clean underwear and put her to bed. Then Ruth tried to feed her some soup.

After that, the woman fell asleep, exhausted.

In the evening, the comrades brought Ruth a few days' worth of food and a few items of clothing.

The stranger awoke and saw Ruth sitting near her bed.

"I want to thank you! You have done so much for me! My name is Rachel and I am a Jew."

Then Rachel told her about all the terrible things that had happened to her until then. When she finished, both cried. They embraced and became friends.

On the following night, Ruth thought about what she could do. After all, she could not hide Rachel indefinitely. If she wanted to save Rachel, then they had no choice but to flee. Ruth decided that first Rachel should flee to Ruth's aunt in Düsseldorf. She, Ruth, would follow a few days later. No sooner said than done! She prepared everything. Rachel rested for another three days after which she was somewhat recovered. She was still weak but was at least able to walk on her own two feet again.

Ruth even managed to find her a wig. Ruth and a few of her comrades brought Rachel to the railway station and put her aboard the train. "I'll follow you soon, Rachel! Good luck!" whispered Ruth into her ear.

After the train had left, Ruth breathed a sigh of relief. So far, everything had worked out. Returning to her room, Ruth removed all the traces of Rachel's stay and lay down to rest, satisfied.

The front moved nearer. All the officers tried saving as many of their "acquired" possessions as they could. Ruth's captain, too, drove his people to hurry. He ordered them to first send home his private belongings.

Ruth revolted against this and tried to stir up her comrades against the captain. But he somehow heard about this and ordered Ruth to be arrested and tried at a military court. Fortunately, Ruth had already packed all her belongings and prepared everything for flight. So she crept away in the dead of the night.

*

Rachel was stunned from everything that had happened to her in the last days. She almost did not dare to breathe. Only a few days earlier she had fled from hell, and now she was already sitting on a train.

She was afraid to fall asleep in case her wig moved without her feeling it.

'Is Yankel still alive?' wondered Rachel, as she huddled in a corner of the compartment, listening to the sound of the train. Tears welled up in her eyes when she thought of her little son Haim, who ended his short life in the gas chamber. Rachel wiped her eyes. Her eyes wandered around the compartment. In addition to her, two other young girls and a few elderly passengers were sitting packed together on the benches. In the passageway, there sat and stood some soldiers who were flirting with the girls.

The woman next to Rachel tried to start a conversation with her, but Rachel closed her eyes and pretended to be asleep. Nevertheless, she followed the conversations in the compartment with interest. Once she really started.

"For the whole war, only the Jews are to blame, only the Jews!" cursed one of the soldiers, an SS man.

"But the Jews are all finished off already! So the war can already be ended!" said the old woman near Rachel, timidly.

Raging, the SS man shouted: "If we meet a Jew, we kill him. We should also kill all Jew friends!"

Rachel opened her eyes wide and uttered a sound of fright. Then she looked around anxiously, but nobody had taken notice of her.

After a short while, the train stopped on an open stretch. It was night. The dark silhouette of a city stood out eerily from the moonlit sky. The chief guard waited for a sign to enter the city. Suddenly the sirens of the city began to wail.

"Air-raid warning! Everybody get off the train!" shouted a conductor, running alongside the train.

The old woman took hold of Rachel's arm and said: "Come, my child! It is an air-raid alarm!" and pulled Rachel with her off the train. Then she pulled a thermos vacuum flask out of her travel bag and poured some warm coffee for Rachel into a cup.

"Where do you travel to, child?" she asked Rachel.

"To Düsseldorf!"

"Düsseldorf! Then you could take a day's rest in Berlin, couldn't you?" The old woman looked into Rachel's big dark eyes and continued: "You know, my husband is a Jew, a very good man. In the past, he was a lawyer, and he had a big practice in Berlin. We lived happily and satisfied until the Nazis came along and dispossessed us of everything; my husband has to work hard now. He was in a labor camp for months and now he is very sick. His heart, liver and stomach are in bad condition. Yes, my child, only a Jew knows how bitter it is to be a Jew."

While she spoke, the woman did not take her eyes off Rachel. So she did not miss that upon the word "Jew" Rachel had started instinctively.

'Aha, so it is then!' thought the old woman with compassion, intending to take Rachel home with her.

The air-raid warning soon ended. There were fires in some places of the city, but the rails were not destroyed. So the train could continue on its way.

At first, Rachel remained reserved. She did not want to reveal herself. But the woman did not let herself be shaken off, and when they arrived at last in Berlin at eleven o'clock, she just took hold of Rachel's hand and pulled her with her.

Rachel did not see much of Berlin but what she did see were ruins. They did not have far to walk in order to reach the house in which the friendly woman lived. There they entered, went through the hallway, crossed a courtyard and climbed up to the second floor. Breathing heavily, Rachel leaned against the doorframe, while the woman took out a key and unlocked the door. Then she led Rachel into the apartment.

On the cupboard, Rachel saw a photograph of an elderly Jew with a long beard, holding a "*Siddur*" (book of prayer) in his hands, and a "*Talit*" (a shawl for prayer) over his shoulders.

The same elderly man entered the room now and greeted his wife lovingly.

"And who do we have here?" he looked at Rachel, astonished, with curiously.

His wife told him how she had met Rachel.

"I am pleased to meet you, my child!" said the man warmly. "My name is Eckstein, Arnold Eckstein, and this is my wife, Sara. You are most kindly welcome to stay, as long as you wish."

Rachel lost her composure with these words. She fell into the man's arms, sobbing, and cried her heart out against his breast.

"Nu, nu, nu! What is it now? Come and tell me everything that tortures you so much!"

Arnold Eckstein led Rachel to the sofa. Then he and his wife listened, shattered, to Rachel's story.

When Rachel had finished, they heard the sound of someone crying in the background. It was Edith, the daughter of the Ecksteins. She had returned home, unnoticed, and had also heard Rachel's words. Now she embraced Rachel and promised to help her.

"We too suffer under the present conditions," said Arnold, "but it is far from what you have gone through, Rachel. A few years ago they took me to forced labor, but at least they let us stay together. And, fortunately, our house has not been hit badly so far. We don't have much to eat, but it is enough for us and also for you. So if you want to stay with us, then you are kindly invited. I wouldn't advise you to go to Düsseldorf, as your life will be in danger there. Bombs are falling there all the time, just the same as here. So it's just as well that you stay here."

"Tell me, Rachel," asked Edith, "what was the name of the girl again, who helped you to escape?"

"Ruth, and she said she was born in Berlin. Do you perhaps know her...?"

"Yes, I think so. We went to school together, and she volunteered to the Wehrmacht just after graduating from the gymnasium. She went to the news unit. Her parents' home is not far from here. Ruth was always a dear person, if it is the Ruth I think."

Sara Eckstein served a simple meal, and everybody ate. After the meal, the mother and her daughter put Rachel to bed. The hardships of the journey had been a little too much for her, and she fell promptly into a deep and sound sleep.

Now they discussed how to help Rachel.

"I have an idea! You, Sara and Edith, you two should go with Rachel to Ingolstadt to Aunt Irene!" suggested Arnold.

"And are we to leave you behind alone? Never!" answered Sara indignantly. "But Edith can go alone with Rachel. I'm staying beside you, as a wife should!"

Arnold took her into his arms, very moved.

"Agreed!" called out Edith. They began to pack immediately. On the following morning, Edith did not go to work. She told Rachel about their plan. Rachel agreed gladly.

On the day of their departure, Sara Eckstein accompanied Edith and Rachel to the railway station. All of them tried very hard to hold back their tears. It was hard for them to say good-bye.

*

Rachel again found herself sitting on a moving train, but this time she had Edith beside her. The train stopped many times, as there were air-raid alarms. So the journey took two full days. At the end of the second day, they were so exhausted that they almost fell out of the train in Ingolstadt. Edith called her uncle by telephone and he met his niece and her friend at the railway station. He was in a hurry, as they had called during his consulting hours.

"You'll tell me everything in detail tonight, why you have come so suddenly and unannounced. Now, just go straight to the house. Your aunt is already so excited and so very curious!" With these words, the uncle dropped the two girls off at the house and disappeared in the direction of his practice.

Edith told her aunt in a few sentences everything about Rachel's experiences.

"My poor child!" said the aunt compassionately, and embraced Rachel. "Of course you will both stay here, until this is all over!"

In the evening, the uncle heard why Edith had left Berlin in such a rush. He, too, invited the girls to stay as long as they wished.

"Don't worry, Rachel, with us you will be safe!" assured Edith's uncle.

The next day, he took Rachel to his practice and examined her from head to toe.

"You are rather run down physically, Rachel. Rest, and try to forget your sorrow. Good care and sufficient food will soon put you on your feet. And the wig, you can put it into the cupboard. You don't need to wear it here with us. But you must not go out into the street without it!"

In the evening, the two girls sat together with Aunt Irene and Uncle Herbert. They talked, and Rachel learned that Herbert Holzner was the senior physician of a hospital in Ingolstadt, where he worked in the mornings, and in the afternoons he had a private practice where he also treated patients without any means.

Both he and Irene loved music. Herbert played the violin and she played the piano. They had a harmonious marriage, lived in a spacious house, surrounded by a big garden, and they did not sympathize with the Nazi regime at all.

They had nothing to fear in that regard. Everybody respected Herbert Holzner because of his occupation and his position.

In these surroundings, Rachel recovered quickly. All of them tried very hard to help her forget her sorrow. Often they sat together in the dining room, and Herbert Holzner played the violin, accompanied on the piano by Edith. But Rachel sat sadly with them, unable to think of anything but her Yankel and little Haim.

*

Ruth was still on the run. She managed to get to Berlin, after a few detours. She left the railway station with joyful anticipation. At last she would see her mother and little brother again.

'I hope they will understand why I have deserted!'

Ruth's parents had always believed in the victory of the Führer. 'Perhaps Mama has changed her belief after father's death!' hoped Ruth as she turned into the street in which she had spent her childhood. Startled to death, she looked upon the horrible picture that presented itself!

Almost all the houses were partly or entirely ruined. Pieces of rubble and ruins lay everywhere. Ruth began to run. But then she stopped and burst into tears. Her mother's house was destroyed down to the foundations. Ruth went on crying, aghast, standing there by herself.

Then, suddenly, a hand touched her shoulder.

"Ruth?" asked the voice of a woman.

Ruth turned around. "Mrs. Eckstein! You are alive?" she asked astounded.

"Yes, child. We are alive, my husband and I and Edith too. Come home with me and I'll tell you everything!"

Mrs. Eckstein led Ruth to their home.

"And…my mother and my brother…?" asked Ruth in a low voice.

"Unfortunately they were killed during a bomb raid," said Mrs. Eckstein with compassion.

Ruth sobbed convulsively out of pain.

In the meantime, they reached the apartment of the Ecksteins. Arnold Eckstein greeted Ruth kindly. Then they told her about Rachel.

"Actually, why do you want to go to your aunt, Ruth? There are as many air raids there as here in Berlin. Why don't you go to Ingolstadt to Edith and Rachel? There you will be safer!"

Ruth stayed for the night with the nice people, and on the following day she set out on her way to Düsseldorf, for she wanted to visit her aunt first, before anything else. She was now her only living relative.

After traveling for twelve hours, interrupted by many air raids, Ruth arrived in Düsseldorf. This city, too, looked like a moonscape. Bizarre mountains of ruins and debris alternated with deep craters. Naturally, there were no streetcars functioning any more. So Ruth went on foot to her aunt's house.

Suddenly a harsh voice said: "Stop! Your identity card, please!" Frightened, Ruth stopped and began to search feverishly in her purse, but the military policeman already had spotted her military passbook.

"So, you have run away?" he grinned, and took hold of Ruth's arm.

"No! I'm just visiting my aunt here and going back to my unit tomorrow!" answered Ruth quickly.

"We know all about that! Let's go!" the officer barked at her and took her away with him. They locked Ruth in a cell, and she was brought before an officer only after three long days of waiting.

"We know everything about you!" he said. "You were given a chance, and you lost it. Now we are putting you before a military court!"

Ruth stared at the man, horrified. 'So that is the end now!' she thought, despairing. She knew that no crying and lamenting would help her now. They locked her into a solitary cell. The guard, who had to watch her, felt sorry for her.

"Why have they arrested you?" he asked.

"Ach, I only wanted to visit my aunt. But I didn't get a leave of absence, so I just went without permission!" answered Ruth.

"Come, quickly give me the address of your aunt. I'll visit her and tell her that you are here," whispered the guard.

Ruth gave him the address, and in the evening he brought her a letter from her aunt, in which she wrote to Ruth:

"Our house has been destroyed by a bomb, and your Uncle Fritz has been seriously wounded. He is in hospital. I have found a sort of shelter in a tiny room at my neighbors' home! So how can I help you now, dear child?"

This news shook her severely, as she had fully believed that her aunt, who had many influential friends in the city, would help her. Tears ran down her face.

"Listen," whispered the guard, "do you want to escape with me?"

"But if we are caught, we will both die!" answered Ruth excitedly.

"You can count on me! Nobody will catch us!" The soldier disappeared and came back a little while later with a uniform.

"Here, put this on! And then we'll get away!"

He held out the uniform to Ruth and helped her to put them on. Then he took her arm and they left the building, as if nothing had happened. Their documents were checked only fleetingly, and then they were already walking on the outside pavement. Ruth could not grasp it. The guard pulled her behind the next corner.

"Go now to your aunt! Tonight I'll come and pick you up from there. Then we will escape together, all right?" he asked.

"Good!" answered Ruth, and hurried to her aunt. She was delighted to see her and tried to convince her to stay at least one night with her.

"It's impossible, Aunt Christel! I must leave here without any delay. I'm not safe here. Please give me some money, and give the soldier also some reward when he comes tonight, will you?"

Ruth kissed her aunt, took the money that she had given her, and parted from her hastily.

"Many heartfelt thanks, Aunt Christel! Please give my warm regards to Uncle Fritz! *Wiedersehen!*"

And she was already out the door. She made her way carefully back to the railway station. There she looked at the mirror in the ladies' washroom and would have laughed aloud, if she hadn't put her hand in front of her mouth just in time.

She really looked so funny! She was dressed in her aunt's clothes and she had made herself look older with some make-up and an old-fashioned hat. Now she looked more like the picture on the identity pass. She could not possibly have fled dressed in her uniform and with her own papers. She knew that she could not have gotten out of Düsseldorf that way. She was sure that they were already searching for her.

Satisfied, she smiled at her reflection and said: "Good night, Auntie!" Then she turned around and walked light-footedly to the ticket counter. After a few steps she stopped, remembering her appearance, and went on with slow measured steps.

"After all, I'm now an elderly lady!" she grinned.

At the ticket counter she asked for a ticket to Frankfurt, for the time being. It was impossible to be sure if somebody had not recognized her already. She passed the barrier slowly, when all of a sudden she heard a voice from behind: "You are traveling to South Germany, madam? May I be allowed to accompany you? I am traveling in the same direction!"

Ruth turned around astonished and saw an SS man standing behind her.

"May I introduce myself? Klingenberg, Hermann Klingenberg!"

"I hope you will not be bored with me," said Ruth, coldly. "Because I'm very tired!"

"Regrettable, very regrettable!" answered Hermann Klingenberg.

"What a fop!" thought Ruth, contemptuously. But perhaps it would be useful to travel together with the fellow.

The train arrived. They boarded it, and Ruth retreated immediately into a corner. After some trivial talk she began to yawn several times.

"Ach, I'm so tired! I'm going to sleep a little. Please see to it that I'm not disturbed, will you?"

"Of course! A gentleman of the old school would not allow anybody to bother the lady!"

While speaking these words, Hermann Klingenberg stood up and clicked his heels.

'This person must really be left over from the previous century!' thought Ruth, and looked at the officer furtively from between half-closed eyelids. She saw an angular face and ice-cold blue eyes and realized that the friendly affected behavior was only a play.

'I wouldn't want to fall into the hands of this one!' she thought, shivering. Then she fell asleep.

A short time later, some officers arrived to check their identity papers. Being still half-asleep, Ruth only vaguely noticed. The SS man said: "This is my companion!"

So the officers went on, without saying another word. In Frankfurt the officer woke Ruth up with reluctance.

"Ach, have we arrived already?" said Ruth, astonished.

She said good-bye to her companion and bought a new ticket at the ticket counter, this time directly to Ingolstadt. She had to wait for the next train, and then she was finally sitting on board the right train to South Germany, traveling without any disturbance straight to Ingolstadt.

There she asked for directions to the given address several times and at last reached the house. She rang the doorbell and Edith opened the door.

"Ruth! How did you get here?" asked a surprised Edith, and embraced her.

"Ach, Edith, it's a long story. Your parents sent me here," explained Ruth.

At that moment Rachel came down the steps, saw Ruth and flung her arms around her neck.

"Ruth! Ruth! How wonderful to see you again!" she called out happily.

"Could I stay with you for the night?" asked Ruth.

"Of course, you can sleep with me in my room!" said Edith. Then the three went to the aunt and introduced the new 'niece.'

"Naturally you can stay here too!" said the uncle, when Ruth was introduced to him. "We feel like we already know you from Rachel's story."

Now the old couple, the doctor and his wife, had a family with three daughters all at once! Rachel was recovering rather well and helped the housewife with her work in the house. Edith helped her uncle in his practice, and Ruth took care of the paperwork in the clinic. So everyone had his own area of responsibility, and all of them lived together in harmony. The three girls formed a tight circle of friends.

While Edith and her uncle were playing music, Rachel sat quietly with them, feeling sad. Herbert Holzner saw that Rachel could not really be joyful. So he sat down beside her and advised her lovingly: "A person should try to make something with his life even in times of physical and spiritual distress. To be passive is like dying. You must not just sit around and mourn, and let your young life drift by in front of you, Rachel! Come, give me your hand!"

He led Rachel to the piano.

"Here, sit down now, and play something for us!"

Rachel sat down and touched the keyboard timidly. Notes sounded, first single and clipped ones, then ones connected to a melody, and finally Rachel played and played; she played all her soul's sorrow and misery.

Her listeners were spellbound. They had rarely been so moved by a piece of music as they were here and now.

"I didn't know that you could play like that!" said Herbert, astonished. "From now on you must play more often, Rachel!"

14.

I N THE FIRST months of 1945, the surviving Jews from the concentration camps were marched at a brutal pace into the interior of the country. Many collapsed, fell down out of hunger and weakness, and did not get up again. Everybody knew what falling down meant. When the exhausted person collapsed but was not dead yet, he received a coup de grâce with a shot or a bayonet. That was why the unfortunates dragged themselves on with their last bit of strength, driven only by their will to survive at any price. And they did not only want to survive, but to stay alive and see the end of the Nazi regime. They wanted to be witness to the ones responsible being called to account for their evil acts.

Numb and almost blind with headaches, Yankel staggered on with his last ounce of strength with a group of prisoners. They dragged themselves through a village. An old farmer was standing in front of his gate, his pipe in his hand, but he did not draw from it. He was too aghast at the sight of the unfortunate people who passed his farm. They were bundles of rags with big heads and enormous grievous eyes, skeletons with skulls, a yellowish skin stretched over the bones contorting the pale lips into a permanent grimace.

The farmer could not continue looking upon this. He stretched out his hand, grasped the next skeleton, pulled it into his yard in a flash and bolted the door from the inside. Then he carried the helpless man to the barn and laid him on a pile of hay. The farmer's wife followed him. She had seen the incident. When she saw the man on the ground, her eyes filled with tears. She left quickly and came back with some coffee and pieces of bread spread with butter, but except for a tiny sip of coffee the weak man could not take in anything.

In the evening they took the man into their house. They bathed him like a small child and dressed him in clean clothes. They burned his striped concentration camp clothes in the oven. Then they let him sip a little beef soup. After this they put him to bed.

By the next morning, he was able to sit up by himself and even speak.

"My name is Yakob Goldenbaum, called Yankel, and I come from Khust," he said. He told them his terrible story. Heinrich, the farmer, his wife Martha and their daughter Elisabeth listened very moved. After Yankel finished, the farmer cried out indignantly: "One has to be ashamed to be a German! How can they do such a thing! I've never believed in the Nazis, but that they could commit such crimes, I would never have believed!"

Heinrich pointed at his wife and his daughter.

"These two also didn't want to believe me. They were just deaf to my words and *followed their Führer*, like most of the people here in the village. None of them wanted to admit that the Jews have attained so many outstanding achievements for Germany, in the economy, in science and in many other areas. Only now most of the Germans see that the senseless war has hit not only the Jews, but, first of all, the Germans themselves. Now, when it is too late, they try to overthrow Hitler! But the wheel of history cannot be turned back again. We must take care to get through the end of the war unscathed. I'm happy, Yankel, that you are feeling better and that I am able to help at least one person!"

The farmer wiped his forehead with a big handkerchief, out of breath. This had been a very long speech for him. He had not said so much for a long time!

Yankel felt much better already. No wonder, with the good treatment he was given there, for which he thanked the old man warmly.

A short while later, they heard somebody knocking on the door. There stood four young people from the German Territorial Army, demanding to come in.

"The enemy is coming nearer, and we have to organize our resistance. We are taking your yard and closing down the street. Here, take this gun, munitions and a few bazookas. You were a soldier in the First World War, so you must know how to use a gun!"

"Such nonsense!" called out the farmer. "Are you mad? If there is going to be even one shot from our side, they will certainly kill us all! Or perhaps you want to win another war, here in our village? The Russians are standing in front of Berlin, and the Allied Forces are advancing! And half of Germany is already conquered!"

"An order is an order!" was the answer. "You are a soldier, and if you do not act according to our orders, we shall take you to be tried by a military court! Heil Hitler!"

The farmer immediately hurried to Yankel and told him about the incident.

They sat together and made a plan of action, the most important part of which was to prepare white flags. So they sewed white flags in feverish haste.

The Nazis in the village tried, up to the last minute of the already lost war, to assemble a resistance group of old men and children.

The Allied Forces came closer; the German Territorial Army group entrenched themselves in the village. The old men and the children were equipped with guns from the First World War. They wanted to hold out to their last breath. Then Heinrich together with Yankel raised the first white flag. All the neighbors followed suit. They formed a group and went together to the Territorial Army unit. "The mayor has sent us. He orders you to give up the village! Lay down your weapons and go home. If there is even one shot from here, our whole village will be destroyed!"

The soldiers did not have to be told this twice. They left their positions hastily, and by the time the first American tanks rolled in, none of them could be seen anywhere.

Heinrich and Yankel walked towards the approaching troops who were marching through the main street of the village. The officer in charge appointed Heinrich the new mayor of the village.

The American soldiers congratulated Yankel on his survival and gave him some presents. The inhabitants of the village came and shook his hand too.

The next day, the American military physician came and examined Yankel. The physician told him: "In München, there is now a Jewish committee, where the Jews who have survived the war list themselves. Why don't you go there? Maybe you can find the name of someone from your family on those lists?"

Nothing could hold Yankel back now. He knew that his parents and siblings had been killed, as had his son Haim. 'But where was Rachel? Perhaps she has also survived?'

Yankel told his new friends of his intentions.

Elisabeth, the farmer's daughter, broke out in tears.

"Please don't cry! If I find my wife Rachel, you can come and visit us!" he consoled her. Then Yankel thanked Heinrich and his wife Martha again for everything they had done for him.

On the following day, he was taken by car to München by an American soldier, a fellow Jew.

Heinrich and Martha waved farewell to him, satisfied.

*

The Polish-Russian army marched swiftly to the west. A short time after the liberation of Warsaw, Beryl and his comrades were ambushed.

Beryl was not hit, but three Jewish comrades were killed. This incident distressed Beryl extremely. Now he wanted to reach the west as quickly as possible. He wanted to fight against the Nazis, but not be shot at from behind, by their own allies. His comrades and he had only one wish left, to fight their way through, to be free.

Just before the river Elbe, they got into an exchange of fire. German troops tried to cross the Elbe to the west. Within this muddle, people tripped over one another. Beryl bumped into his comrade Nathan, who was seriously wounded.

"Nathan, Nathan! What happened to you?"

Beryl shook his friend, but Nathan only heaved with pain once more, and then his head fell to the side and his eyes froze.

Tears rose to Beryl's eyes, as he closed his old friend's eyes. He could do no more for him. Beryl turned around and stared at the river. Suddenly everything was silent. They had stopped firing. Then, on the opposite bank some soldiers appeared, waving their guns in the air.

Beryl recognized them by their uniforms. They were Americans. Beryl and his friends jumped up.

"Come on!" called out Beryl. "Let's cross over to the other side!"

He ran down to the riverbank and indicated to the Americans, through signs, that they wanted to cross over. Thereupon, the American soldiers lowered some boats into the river and brought Beryl and his friends over to them. They took them to the American camp and supplied them with civil clothing, refugee identity cards and some money. Now they were free people.

After finishing all the formalities, they rode with a refugee transport to München.

At the railway station, they met other survivors who were arriving from different places. The information about the Jewish committee had spread already, so they went together and added their names to the list of the survivors. Then they stood around there for days, or wandered hopelessly through the streets, searching for their family members or friends. Day after day, their hope turned to disappointment, again and again. And so it went on for weeks.

Many Jews who had lived miraculously through their time in the concentration camps perished now because of their terrible anguish and the aftermath of their physical injuries.

Beryl, though physically healthy, was also deeply depressed. He had been in München for weeks already and still had not found any of his family members. He roamed the streets aimlessly.

Suddenly, a voice tore him out of his lethargy: "Hey, Beryl! You are Beryl, aren't you? Yes, I wasn't mistaken! How are you?"

"Yes, Baruch! I wouldn't have recognized you from a distance!" Beryl embraced the friend and they clapped each other joyfully on the shoulder. Then they looked into each other's eyes, silently. Yes, each of them stood up to the other's scrutiny, without batting an eyelid. They had remained their old selves, although, since they had seen each other last, they had turned from young boys into mature, sorely afflicted men. And they had much to tell each other.

"Come," said Beryl, "let's go to my lodgings."

"Do you have a room?" asked Baruch.

"No, I'm staying in a camp!" explained Beryl. "In a transit camp for emigrants to Israel."

"Then let's go to my place!" said Baruch.

He took hold of Beryl's arm and led him to his room. There he began to tell his eventful story.

"I arrived in Khust just after the Russians marched in, but except for two Jews, none of the others were there any more. The Swabians and Hungarians had escaped, leaving only the Ruthenes, who told us that Jews were not wanted there!"

Baruch wiped his eyes, and Beryl sighed.

"Then I went away," continued Baruch, "and crossed the Hungarian border. In Miklosh, the inhabitants demonstrated openly against the Jews coming home, who only wanted to get back their legal properties, and the Russian army did nothing to intervene. But it gets even worse! On the way to Budapest, near the little town of Gödölö, the Soviets set up a so-called 'refugee-camp,' surrounded with high barbed wire, for 'safeguarding,' where they brought Jews from Budapest or those coming home from the concentration camps. They caught me too and put me in there."

"This cannot be true! This cannot be for real!" said Beryl with a sigh. "How can one lock up people who have just escaped from the hell of the concentration camps?"

"But they can!" answered Baruch. "We even had to sleep in the open air, since there was no accommodation prepared. Many of the inmates who came from the ghettos or from the camps died of hunger and weakness. Some other strong young men and I managed to cut the barbed wire and escape. I don't know what happened to the people who remained behind. Anyhow, I went to the Jewish community and spoke with the newly-appointed head of the community in Budapest. He promised me to devote himself to the release of those unfortunates and to the dispersal of the camp.

"After that, I didn't stay in Budapest for long, but carried on west. And imagine, Beryl, there I met Mendel! I was just by the border between the Russian Zone and the American one, when I saw two Russian soldiers with Mendel between them. A crying girl was walking behind them. I wanted to stop the soldiers and talk with Mendel, but they shoved me aside. So I stopped the girl. Her name was Annerl and she was an Austrian. She told me that her parents had taken in Mendel and had hid him. When he was found out, she fled together with him to relatives in South Germany, and they lived there through the end of the war.

"Then they set out on their way to Austria to return to her parents. When they entered the Russian Zone of Austria, the Russians stopped them, and led Mendel away, claiming that all Jews were American spies!

"The girl protested that Mendel had been with her the whole time, but in vain. Nobody listened to her at all. On the contrary, they even threatened that they would put her into a labor camp if she did not get lost immediately!"

Beryl and Baruch sat silently for a while. Both thought about what had happened to them. Then Beryl asked: "Did you meet any other fellow countrymen?"

"Yes," Baruch now said. "I met Haim and Feigele. I escaped together with them from the train. They made it through the end of the war in Czernovitz and then left for Bucharest. From there, they planned to go to Israel. They also had Esther with them, the daughter of the locksmith, do you remember her?"

"Sure!" said Beryl. "I remember the girl."

Baruch and Beryl talked on for quite awhile, and then Beryl asked: "Baruch, I still have to go to the committee. I haven't been there yet today. Would you like to join me?"

"Why not? Perhaps there will be something new!"

The two friends set out together. As they arrived at the front of the building in which the Jewish committee was situated, a figure stumbled out, looked at them, stopped short and called out: "*Haverim! Haverim!*"

Baruch and Beryl could not believe their eyes. Before them – hardly recognizable – stood Yankel! The sight of their emaciated and weakened friend moved the two of them to tears.

"Yankel, Yankel! How good to see you again!"

Baruch and Beryl immediately turned around and took Yankel with them to Baruch's lodgings.

Baruch was a partner in a business and had good connections. He organized rooms for the two friends and took Beryl into his business as an additional partner.

A few days later, Yankel found a position at the Jewish committee. He organized groups for the *Aliya* to Palestine again.

Baruch and Beryl earned a lot of money with their second-hand shop. Yet this could not drive away their innermost unease. They just did not know what to do with their lives. At home, in Khust, they had worked hard, but they had had their relatives who had given them the necessary balance. But here, they did not have anything worthwhile to live for. So the friends kept searching for new ways to amuse themselves. They spent a lot of time in cafés and questionable bars, met women and learned to drink alcohol copiously. Yet nothing fulfilled them, or brought them real satisfaction. In their thoughts, they still lived together with their families.

Beryl often dreamed about his past, even in full daylight, and for this he had to put up with many mocking remarks. But it was not a member of his family that he dreamt about. He still searched for a pair of eyes that had looked at him so intensely...at that time, on a small misty glade in the woods...

15.

Time went on, and one day the news of the German capitulation reached Ingolstadt as well.

"Rachel, Rachel!" called Ruth excitedly. "The war is over! The Germans have surrendered!"

Edith and Rachel could hardly believe it! But it was true. Uncle Herbert had also heard it.

Now there was nothing to hold the girls back any more; a few days later they set out on their way. Edith went to Berlin. She wanted to find out as quickly as she could whether her parents had survived the terrible time. Ruth wanted to accompany her.

"And what are your plans, Rachel?" the two girls asked their friend. "Are you coming with us to Berlin, too?"

"No! I'll go to München. I was told that there is a Jewish committee, where all the Jews who have survived the war are being listed. Perhaps I will find relatives there. If not, I'll go from there to Israel. What is there for me to do here now?"

"But child!" called out Uncle Herbert with a start. "What do you want to do over there, entirely on your own? Please stay here with us!"

"No, it's impossible for me, after all that has happened here! I am a Jew, and they have destroyed my whole family, yes, almost all my people have been exterminated! You were spared by the war! You can live on now, as if nothing has happened; you have remained in your own land. In my homeland, there are only empty houses and endless rows of graves waiting for me. With every step, the souls of the dead walk beside me!"

Rachel bent down and hid her face within her hands.

"Ach, Yankel, and Haim, my little darling! Why did you leave me alone...?"

Rachel wept.

"We did not want the war," she continued, "and we did not wage war against anybody! Nevertheless, they have destroyed us in Europe!"

Rachel looked with an accusing glance at the others, who kept silent awkwardly.

"Those who have stayed alive, miraculously like I have, have neither a home nor a homeland anymore. We are going to stay defenseless and unprotected. Who knows, perhaps in a few years' time we are going to be persecuted again! As long as we don't have our own land, we are going to be nomads forever!"

"Calm down, Rachel," said Uncle Herbert, and stroked the girl's hands. "Go to Palestine. It will be the right thing for you to do. But promise me one thing: Don't think of us as being so bad. Not all the Germans were fanatic Nazis. Look at me! You can take me as an example. And there are many others like me."

"It's a pity that there were not enough such good people like you," said Rachel regretfully.

"I know, Rachel, the dead cannot be brought back to life anymore, but those who are responsible for the suffering of countless people, and those who often with a single stroke of their pen sent hundreds of people to their deaths, must be brought to account for it!"

Rachel embraced the old man.

"I thank you, Uncle Herbert, for that, that you do understand me!"

"Come, let's drink another bottle of wine together!" offered Aunt Irene now, and with that she broke the spell which had taken hold of them all.

The next morning, the three girls said good-bye to Irene Holzner. Uncle Herbert brought them to the railway station. Then they boarded the trains and went their separate ways, Edith and Ruth to Berlin, Rachel to München.

*

On the following day, Rachel arrived in München and asked for directions to the Jewish committee. There, in the courtyard and on the staircase, countless people stood together in knots and talked. Rachel looked at all of them but did not see any familiar face. From their conversation she understood that people came there every day and searched for their missing relatives.

Rachel's heart raced, as she entered the office, shivering. She took a deep breath and said in a breaking voice: "I am looking for my husband, Yakob Goldenbaum!"

The committee's clerk lay out the name lists before her. In a feverish hurry, she glanced over the pages again and again, but she couldn't find her husband's name on them. Rachel broke out in tears.

"Please calm down!" said the employee, who was already used to such scenes. "Every day, new survivors are coming to be put on the list. Give me your address, so that I can inform you when your husband arrives!"

"I have just arrived here and don't have any address," said Rachel, discouraged.

"Then I'm going to fill out a certificate for your admission into the assembly camp!" said the young man. "Don't fret, the camp is set up in a former school, and you may come and go as you wish," he added, when he saw that Rachel had started upon hearing the word 'camp.'

With the certificate in her hand, Rachel left the office and then stood helpless and lost on the street.

"What shall I do now?" she thought, in despair. "There is no one I know here!"

Tears fell down her cheeks. She stopped in the middle of the pavement to search for a handkerchief in her handbag, dropping the note she had just received in the office onto the pavement.

A man bent down for the piece of paper. "Here, please!" he said, and straightened up. His look fell on the note, and he read Rachel's name and birthplace.

"Khust? You are from Khust?" cried the surprised man, and embraced the girl. "Well, don't you recognize me?"

Rachel wiped the tears out of her eyes.

"Rachel, Rachel. It's me, Beryl," she heard.

"Beryl!" she then called out with joy. "I wouldn't have recognized you, really!"

"When did you arrive?" asked Beryl, and continued without waiting for an answer: "Have you already seen Yankel? It was only yesterday that we spoke of you and…"

Rachel interrupted him: "Where…where is Yankel, Beryl? Tell me, is he well?"

"But didn't you meet him yet?" asked Beryl, astonished. "He is working here in this building at the Jewish committee!"

"They told me that they didn't know him," said Rachel, disconcerted, "and his name doesn't appear on the name lists!"

"I don't understand! Come, I'll take you to him!"

A few minutes later, Beryl was witness to a very moving reunion. Rachel and Yankel stood closely embracing in front of him, with tears of unspeakable joy in their eyes.

"Rachel, my dearest! I still cannot believe it! You are alive and here in my arms!"

Rachel could not utter a word. Then they stepped apart and told each other how they had managed to survive.

*

A few days later, Beryl and Baruch were sitting in the room of the happily united couple, listening to Rachel's story. Rachel told about the family in Ingolstadt, about Edith and Ruth and about the time they had spent in Ingolstadt. She had a picture of herself, Ruth and Edith.

Beryl took just one look at the picture, when he let out a cry and went over to the window.

"Baruch, it's her! It's the girl from the glade in the woods!"

Beryl told them now about his encounter with the Wehrmacht news reporter.

"The girl's name is Ruth," said Rachel, and described Ruth's appearance and height.

Beryl was very excited and he decided to go to Berlin together with Baruch, as soon as possible.

*

In Berlin, the black market business was flourishing. At the Brandenburger Tor, there was a lively hustle and bustle. Just about everything could be bought and exchanged. Men in uniforms, civilians, men and women, Allied and Germans bought, exchanged and sold everything. The black market joined together winners and losers, friends and foes.

Ruth and Edith stared aghast at the turbulent crowd. They had not expected this. But actually, they should have been used to masses of people, because they had seen them on their way from Ingolstadt to Berlin often enough. From the time they had arrived in Stuttgart, there were clusters of people hanging out of the train. Everywhere, people were holding on and dangling or sitting, at the doors, on the roofs and on the steps. And then, the train could not go any further, because the rails had been destroyed. Edith and Ruth had to go the rest of the way on foot. But after a short walk on the road, they were picked up by a horse cart and then went on with a tractor, after which they were lucky and got a ride in a truck. Traveling like this, they managed to get themselves through to Berlin. It took them exactly eight days for the stretch from Ingolstadt to Berlin.

Then, at last, they arrived at Edith's parents house. Miraculously, this house had only been partly destroyed.

The Ecksteins embraced them happily and brought them into their apartment. The girls rested for one day only, and then they wanted to look at Berlin. And now they stood in front of the Brandenburger Tor and looked upon the black market muddle.

"Ruth, look at the two Russians and the American over there!" said Edith, pointing.

An American was sitting on the ground, and in front of him stood two Russians. One of the Russians took a watch out of the American's hand and held it near his ear. Unnoticed, the other Russian took the watch from him, quick as lightning, and ran away. The first Russian laughed loudly and showed the American his empty hands. The American soldier spit out his chewing gum and pulled at his hair.

Ruth and Edith laughed and went on. There were ruins everywhere, ruins, nothing but ruins and rubble!

Out of one of the ruined courtyards, two black American soldiers suddenly appeared in front of them. Proudly, one of them pointed with an expansive gesture upon the landscape of the ruins and called out to them: "You see, Hitler *kaput*!" smiling and showing his snow-white teeth.

Startled, Ruth grabbed Edith's arm and quickened her steps.

"Perhaps they are going to look upon us as fair game, or they hate us, like the Nazis hated the Jews!"

Edith calmed her: "Come on, you see, they didn't do anything to us!"

"Well, you never know!" answered Ruth carefully.

That evening, the family was sitting comfortably together, when the doorbell rang. Sara Eckstein opened the door and let in two young men who said that they had come after seeing Rachel. The two told them that Rachel and Yankel had been reunited in München, and that they were helping others to emigrate to Israel.

While Beryl spoke, Ruth recognized him and came closer to the guests.

He had also recognized her.

"Are you the girl from the front, Ruth?"

"Yes I am, Beryl!"

Saying this, they embraced and kissed each other for a long minute, forgetting the world around them. Only then did they begin to tell one another about the hardships they had gone through since that time in the woods. Both were convinced that they had found each other for life.

Of course, this had to be celebrated. They drank wine, laughed and danced. Then, the old Ecksteins went to their room and left the 'young people,' as they jokingly said, on their own.

*

In the following days, Baruch and Beryl wandered through Berlin. Seeing the ruins, their hearts became heavy. But then they thought about the millions of Jewish people, whose extermination and destruction had been planned in this city. Nevertheless, the Berliners' fate touched them. After all, under the mountains of rubble lay not only criminals, but also many innocent people. The sight of this huge mass grave made Baruch and Beryl sad.

The men set out for the home of the Ecksteins. Beryl was silent the whole time. Inside him, a fight was raging between his reason and his emotions. His emotions pushed him to ask Ruth for her hand. But his reason told him: "If you really love her, you must not shackle her to you!"

'That is true,' thought Beryl. 'Before the war, I wasn't so religious, but now, I couldn't live without the religion of my forefathers. And therefore I want to go to Israel. But how could I expect Ruth to go there with me?' Beryl racked his brains in order to find a solution, but he could find none.

After a short while, they reached the home of the Ecksteins. "Just listen to what I've been told," said Arnold Eckstein excitedly. "The British have sent a ship back to Hamburg, full of Jewish emigrants. They were not allowed to land!"

Baruch and Beryl were deeply excited.

"I must go immediately to Hamburg!" cried out Beryl.

"But what do you want to do there?" asked Baruch. "You cannot help them!"

"All the same, I must go there!" answered Beryl, fiercely.

Ruth looked at him sadly.

Next morning, Beryl set out on his way to Hamburg. Baruch, too, said good-bye to the Ecksteins, as he wanted to return to München.

In Hamburg, they had already organized demonstrations. Beryl joined the demonstration march. He was one of the loudest and most zealous of the marchers.

But the British sent a whole unit of soldiers to restrain the protesters harshly. Beryl, too, was arrested.

Soon after, Ruth heard indirectly about Beryl's arrest and immediately made her way to Hamburg. She obtained a visiting permit and stood opposite a surprised Beryl.

"Ruth!" he called out. "What are you doing here?"

"I was told that you had been arrested. So I came straight here." Ruth smiled at Beryl. "Surely you don't have to stay here for long. I shall move heaven and earth in order to set you free."

"I can only tell you one thing: I'm innocent! I didn't do anything!"

Beryl couldn't say anything more, as they took him away to his cell. Ruth gazed after him, until the barred door closed behind him. Then she turned around and asked to be led to the officer in charge.

"I'm sorry, I cannot help you. Only the military judge can decide to discharge an arrested man," said the officer, bored.

Ruth went out sadly. Now there remained only one possibility: a lawyer. Arriving at her hotel, she asked for the address of a good lawyer. She went to see him that same day and discussed the case with him. Dr. Heidenreich, the lawyer, called the judge on the telephone and managed to arrange for Beryl to be released on bail.

Ruth was dumbfounded. How could she raise the money for bail? She thanked the lawyer and said good-bye. For hours she walked and walked through the city, and suddenly she knew what to do. She went to the post office and sent a telegram to Edith, saying: "Come immediately to Hamburg and bring the blue case from my bedside table. Ruth."

A few hours later she received a telegram.

"Arriving tomorrow Tuesday one o'clock P.M. Edith."

Ruth could hardly await the arrival of the train now. Finally, the moment had arrived! The train from Berlin entered the railway station. But it took almost half an hour more until Ruth at last found Edith in the crowd of people.

"Hello, Edith! Thank you for coming. Did you bring the blue box?" were her words of greeting.

"Well, would you listen to that! Your greeting is not very friendly, is it?" answered Edith, grinning. "What do you actually want to do with the box? Your entire jewelry collection is in it! Are you going to a ball?"

"No, I want to sell the jewelry! I need the money in order to free Beryl!" Ruth sighed. "Come, Edith, let's search for a jeweler who will buy the jewelry from us."

The jewelry box contained a diamond necklace and a matching ring and bracelet. Ruth had inherited these pieces of jewelry from her grandmother.

The two girls went from one shop to another, until they found at last a jeweler who had sufficient money in cash for the payment. Then, a short time later, an overjoyed Ruth paid the bail and took her Beryl with her.

"You?" he called out astonished. "You have paid the bail for me?"

"Yes!" she answered. "I've sold my jewelry, what do I need diamonds for? You are more important to me!"

"I love you, Ruth. From the moment I saw you for the first time, I couldn't get you out of my mind. But I'm afraid that you don't understand me!"

"But why, Beryl?" asked Ruth, insistently. "You can tell me everything!"

But Beryl remained silent. He led her to the exit, and then they walked for a while through the streets of Hamburg. Finally they arrived at the railway station. Ruth bought three tickets to Berlin.

"Why three?" asked Beryl astonished.

"Edith is also here," explained Ruth, and told him about the telegram. Later they met with Edith at the hotel, and on the next day they traveled together back to Berlin.

Arriving there, Ruth and Edith went straight to the kitchen to prepare some food. Beryl was sent to rest. He felt really good. Ever since he was with Ruth, he did not feel any loneliness. Living with her gave him a feeling of safety he had not felt since he had left his parents' home.

He let his life, up to now, pass in his mind's eye in review – his period of battle as a communist, the Soviet Union, his comrades who argued about their communistic ideals…! These memories excited him.

Just then, Ruth entered the room and sat down beside him. Beryl told her about everything that was going through his mind. He told her about his past life, about his friends, about Khust, the Zionistic struggle for Israel and about his experiences as a soldier in the Polish-Russian liberation army.

"And now," Ruth continued when he had stopped, "we will go together to Israel and help establish a homeland for the persecuted Jewish people. We shall be very happy there, right?"

"Ruth!" called out Beryl excitedly. "You really want to come to *Eretz Israel* with me?"

"Yes, yes, my love! How do they say so beautifully: 'Wherever you go, I shall go too!'" said Ruth with a smile.

That took a load off Beryl's mind.

"Come, dearest!" he cried, high-spirited, and led Ruth into the living room.

"Dear friends, you are looking at my future bride!" he gasped breathlessly. "We have just become engaged!"

"*Mazel-Tov!*" the Ecksteins said, embracing the two.

"And we are going together to Israel!" Beryl took Ruth's hand into his own. "We want to build us a new homeland there!"

16.

WHILE RUTH AND Beryl prepared themselves for their emigration to Israel, Bernhard and Judith arrived in Berlin. Their journey from Bucharest to Berlin had taken them weeks. The entire stretch was neverending. They were both dead tired and exhausted, and Judith could hardly hold herself on her feet.

The two left the railway station slowly. They looked around horrified. Bernhard's blood almost froze, standing there. Ruins, rubble, craters on the streets, devastation everywhere one looked. Tears rose to Bernhard's eyes.

"Where are we, *Vati*?" asked seven-year-old Judith. "Is this Berlin?"

"Yes, Judith! This is Berlin!"

Bernhard took the girl by her hand and went further down the street. Everything was submerged in debris. It was hard for him to orientate himself here. Everywhere they saw people poking around in heaps of rubble searching for their lost belongings. Many of them were also busy, taking apart the rubble, carrying parts of it away to rebuild or somehow restore their houses.

Endless queues of people stood in front of the reopened shops, their faces showing hopelessness and exhaustion. The children looked at the world with big serious eyes. The little ones knew only hunger, air-raid shelters, air raids, emergency accommodations and queues for all the daily necessities.

'My God', thought Bernhard, 'what kind of adults are these children going to be, if they have to grow up in these circumstances?'

For hours Bernhard and Judith drifted through the city of Berlin. They were searching for possible survivors, for former friends or relatives, but it was in vain. Wherever they went, they saw only blackened ruins yawning towards them and admonishing, windowless ruins of houses looming up towards the sky. The house in which their family had lived was destroyed, as well as the building in which his shop had once been. Piece after piece of his past crumbled away before his eyes, as Bernhard stumbled with his little daughter through the paths in the debris, searching for a friend, relative or acquaintance who had possibly survived the war, who would give them shelter for one night or more. Each disappointment stabbed at his innermost being and he became more and more convinced that there was not a single thing to connect him with this city anymore. The past was dead.

Deeply saddened, Bernhard kept walking. 'Why have I come here?' he asked himself. 'Had I gone straight from Bucharest to Israel, I would have remembered Berlin as it was before!"

But something had driven him here; he just had to come here. Even the hardships of the long journey from Bucharest to Berlin had not frightened him. And now this…!

At that moment, Bernhard saw a man walking towards him. Somehow, the young man looked familiar to him.

'Where have I seen this man before?' he thought. Then he took a step towards the man.

"I know! Beryl! You are Beryl, aren't you?" called out Bernhard joyfully. "Beryl, the communist from Khust!"

"Yes, that I am!" answered Beryl, astonished. "And who are you?"

"I'm Bernhard Rosen, a friend of David Gutmann. I met you in Khust. Yankel Goldenbaum and I visited your aunt that time!"

"Oh yes, now I remember!" A smile spread over Beryl's face. "You were the man who came to us for a vacation, despite the bad time!"

"Yes, that's correct! And you were so upset about it."

"So what do you do now? Was your house destroyed by the bombs?"

"Yes, but I've just come back today. I was with my child in Hungary, as it was too dangerous for us here in Berlin. You know, I met some friends of yours in Budapest: Yankel and Rachel."

"Then you must be the Bernhard whom Yankel mentioned?"

"Yes, probably. But where did you meet Yankel? If I remember correctly, he was going to Khust in order to bring his wife and his son to safety. And since then I haven't heard anything from him."

"Yankel is in München, together with Rachel. But they've been through a lot. It is a sad story! Tell me, Bernhard, do you have a place to stay for the night?"

"No, all the houses of my friends and acquaintances have been bombed, destroyed to the ground. I don't know what has happened to any of them."

"Then come with me to the Eckstein family, where I'm staying at the moment. I'm sure that they will somehow manage to take you and your child in too."

So Beryl, Bernhard and little Judith went to the Ecksteins. They were greeted with open arms, and Bernhard had to tell his dreadful story again. Judith was put to bed right away.

Hearing about Bernhard's wish to emigrate to Israel too, Beryl said: "Then we can go together."

The Ecksteins gladly agreed to accommodate Bernhard and Judith for the remaining time.

Beryl was occupied with concluding his business, and Ruth prepared everything for their emigration. She had thought up an additional special present for her Beryl. She wanted to convert to Judaism.

She secretly bought a German-Hebrew dictionary, in order to learn the basic words and principles of the Hebrew language. Without telling Beryl a word, she visited a rabbi and learned from him everything a Jewish woman needs to know about the Jewish rituals.

Mrs. Eckstein was like a second mother to her and helped her with her plan in word and deed.

"I love Beryl and my innermost wish is, above everything else, to make him happy. Therefore I've decided to join his faith and convert to Judaism. I don't want us to live in two different worlds of religion. Now I know only one world, the world of Beryl, and I wish to live in it and be happy! That way, Beryl doesn't have to be inhibited before his fellow Jews upon introducing his German wife to them," said Ruth to Mrs. Eckstein.

Ruth's request and admission into the Jewish faith was examined strictly, but after a lengthy consultation of the three rabbis and the test afterwards, she stepped into the water of the *Mikve*, for purification, and became a Jew.

She left the rabbinate, radiant with happiness.

On Friday evening, Ruth set the table according to the Jewish tradition for the first time. Mrs. Eckstein had given her a little tablecloth, embroidered with Hebrew letters, as a present. With that Ruth covered the two *Challahs*. She had also bought a bottle of kosher wine and a silver cup, and now she put both on the table. Two Sabbath candles and the Hebrew prayer books completed the setting. Ruth had even matched her clothes festively for the Sabbath: she wore a dark blue silk dress, set off with white trim, and as a sole adornment a small Star of David, studded with diamonds.

Beryl returned from the synagogue, unsuspecting. Ruth walked towards him, kissed him tenderly and said: "I wish you a 'Sabbath Shalom,' or as you say '*Gut Shabbes,*' Beryl!" Beryl looked at her, astonished. Then he pulled her to him, kissed her and answered. "You look beautiful in your new dress."

Ruth led him solemnly into the living room. Beryl's eyes opened wide. He thought he was dreaming. He hadn't seen such a festive Sabbath table since he was a child in his parents' home. Disbelieving, he looked at Ruth and became aware of the Star of David at her neck. He could not grasp it.

"Ruth! You are wearing the '*Magen David*'? But do you want to....?" stammered Beryl.

"I already am a Jew!" answered Ruth happily, and wrapped her arms around his neck. "I went secretly to a rabbi and have learned everything. I wanted to surprise you with it!"

"Ruth, my darling! You don't have any idea how utterly happy this makes me!" Beryl kissed her again and again. "I've already had thoughts about our life together in Israel, dearest! I saw insurmountable difficulties approaching us, because I wanted to hold on to the faith of my forefathers and later to bring up our children in the same spirit and thought that you would be against it...!"

"No, no!" Ruth removed herself from his arms. "On the contrary. I want to belong to you entirely. But now you have to make the '*Kiddush*'!"

With these words, Ruth put a *yarmulke* upon her Beryl's head, took hold of a prayer book and prayed from it. Then she lit the Sabbath candles.

In Beryl's mind's eye, he saw Friday evening in his parents' home. How festive and wonderful the evening had been, when his father had made the *Kiddush*. He had liked the beginning of the Sabbath most, when his father had sung the lovely verses in which he had praised and thanked the Lord for his wife, and with these words for his whole happiness.

'This joins together the whole family, preserves peace and happiness', thought Beryl, and took hold of his prayer book. But he was too moved and could not utter a word, as tears filled his eyes, out of joy and emotion. He sat down and pulled Ruth upon his lap. Ruth rested her head against his chest; then she kissed away his tears and asked him: "Do you really love me?"

"Now you are a Jewish woman, and my people are your people too! I love you very much and wish only that you should be my wife very soon!"

"Yes, Beryl. We can marry under a *Huppah* in Israel."

"No, that will take too long!" said Beryl excitedly. "Let's marry while we're still here, at our friends' place. Here we can arrange the formalities much more quickly."

They sealed their decision with a passionate kiss. Startled, they jumped apart from each other when somebody knocked on the door.

It was the Ecksteins and Bernhard with Judith. "We wanted to hear the *Kiddush*!" they said, and greeted the couple. "*Guten Shabbes!*"

Beryl washed his hands and made the *Kiddush*, just as he had learned it from his father. The others stood around with shining eyes.

"Amen," said Ruth first.

One week later, Beryl and Ruth stepped under the *Huppah* and took their marriage vows. Two days later, they embraced their friends warmly and set out together with Bernhard and Judith on their way to München.

The train left the railway station, and Bernhard looked, with a heavy heart, at the last houses of Berlin passing by him.

'Lea!' he thought, tears coming to his eyes. 'I have to leave you here now, but in my heart I'm taking you with me. There you shall stay forever!'

"Papa," asked little Judith, "are we going away from Berlin now forever and never ever coming home again?"

Bernhard looked thoughtfully upon the silhouette of the wrecked Berlin, which grew smaller and smaller and finally disappeared behind the horizon. He turned to Judith with a sigh and said: "Listen, my child. We are now going to Israel, to your brother Daniel. There we are going to build us a new home. Perhaps, some day we shall come here to visit, when the ruins will be removed and all the houses of Berlin will be rebuilt."

In his heart, Bernhard thought: 'I think I shall never be able to live here again.'

One week later, the friends arrived in München and continued their journey from there to *Eretz Israel*, with a one-week stop in Italy. Yankel, Rachel and Baruch accompanied them, together with a group of Jewish orphans.

They all left Europe, where they had suffered so much sorrow. But they did not bear hatred in their hearts.

They were fulfilled with the spirit of Theodor Herzl and inspired by the courage and the power which they drew out of their strong belief. They were ready to take anything upon themselves in order for the Land of Israel to rise again, as it had been promised to their people thousands of years before.

Shalom!

Bernhard, a Jewish man from Berlin, who escaped to Budapest with his two children, on a train with a fake passport.

Yankel, the son of an Orthodox Jewish family in Khust, and his beloved girlfriend **Rachel**. Both escaped the horror of a massacre and fled into the woods, to a group of escapees who tried to survive there through the war.

Beryl, a young communist laborer from Khust, who went to join the Red Army and took part in the liberation of Poland. He fell in love with **Ruth**, a German military journalist of the Wehrmacht.

Baruch, the carpenter from Khust, who helped **Haim**, the medical student, and his girlfriend **Feigele** to jump from a moving train taking the Jews of Khust to the massacre.

Mendel, a young musician from Khust, whose violin cried while playing for the partisans.

Nikolai, a giant black-bearded partisan who helped the refugees to join the partisans in the wood. He also rescued **Esther**, a young girl from Khust.

www.ingramcontent.com/pod-product-compliance
Lightning Source LLC
Chambersburg PA
CBHW082225140626
46556CB00020B/3327